GRACE

AND

FURY

TRACY BANGHART

GRACE AND FURY

GRACE

AND

FURY

TRACY BANGHART

LITTLE, BROWN AND COMPANY

NEW YORK   BOSTON

Little, Brown and Company
Hachette Book Group
1290 Avenue of the Americas, New York, NY 10104
Visit us at LBYR.com

First Edition: July 2018

Little, Brown and Company is a division of Hachette Book Group, Inc. The Little, Brown name and logo are trademarks of Hachette Book Group, Inc.

The publisher is not responsible for websites (or their content) that are not owned by the publisher.

Produced by Alloy Entertainment
1325 Avenue of the Americas
New York, NY 10019

Book design by Liz Dresner

Library of Congress Cataloging-in-Publication Data
Names: Banghart, Tracy E., author.
Title: Grace and fury / Tracy Banghart.
Description: First edition. | New York: Little, Brown and Company, 2018. |
Summary: In an alternate world where women have no rights, two sisters face very different fates after an attempt to win the favor of the heir to the throne—one in the palace, the other on a volcanic prison island.
Identifiers: LCCN 2017043582| ISBN 9780316471411 (hardcover) |
ISBN 9780316471398 (ebook) | ISBN 9780316471404 (library edition ebook)
Subjects: | CYAC: Sisters—Fiction. | Women's rights—Fiction. |
Sex role—Fiction. | Princes—Fiction. | Fantasy.
Classification: LCC PZ7.B223 Gr 2018 | DDC [Fic]—dc23
LC record available at https://lccn.loc.gov/2017043582

ISBNs: 978-0-316-47141-1 (hardcover), 978-0-316-47139-8 (ebook),
978-0-316-48726-9 (OwlCrate), 978-0-316-52909-9 (Target)

Printed in the United States of America

LSC-C

10 9 8 7 6 5 4 3 2 1

For every woman who has been told to sit down and be quiet . . . and who has stood up anyway

ONE

SERINA

SERINA TESSARO STOOD on the steps of the fountain in Lanos's central piazza flanked by nine other girls her age, all in their finest gowns. Her brilliant smile never dimmed, even as the thick, coal-hazed twilight tried to choke her.

Signor Pietro gave each girl his narrow-eyed appraisal. He had known all of them from birth, watching and gauging and critiquing their potential. His salt-and-pepper mustache twitched as he pursed his lips.

The dark hulk of the mountains loomed over the soot-stained city, blocking all but a few final rays of daylight. Serina's family stood in shadow at the edge of the crowd. Only Nomi's flushed cheeks caught the light. Serina could see plainly, even from this distance, the fury in her sister's eyes. Their brother, Renzo, kept a hand on Nomi's arm, as if to hold her back. Serina couldn't read his expression, but she was sure it didn't echo their parents' open anticipation.

Signor Pietro turned away from the girls on the steps of the fountain to address the people gathered in the piazza. As Serina waited for his decree, her heart clamored in her throat, but she hid her excitement beneath a veneer of serenity. Her mother had taught her the importance of masks.

"This year the Heir will choose his first Graces. Each province is allowed to send one girl to vie for this honor. As magistrate for Lanos, it falls to me to choose which of our daughters will travel to Bellaqua." Maybe he paused. Maybe he drew out the suspense. But time didn't slow the way Serina expected it to. He just kept saying words in his even, methodical voice, and the words were, "I have chosen Serina Tessaro."

The crowd applauded. Mama Tessaro's eyes lit with hope. Nomi's face fell.

Numb, Serina stepped forward and curtsied deeply. She couldn't believe it. She was going to Bellaqua. She was getting out of grimy, stifling Lanos.

Serina had imagined it so many times. Riding the train for the first time, down through the lush countryside of Viridia. Seeing the Superior's city, with its canals and vast marble palazzo. Meeting the Heir. He would be handsome, like a prince in a fairy tale.

And if he chose her, she'd live in a beautiful palace for all her days. She'd never have to work in a textile factory like her mother did, or become a servant like her cousin. Nor would she be forced into a marriage with whichever man could pay the most for her hand. She would go to glittering balls and want for nothing. Her family would want for nothing, and even Nomi would live a better life, for all her resistance. As Serina's handmaiden, Nomi would get to leave Lanos too.

Signor Pietro shook her father's hand as Serina descended the stairs. The crowd slowly dispersed. The other girls didn't speak to her as they rejoined their families. By the time Serina reached hers, Mama Tessaro was quivering with excitement. She'd once been as tall as Serina, but decades of hunching over her sewing machine at the textile factory had twisted her back.

"My flower, I am so proud of you." She hugged Serina tightly. "You have brought our family great honor."

Nomi made a noise in her throat.

Serina shot her a quelling look. If Signor Pietro heard Nomi speak out against the Heir or the Superior in any way, he'd have her flogged. He'd already threatened to do so during one of Serina's physical examinations last month, when Nomi had muttered, "This is ridiculous," under her breath as she watched the signor inspect Serina in her shift.

"Thank you, Signor," Papa said, bowing.

The magistrate strode off to his carriage, his short scarlet cape fluttering in the sallow glare of lamplight.

"Let's go," Papa said. "We've only two days to prepare for your journey." He led the way to a street in the opposite direction of the signor. They only lived a few blocks away from the central piazza.

Serina drew in a breath of dingy Lanos air and turned to follow. Papa hadn't even looked at her. She tried to gauge his mood from his stiff shoulders. Was he proud of her, like Mama was?

She couldn't tell. She never could with him.

Renzo bumped her arm. "You look beautiful," he said. "The Heir would be a fool not to choose you." She shot him a grateful

3

smile. Renzo understood how much this meant to her. To all of them.

With his tall, sturdy form, it was easy to forget he was younger than Serina by almost two years. He and Nomi were twins but didn't look much alike, except for their amber-brown eyes, several shades lighter than Serina's.

Nomi lagged behind her siblings, scuffing her feet like a sulking child. Serina dropped back so she could walk with her sister.

"This is *good* news," Serina murmured, too quiet for their parents to hear. The streets they walked were empty now; everyone else had already returned to their homes after the big announcement. Flickers of lamplight threw splotches of yellow against the rough stone walls of the houses they passed. The dirty cobbles were uneven underfoot, but Serina never faltered. Her copper-colored gown whispered against the stone.

"I don't want to talk right now," Nomi growled, obviously not as worried about keeping her voice down.

Serina wanted to throttle her. "How can you not be pleased? I truly don't understand. We get to leave this ugly city. We might get to live in the *palace*. Being my handmaiden will be easier than taking care of the whole family the way you do now, and we won't have to worry about having enough food. Mama will be able to stop working. . . ."

Nomi walked faster, as if trying to physically escape Serina's words. "That's the difference between you and me," she said, her hands clenched at her sides. A dusky pink flush bloomed across her face. "I don't think this city is ugly. And I don't believe in fairy tales. I don't *want*—"

"Everything you *do* want is beyond our reach," Serina

4

snapped, tired of Nomi's anger. "You will never be able to choose your own job or your own husband, or . . . or anything else. It just doesn't work that way." It wasn't *Serina's* fault that Viridia gave women so few choices. Serina had learned long ago that fighting didn't change anything, so she made the best of what she had.

And what she had was the chance to become one of the most revered women in the whole country. If the Heir chose her, she could become the mother of a future Superior.

"Nothing should be beyond our reach. That's my whole point," Nomi said.

They were still swept up in the tide of their argument when they reached the creaking door of the family's small apartment. Renzo held it open for them, his sardonic look making it clear he'd heard them. "Nomi, Papa wants you to start dinner."

Nomi stormed into the small living room without answering. Serina followed, pulling her skirts close so they wouldn't catch on the doorframe. Serina saw her sister's gaze linger on Renzo's schoolbooks, still open on the rough-hewn dining table. She nudged Nomi's arm in warning. When she didn't move, Serina cleared her throat.

Nomi looked up at her sister, but it took a split second for her eyes to focus. Then she shook her head, as if to clear it, and hurried to the sink.

Serina glanced over at their parents, but they were speaking quietly by the little potbellied stove. They hadn't noticed the exchange. There was a lot they didn't notice.

Serina and Nomi were like any other daughters in the cold, industrial town of Lanos.

5

But Serina had her beauty.

And Nomi had her secret.

Serina prayed she was enough to catch the eye of the Heir, for her sake as well as her sister's. But as Renzo closed the door, the hollow thud echoed into Serina's bones. She shivered, suddenly filled with fears she couldn't name.

TWO

NOMI

THE RICKSHAW DRIVER pedaled madly, undeterred by jarring gaps in the cobbles and wide-eyed pedestrians. All the rocking and bumping unsettled Nomi's stomach. Or maybe it was the heavy, humid air that smelled of rotting fish.

No. She knew what twisted every muscle and sucked all the breath from her lungs. The closer they got to the palazzo, the more fervently she wished they were heading the other way. It had been less than a fortnight since Signor Pietro had chosen Serina, and the days had skittered by as quickly and painfully as this last, rickety ride.

Nomi winced as Serina's grip on her arm tightened, her nails digging in as the carriage careened over a small bridge, teetering frighteningly close to the edge. Renzo's cheeks paled. He took up the entire seat across from them, his long legs folded up like a spider's to fit in the small space.

Too soon, the rickshaw slammed to a halt at the edge of the grand piazza. Nomi's stomach gave a sickening lurch.

At the far edge of the teeming square, a wide canal glittered in the sun, dotted with flocks of long black boats. Beyond it, on its own island, the Superior's palazzo rose into the sky like a golden sunrise. Nomi took a few deep breaths. Under different circumstances, she would have enjoyed seeing Bellaqua. But not like this. Not today.

Renzo shoved some money at their driver before helping Nomi and Serina out of the rickshaw. Nomi's knees trembled even after she'd made it to solid ground.

"Time to say goodbye," Renzo said. He was trying to sound strong, but his voice shook. Of course, Serina kept her head bent, the dutiful sister, as he pulled her into a polite, fleeting embrace.

But Nomi would have none of that. She hugged her brother tightly, burying herself in his jacket, breathing in his familiar, reassuring scent. Her legs and stomach settled, but only a little. He would wait in Bellaqua until the announcement. She might see him again in a few hours, or never. She couldn't bear the uncertainty.

"Should I plan to spirit you two to freedom, if Serina is chosen?" Renzo whispered jokingly, but with an edge to his voice.

If only. Nomi tightened her arms around him before drawing away. They shared an agonized look.

"Come on, Nomi," Serina said quietly. A man in black-and-gold livery was holding out a hand to her. With bowed head, she placed her fingers on his arm.

Nomi's breath seized. She wasn't ready.

Renzo seemed to understand. With an attempt at a smile, he

kissed her cheek and hurried away so she didn't have to be the one to leave him. The parting cut her like a blade.

"Come on," Serina murmured again.

Reluctantly, Nomi turned to follow her sister through the crowd. The black-and-gold-clad gondolier led them across the piazza to the grand canal, where his gondola bobbed gently with the others. He helped Serina and then Nomi into his boat, settling them onto soft, gold-threaded cushions. All around them, scores of other girls floated over the water in their own gondolas, their colorful dresses marking them as prospects.

The crowd watching the procession of girls laughed and cheered. A child threw handfuls of flowers into the air as Nomi and Serina pushed away from the edge of the canal. Serina smiled at the attention, at the soaring pink petals.

Nomi couldn't stand her sister's serene expression. It was so at odds with the turmoil twisting her stomach. She wanted to leap onto shore, run back to Renzo, and flee the city. She wanted to do anything but float toward the Superior's palace like an unwilling sacrifice to an ancient god. But that was the problem: Serina *was* willing.

Nomi wiped at her eyes, trying to keep her tears in check. Her other hand grasped their small bag of belongings in a death grip. "What if we never see Renzo again?"

"It'll be a blessing," Serina replied. But there was a tremble in her voice. Nomi noted the furrow between her sister's brows as she stared at the approaching palace, the hint of tension at the corner of her mouth. Maybe she wasn't as serene as she appeared. More softly, Serina added, "You know that."

"But I can wish things were different," Nomi muttered just

as the gondola bumped against the rim of the canal. Some of the girls had already disembarked at the base of the steps leading to the Superior's palazzo. The cypress trees lining the canal were hung with tiny bells that tinkled in the breeze.

As Nomi climbed the massive staircase to the palazzo, the last in a long line of girls in bright, fine dresses, she cursed the Heir waiting at the top. He wouldn't notice her—or any of the other handmaidens—but her whole life hinged on whether he noticed her sister.

In front of Nomi, Serina floated up the stairs, her waist-length chestnut hair loose and shining. Her gown, an intricate patchwork of different fabrics that their mother had painstakingly made, rippled like water. She betrayed no hint of weariness, no indication that they'd just spent six long days on a shuddering train, a night in a threadbare hotel room, and a day frantically preparing her for the Heir's ball.

Nomi clutched her bag tighter. She tried not to trip on the marble stairs as she snuck a glance up at the Superior, sickly thin and severe, and his two sons. Malachi, the Heir, wore a white uniform embroidered in gold that accentuated his muscular frame. His broad cheekbones and trim brown hair gave his face a hard edge, but his full lips eased its severity. Even she had to concede he was handsome, if terrifying. He watched his prospective Graces closely, his dark eyes boring into the tops of their heads as they passed.

The younger son, Asa, gazed out toward the canal. His dark hair was longer than his brother's, and disheveled, as if he frequently ran his hands through it.

Nomi should have bowed her head when she reached the

men, but she didn't bother. As she'd expected, no one noticed her. All three stared at Serina's gleaming hair and swaying hips as she passed. Sometimes it irked Nomi, the way Serina drew every gaze. But this time, Nomi was happy to be invisible. She didn't envy her sister's task or the weight of the Superior's icy glare.

When Nomi reached the shade of the veranda, out of sight of the men, she relaxed a fraction. The prospective Graces and their handmaidens proceeded into an ornate gallery with a set of heavy carved wooden doors at its end.

Nomi and Serina picked a spot next to the wall.

"Let me check your makeup one more time," Nomi said. As much as she wished she were anywhere else, she still had a job to do. They both did.

"What do you think of our chances?" Serina murmured, glancing sidelong at the nearest girl, whose handmaiden was re-arranging her vivid orange gown.

Nomi was tempted to tell Serina what she really thought: that they should leave, right now, without a word. That they should go back to Lanos, or better yet, somewhere else entirely, somewhere *they* could decide what they wanted to do all day, instead of Nomi's endless chores and Serina's hours of training in etiquette and dancing. But Nomi knew the truth as well as Serina did: A place like that didn't exist. No matter where they went, their choices were the same: They could be factory work-ers, or servants, or wives. Unless Serina became a Grace.

In Viridia, Graces were held as the highest standard of beauty, elegance, and obedience. What all little girls were meant to aspire to.

For Nomi and Serina, becoming a Grace and a handmaiden was a ticket to a different life, but in this they disagreed: Serina believed *this* different would be better, and Nomi did not.

"I think we're going to lose something either way," Nomi said as she rubbed out a tiny smudge of kohl at the corner of Serina's eye.

"Don't say that," Serina said warningly. "Don't—"

"Don't think about you parading before the Heir, a possession for him to own?" she whispered. She smoothed a section of Serina's hair, her hands trembling. She and her sister both had brown hair, olive skin, and their mother's high cheekbones. But somehow, their shared features combined to make Serina as rich and lovely as Nomi was slight and inelegant. Serina was extraordinary; Nomi was not.

"It's not about becoming his possession, it's about winning his admiration and desire," Serina said through an artificial smile, for the benefit of the girls who'd glanced their way. "This is our chance to have a better life."

"What makes it better?" Nomi shook her head. Anger surged uselessly in her chest. "Serina, we shouldn't *have* to—"

Serina stepped even closer. "Smile at me, like you're happy. Like you're just like the rest of these girls."

Nomi stared into her sister's eyes. Serina was so beautiful like this, with anger staining her cheeks. She was so much more interesting when she wasn't strapping herself into a corset and a demure, downcast grin.

The hushed murmurs of the prospects and their handmaidens died down suddenly, as a woman stepped onto a small raised dais at the far end of the room. Her gown of cream silk highlighted her refined, statuesque air. "My name is Ines. I am the Head Grace." The woman's words were soft as a song. "The Heir is honored that you have journeyed so far. He regrets that he can only choose three of you to remain. But be assured, you are all blessed."

Nomi had always found it odd that Superiors and their Heirs chose three Graces every three years, rather than one a year. Then again, the choosing did consume the whole country, with magistrates spending months observing their province's prospects, and the Superior organizing balls and other events to show off the new Graces once they were chosen.

The current Superior had nearly forty Graces now. But rumors swirled about his health, and this year he had announced no plans to choose Graces for himself. Instead, the Heir would make his first choice. Many assumed this meant the Superior would soon step aside and allow the Heir to rule Viridia in his place.

"The ball is about to begin," Ines said, her thick gold bangles clinking as she raised her hands. "Prospects, it's time."

Serina hugged Nomi tightly. "Be good," she admonished.

"It's not me I'm worried about," Nomi replied, holding on to her sister just as tightly.

One by one, the girls were announced, the doors to the ballroom opening and closing between them. When Serina's moment came, two of the Superior's men pulled the massive doors wide, exposing the swirling brightness within. A deep voice stated, "Serina Tessaro, of Lanos." Without a backward glance, Serina stepped into the light.

Nomi's heart did a painful flip when her sister disappeared from view.

She placed her bag against the wall where the other hand-maidens had left their things and stood awkwardly in the corner. Some of the girls grouped themselves on the balcony to talk. The rest sank into chairs or meandered around, taking in their opulent surroundings.

The walls pressed in on her, the gilt and sparkle heavy as iron. Everything was so different from home. She'd only been gone a week, but she already missed waking up to the sound of Renzo gathering his books for the long walk to school. Missed the stolen moments after her chores were done, when she could sit and rest without Mama scolding her. Missed the taste of the sharp, snow-edged wind at twilight, knowing the world would look entirely different by morning. Even the groaning pipes and tiny soot-crusted windows of their family's apartment on Factory Row.

A part of her desperately hoped they would be sent home. That she could return to their small, shabby apartment. But she knew that would only delay the inevitable separation from her family.

It struck her that she might spend the rest of her days like this: trapped in a beautiful room waiting for Serina to return, her own life a footnote. Unremarkable. Invisible. Forgotten.

Her eyes burned with unshed tears. She glanced around, self-conscious, but no one was paying attention to her. Maybe if she splashed some cold water on her face, took a moment to herself, she'd feel better.

She made her way out into the hallway in search of the lavatory. With each step, the tightness in her chest lessened.

As Nomi rounded a corner, the interior of a room caught her

eye. Deep upholstered chairs, a finely patterned rug. And endless bookcases of rich mahogany, stacked toweringly high with bound volumes edged in gold. *Books.* More than she'd ever seen in her life. Before Nomi could fully grasp what she was doing, she strode toward the room. She paused outside the half-open door for as long as she dared, listening for movement. Then, with a deep breath, she slipped inside.

The whole world opened up before her. Rows and rows of bookshelves climbed to the ceiling. The scent of pipe smoke hung thick in the air. Nomi breathed deeply, letting the room's stillness, its promise, wash over her. On trembling legs, she sidled up to the shelves and ran tingling fingers across the thick leather spines. The gold-leaf titles shone in the low light. She traced the words, many of them unfamiliar to her. Her hand caught on a slight volume nearly swallowed between two thick black tomes. She gasped in recognition. *The Legends of Viridia.*

Immediately, a memory rose in her mind. The autumn Nomi and Renzo had turned twelve, he was given this same book of legends to study, and she'd demanded to know what it said.

It was against the law for women to read. It was against the law for women to do almost anything, really, except birth babies and toil in factories and clean the houses of rich men.

But Nomi couldn't let it go. And Renzo couldn't resist showing off what he knew. Slowly, surely, he had taught her to read.

It had been the best few months of Nomi's life. They'd spent their nights hunched by a guttering candle as Nomi haltingly read and reread the story of the moon and her lover, the terrors of the deep, and—her favorite—the tale of two brothers driven apart by a mysterious tattooed woman with a golden eye.

Only Serina knew their secret. Renzo once asked if she wanted to learn too. But Serina preferred to be read to, the same stories over and over, while she practiced her embroidery. When spring had come and Renzo's school had exchanged the book of legends for one of math equations, Nomi and Serina had continued to tell each other the stories from memory. But it was never quite the same.

She drew the book from the shelf, caressing the embossed letters on the cover. It was made of the same soft leather, only without the battered corners and bent cover. She hugged the book to her, remembering every night she and her brother had pored over the pages, teasing out the pronunciation and meaning of each word.

This book was home to her, more than the palazzo and its fine furnishings could ever be.

She couldn't bear to leave it behind. Surely no one would miss a small book of stories. It slipped down the front of her dress so quickly, so easily, she could almost convince herself it had been the book's desire, not her own. She hurried into the corridor, arms crossed protectively over her chest.

She was nearly back to the gallery when two men rounded the corner right in front of her.

The Heir and his brother.

Nomi bowed her head and waited for them to pass, arms tightening over the hidden book.

"—should be up to *me*, not the magistrates," the Heir was saying, anger edging his words. He stopped speaking when he saw her.

Nomi should have curtsied. She should have kept her head

down, like any other handmaiden. But she was caught off guard, unprepared, and without meaning to, she met his gaze.

The Heir's eyes were deep brown and held a silent intensity. He stared at her as if he could puzzle out her history, her secret hopes, everything. With one look, he laid her bare.

Cheeks burning, she finally tore her gaze away.

"Who are you?" Malachi demanded.

"Nomi Tessaro," she murmured.

"And what exactly are you doing here, Nomi Tessaro?" The Heir's voice filled with suspicion.

Nomi bowed her head. "I'm—I'm a handmaiden. I was just . . ." Her voice petered out. She couldn't remember what she was supposed to have been doing. The book burned through her skin.

"Come on, Malachi, we're late," Asa said, running an impatient hand through his hair. His black suit shadowed Malachi's white one, down to the gold embroidery, but there was something more relaxed, almost untidy about him.

Malachi ignored his brother and stepped closer to Nomi, his muscled frame trapping her against the wall. "You were just what?"

The attempt at intimidation had the opposite effect. Nomi bristled, a familiar, instinctive fury momentarily squashing her panic.

Her spine straightened. She lifted her chin and faced the Heir's steely gaze with one of her own. Defiance radiated from her in waves. "I was using the lavatory," she said clearly. "It's just there," she added, nodding toward the other end of the hall, "if you need to go."

Asa snorted, but the Heir did not look amused. His cheeks flushed an angry red.

Horror rose, bitter at the back of Nomi's throat. She dropped her gaze. Serina had asked her to behave. And she couldn't, not even for ten minutes. The audacity of what she'd just said . . . the expression the Heir had no doubt seen in her eyes. . . .

"You may go," Malachi said at last, but it sounded more like a sentence than a reprieve.

Nomi scurried into the gallery as the men continued on their way, her heart beating a panicked rhythm. The sharp edges of the book she'd stolen dug into her skin.

She hurried to the corner where she'd left her bag, and slipped the book in among her things. She was almost certain the Heir hadn't seen it. But her impertinence had been damning enough.

The rest of the evening she waited, eyes pinned to the open doorway, wondering when her world would end.

THREE

SERINA

SERINA'S FIRST BALL was almost exactly as she'd imagined. The long, gleaming ballroom teemed with movement, the prospective Graces as glittering and colorful as a school of fish. The mirrored walls and endless gold filigree caught the light of a dozen crystal chandeliers. Musicians sat in a corner by a wall of arches leading to the terrace, their fingers flitting so fast across their instruments Serina couldn't follow them.

It was a far cry from her cramped living room, where an instructor had taught her to dance with Renzo as her partner. They'd had no music—only the dogged beat of the instructor clapping his hands.

Here, the sparkling music curled and spun, and Serina twirled and smiled in the arms of the Superior's finely dressed dignitaries, thrilled to be at the center of the glamour, one of the glittering, colorful fish.

But there was a flaw in the fairy tale. The Heir didn't appear. When the musicians took a short break, Serina slipped into a corner to catch her breath. The strain of her corset against her lungs had become suffocating. As she rested, she scanned the ballroom. It wasn't hard to pick out the Superior's Graces. Unlike the prospects, they moved as if they wholly belonged, taking the attention in stride. Several posed on tall, circular platforms, draped in shining purple satin, raised up—literally—as the epitome of female perfection. Serina stared at them, awed by the control it took to stand so perfectly still.

She had been groomed for this, her training beginning before she was old enough to truly understand a Grace's role. From the moment she first danced across the dusty floor with Renzo, the weight of expectation was upon her shoulders. Even then she knew that being chosen would change her family's fortune, that it was the highest honor for any girl in Viridia, that it would allow her mother—nearly blind from years of squinting over her sewing in the factory—to finally stop working. That it would allow her brother to someday afford a bride.

Most important, she could keep headstrong Nomi by her side. Nomi was smart, *too* smart: too challenging of authority and the rules. Where Nomi was a dreamer, Serina was a realist, and she would do everything in her power to keep it that way—protecting Nomi's fiery spirit and her safety at the same time. Nothing scared Serina more than the thought that her sister might someday take too great a risk, and be caught.

Nomi didn't see this chance as a gift, but Serina did. She wanted more than anything to become a Grace and keep Nomi by her side as her handmaiden.

A girl paused next to Serina, her floral dress swishing delicately. "It's all quite incredible, isn't it?"

Serina appraised the girl with a quick glance: soft features, pretty blue eyes, hair a peculiar blond-silver that almost seemed to shimmer in the low light.

"I've never seen anything like it," Serina replied. She scanned the room again. Surely the Heir was about to make his entrance.

"*I've* never seen anything like your dress," the girl said. "Did your mother make it for you?" It took Serina a moment to recognize the barb hidden in the girl's sweet voice.

She smiled benignly. She wasn't about to admit that her mother *had*.

"It's so . . . *interesting*," the girl continued. "In Bellaqua, no one's worn blue in years." She cast a glance across the dance floor.

Serina followed the girl's gaze. It was true; the room was a sea of pinks and purples and yellows. And most of the gowns were full length, some heavy with brocade. More formal than her calf-length, swirling dress and golden sandals.

Serina raised her chin and said with a casual shrug, "I suppose that's lucky for me, then, seeing as blue is the Heir's favorite color." It was a lie, of course; Serina had no idea what his favorite color was. But the flabbergasted look on the girl's face was worth it. Serina walked away, leaving the girl gaping.

A sudden ripple of excitement passed through the ballroom. Serina turned in time to see the Heir arrive at last, with his brother beside him.

The Heir surveyed the ball, his eyes picking out each of his prospects. Serina lowered her gaze long before his scrutiny reached her. A handful of prospective Graces drifted closer to him. Ines appeared at his side. The girl who'd talked to Serina

21

hurried toward them, but Serina stayed where she was. She didn't want to cluster in with the others and risk being lost in the crowd. Instead, she made her way to the terrace to watch the last streaks of sunset stretch across the sky. The light was lovely, rich and golden, and she knew it would make her skin glow.

Far below the terrace, the canals shimmered with the pink and orange of the fading light. Serina had heard stories about Bellaqua her whole life. Perched at the southern tip of Viridia, the capital was the royal family's stronghold and its greatest achievement. The first Superior had designed it to resemble an ancient northern city that had been destroyed in the Floods. Seeing it herself for the first time, she couldn't deny the city's beauty; but it also had a cold quality to it—untouchable, removed.

Ines reached her at last. "Malachi, this is Serina Tessaro, of Lanos."

Serina turned away from the balustrade and dipped into her lowest, most graceful curtsy. As she straightened, she raised her gaze just to the Heir's lips, which were full and soft in contrast to the hard lines of his jaw. It would be impolite to meet his eyes.

"I am honored to be here and eager to serve you, Your Eminence." She smiled.

"Serina Tessaro? That's your name?" he asked, with a gruffness she wasn't expecting.

She bowed her head gently, just as she'd been taught, like a flower nodding in the wind. "Yes, Your Eminence," she replied, then shifted slightly so the light would fall just so along her cheekbones.

"Dance with me," he ordered.

A bolt of nervous heat shot through her. "I would be honored, Your Eminence."

His hand closed around hers, and he drew her onto the dance floor, where the musicians were beginning a fast, wild song. She spun away from him and then back into his arms. As Serina dipped and twirled, it was impossible to miss the envious stares of the other prospects. Her feet flew through the steps of the dance, and her skin prickled everywhere the Heir touched.

"You're from Lanos?" Malachi asked when the music slowed. She expected him to move on to the next girl, but he didn't. Instead he pulled her closer. He smelled delicious, like spun sugar and spiced wine.

"I am, Your Eminence," she replied. "Up in the mountains. It's still cold this time of year."

"You live with your parents? Brothers? Sisters?" By now, they were barely moving, just the slightest sway to the beat of the music. His hands were on her hips, his heat passing through the filmy layers of her dress.

"Parents. A younger brother and sister. My sister's here with me as my handmaiden, Your Eminence."

The song ended, and this time the Heir released her. The warmth of his hands remained long after he let go, imprinted against her skin.

She curtsied again, unable to contain her smile. "Thank you for the dance, Your Eminence."

"It was my pleasure," he replied. Then he wove through the other dancers and disappeared from view.

As Serina returned to her spot on the terrace, she ran through every sentence, every touch, analyzing her performance. He'd seemed engaged. He'd held her close. She'd kept to the flattering light. For the first time in a week, since they'd begun the long journey from Lanos, Serina felt her shoulders relax. She'd done her job. Done it well, even. Maybe he *would* choose her.

And if he did?

A slow smile bloomed across her face. He was just as handsome as she'd imagined.

A murmur ran through the ballroom, pulling her from her thoughts. She scoured the dance floor with her gaze, searching for the Heir. But it was all dignitaries and Graces, no sight of his white jacket anywhere. A few of the prospective Graces were glaring at her.

The realization shot through her like the last rays of the sun: Prince Malachi had left for the evening, and she was the only one he'd asked to dance.

————————

As the prospects returned to the waiting area, Serina barely had a moment to catch her breath before Nomi was upon her. She grabbed Serina's arm and dragged her to a corner half-hidden by a massive plant in a painted urn. She looked anxious, and a little bit ill.

Serina squeezed both of her hands, hoping to calm her. "It's okay," she said breathlessly. "It went well—even better than I'd hoped. We have nothing to worry about."

Nomi looked pained rather than relieved, but before Serina had a chance to ask what was wrong, Ines entered the room and a hush spread over everyone. "My flowers," she began. "The Heir was greatly pleased to have met all of you. Your unparalleled beauty and poise made his choice very difficult, but after a consultation with the magistrates from your provinces and much consideration, he has made his decision.

"Once I've announced those chosen, I'll show them to their quarters. The rest of you will remain here while we arrange for your transportation back to Bellaqua's central piazza, where your families are waiting. Those of you staying with us, your families will be notified of your good fortune. And you may, of course, send a message to them as soon as you wish through the palazzo's scribes."

Serina squeezed her sister's hand. The time had come. Her old life was ending, and her new one was about to begin. The other girls shifted and whispered to their handmaidens. Serina's pulse fluttered in her throat.

"Maris Azaria, the Heir has chosen you."

Serina searched the crowd of girls, but it wasn't hard to find Maris—she burst into tears, hugging her arms close to her sparkling pink dress. Her straight, waist-length black hair flowed forward to curtain her face. Whether they were tears of joy, Serina couldn't tell.

"Two more," she whispered to Nomi. Two more chances.

Ines waited until the room settled. "Cassia Runetti, you have been chosen." She nodded to a girl near the dais.

It was the girl who'd spoken to Serina. Cassia's delicate jaw went slack, her eyes widened, and then she laughed out loud, her silver-blond hair rippling. Serina could tell that her dress was of very fine quality, as were her precariously high heels. She was probably from one of the wealthy eastern cities, like Sola or Golden Isle.

The other girls shifted and whispered to their handmaidens. Only one name left. When Ines cleared her throat, Serina held her breath.

"The Heir's final Grace will be . . . Nomi Tessaro."

A weight lifted from Serina's shoulders in a great rush. *I did it!* The thought filled her with relief and joy. But, she realized, they'd made a mistake. She smiled at Ines. "It's *Serina* Tessaro, actually."

The older woman shook her head. "No, my flower. You were not chosen," she said, her words dropping into the wondering quiet of the room. Every gaze turned toward Nomi.

Serina's vision went spotty; she was holding her breath again. Ines stared straight at her as she said, "Your handmaiden was. Your sister. *Nomi* Tessaro."

The room erupted with voices raised in confusion and anger.

Serina stared at Ines, then her sister, her heart beating a frantic rhythm. Nomi's eyes were wild, and her hair was escaping its long braid. Her simple brown dress was hiked awkwardly up on one hip, making the hem uneven. Even here, dressed in her nicest clothes, Nomi looked as untamable as ever. A girl who hated everything about the Graces and what they represented—and now she was one of them.

FOUR

NOMI

NOMI SWAYED, UNABLE to breathe. This was a mistake. How could this possibly *not* be a mistake?

All around her, people were moving. Some prospects had started to cry. Others were glaring at her. Ines headed for the door, followed by the other newly chosen Graces and their handmaidens.

Ines turned back to give her an impatient look. Woodenly, Nomi bent to pick up her bag. Serina grabbed it out of her hand.

"But I—"

"Nomi, you're a *Grace* now," Serina hissed. She headed for the door.

Nomi followed because she couldn't think and she didn't know what else to do. *I am not a Grace.* This was a hallucination. A fever dream.

A nightmare.

Ines led them down the corridor, the opposite direction from the library.

"What happened?" Serina muttered. Her cheeks were stained a violent red.

"I don't know." Nomi rubbed at the skin of her neck. It felt as if it were stretched too tight. Choking her. "Is this even allowed? Signor Pietro chose you, not me."

"It is the Heir's will." The snap of Ines's voice silenced them both.

Nomi faltered, nearly tripping on her own feet. She'd been rude to the Heir. Defiant. He'd *known* she was a servant, and somehow out of a ballroom full of beautiful women, he'd chosen *her*?

Nomi wasn't flattered. She was terrified.

Ines led the group of girls down endless corridors, up several staircases, until the blood was humming in Nomi's ears and she could barely breathe without gasping. At some point, Serina grabbed her arm, maybe to hold her up.

They finally came to a set of double doors carved with huge peonies and twisting vines, guarded by a man in a black uniform. He swept open the doors for them, his expression blank.

Inside, golden light warmed a circular room, edged in gilt and ivory. Marble archways gave hints at the labyrinth beyond. Each was framed by spidery ferns set in painted urns. In the center of the room, cream divans were piled with crimson velvet pillows. One of the new Graces, Cassia, sighed and clasped her hands at her chest.

"We meet here before events," Ines said. "And this is where the Heir's emissary will wait for you if you've been summoned to see him alone."

Nomi swallowed hard. Lending elegance to functions at the

palazzo was not a Grace's only job. She and the others would be expected to please the Heir privately as well.

Nomi fought back a wave of nausea. She was supposed to serve Serina, not the Heir. That's what she'd prepared for, all those years Serina was learning to dance and play the harp.

She hadn't prepared for this. She didn't *want* this.

"Our chambers are extensive," Ines continued. "You are allowed to enjoy the gardens and beaches of the palace, but you're not to wander beyond these rooms without an escort. I can arrange such excursions for you. Once in a while, we venture into Bellaqua, but only on special outings that the Heir or the Superior has arranged.

"As Graces, it is our job to please, but it is also important to lift each other up. We *need* each other here. You'll see that." An odd undercurrent ran through Ines's words, but Nomi was too overwhelmed to decipher what deeper message—if any—the woman was trying to give.

Ines led them into a maze of sitting rooms decorated in pale yellows and pinks, with heavy damask curtains and delicate furniture. Arched doorways led to tiled bathing areas, wide balconies with marble balustrades, a large dining room, and massive walk-in closets full of the most beautiful gowns and negligees the textile workers in Lanos could create. Nomi knew just how precious these clothes were; her mother, and others like her, had worked themselves to the bone to make them. Serina had told her that the Graces lived in luxury, but this was beyond anything she had imagined.

In each room, groups of Graces played Saints and Sailors or embroidered, silently overseen by men in white livery. Nomi had no doubt these men listened, watched, and reported back to the Superior. Some of the Graces walked along the terraces, or spoke quietly over tiny cups of steaming espresso. Despite the dozens of women she saw, the endless rooms remained quiet and serene, unmarred by laughter or raised voices.

Nomi hated it all. The excess. The silence. The fake smiles the women wore, even here. She could have survived in this world as a servant—invisibility had an element of freedom to it—but she would never be able to school herself to serenity the way these Graces did. The way Serina could.

By the time Ines showed each Grace and handmaiden to their respective rooms, Nomi was wobbling with exhaustion, overfilled with questions that threatened to spill out into the silence.

"There are refreshments in your rooms," Ines said. "Someone will wake you for breakfast. Handmaidens, I'll introduce you to our Head Maiden in the morning. She'll explain your duties." Her eyes narrowed on Nomi. "I assume your sister will become your handmaiden? Otherwise, a handmaiden can be assigned by the palace."

Nomi's tongue stuck to the roof of her mouth, dry as sand, but she managed a choked "I want Serina."

At last, the sisters were alone. Their bedroom was cool, a steady breeze slipping in from the open window. A feather bed had been set underneath it, its thick golden drapes doubling as window curtains. Candles flickered on the dressing table, scenting the room with rose and vanilla. A plate of fresh fruit and bread rested beside the candles. Outside, the crescent moon hung near the horizon, its reflection dancing along the restless ocean. On this side of the palazzo, only the endless water was visible, instead of the city's gleam and glitter.

Nomi turned to her sister. She had so much she wanted to say, but it was all trapped in a tight knot in her throat. She sank to the edge of the bed.

"What happened?" Serina bent down and yanked her sandals off, pulling savagely at the straps.

Nomi's eyes filled. "I was in the hallway . . . and the Heir and his brother rounded the corner. They were right there, right in front of me, and—" She broke off, took a deep breath, and then continued haltingly. "They caught me off guard, and I—I didn't mean to—I said something I shouldn't have."

"Oh, Nomi. How could you?" Serina's reply was harsh.

And of course she was angry. Nomi had never gone this far before, never put them so much at risk. Nomi punched her fist into the soft bedding. "I wish I'd never seen him. It was just such a shock. Especially, well, especially because . . ." Reluctantly, she retrieved the book of legends from their bag. Serina would be furious, but it was better to lay everything out now so they could work through it. Come up with a plan. "There's this too."

Serina's whole body stilled. Her sandals dangled from her fingers, forgotten. "Where did you get *that*?"

"There was a library near the lavatory. I saw it, and I just . . . I went in. It was amazing. There were so many books, bookshelves to the ceiling. . . ." Nomi's eyes glazed over just thinking about it.

"So you what? Thought you'd take one for yourself?" Serina's voice shook with rage. "This is so much worse than what you've done before. Speaking your mind, sneaking out of the house . . .

31

that was bad. But *this* . . . carrying a book through the halls of the palazzo as if there wouldn't be hell to pay. . . . Did the Heir see it?" Serina's anger turned to panic.

"No. I had it hidden." Nomi swallowed against the lump in her throat, shame boiling in her veins. "But my impertinence was bad enough. I expected *punishment*, not—not this. . . ."

"It doesn't matter what you expected." Serina opened the tiny armoire next to the handmaiden's cot and threw her shoes inside. They thudded hollowly against the wood. Nomi flinched. "You caught his attention. You are a Grace now. Congratulations."

Nomi's tears spilled, burning her cheeks. "I didn't *want* this. This isn't a *prize*, Serina. We should have a *choice*!"

"This *was* my choice," Serina blazed.

"*No.*" Nomi's heart wrenched. "It isn't a choice when you don't have the freedom to say no. A yes doesn't mean the same thing when it's the only answer you're allowed!"

"You are so naive." The fire snuffed from Serina's eyes. She reached back to fiddle with the clasps of her dress. Nomi hurried to help her, releasing the tight laces of her sister's corset.

Serina pulled off her clothes and put on one of the threadbare nightgowns from Nomi's bag. Then she sank onto the handmaiden's cot. "I can't believe this happened."

"If you can't bear it, go home," Nomi said. Her heart ached for her sister, but that didn't mean she understood her. Why wasn't she *relieved*? Nomi slipped out of her dress and pulled on the other nightgown. "You don't have to be my handmaiden." The thought sent icy spears of fear through her. She wanted Serina to stay. She needed her sister if she was going to survive here. "For once, you have a choice."

"You see *this* as a choice?" Serina laughed bitterly. "I love you, Sister, as maddening as you are. I would never leave you to face this alone."

"Father would find a wealthy man to marry you," Nomi persisted. "You could have children."

Serina stretched out on the cot and closed her eyes. "I won't leave you," she said again, with finality.

Nomi's heart ached with fear and regret. She glanced at the bed by the window and then at her sister. More than anything in the world she wished they were back in their small room in Lanos, curled in the bed side by side. "Do you want to sleep up here with me? There's plenty of room."

But Serina turned onto her side, her back to Nomi. Her meaning was clear: She wouldn't abandon her sister, but she hadn't forgiven her either.

Nomi climbed into bed alone.

All night, her breath strained in her lungs as if her chest were bound in iron.

I am a Grace.

FIVE

SERINA

BY THE TIME dawn broke, Serina was already dressed, bleary eyed and hungry, listening to the Head Maiden talk about how to return dirty dishes, what she was allowed to request from the kitchen for Nomi, and where to find the supplies to clean the bedroom. Each handmaiden also had tasks assigned for the common areas—dusting, sweeping, sending clothes out for cleaning—the list went on and on. Serina spent the lecture staving off panic. She reminded herself that she was a quick study. She could learn to be a handmaiden, just as she'd learned to be a Grace.

The Head Maiden led Serina and the other new handmaidens to a large room filled with hundreds of dresses, shelves of shoes, and trunks of fine lingerie. "Find clothes that will suit your Grace," she ordered. "There are a variety of sizes; anything that needs to be altered should be brought to my attention so I can schedule a fitting with our seamstresses." She opened a door at the far end of the room, revealing a small annex lined with shelves. "You'll find your uniforms here. You may each take three sets. Once a week, you may send them out for cleaning."

Serina walked through the rows of fine clothes, letting her fingers drift along the silk and lace. She picked out a soft green dress that would complement Nomi's skin tone, and a black gown shot through with silver thread. She piled dress after dress onto her arm, hugging the fine fabrics close, thinking of her mother.

Mama Tessaro had pushed Serina so hard, since the first moment she'd realized her daughter would be a beauty. She'd never allowed Serina to doubt herself or her ability to do what was necessary to become a Grace. Never let her lower her guard, raise her gaze, be anything but graceful and obedient and poised. While Mama's focus was so tightly set on Serina, she'd missed who Nomi had become.

She'd missed Nomi's outrage that she wasn't allowed to go to school when Renzo did. She'd missed Nomi's rebellious streak, her belief that she deserved the same treatment and rights as her brother, who'd been born minutes after her. Nomi had wanted to be Renzo, had wanted the freedoms of Renzo's life. If Mama had realized, Serina wasn't sure what she would have done. Punished Nomi privately at home or, worse, turned her in. But Mama Tessaro had only seen what she wanted to see: Serina's beauty. Nomi's usefulness.

Serina had seen, though. She knew her sister had learned more than how to be a handmaiden. But Nomi had never learned how to be a Grace. It went deeper than the dancing and embroidery and harp playing. Nomi had never learned the temperament of submission.

Not as Serina had.

He should have chosen me.

Serina grabbed three uniforms for herself and stacked several pairs of shoes on top. Back in the bedroom, she hung the dresses carefully in their armoire, laying a flowing flowered dress out on the foot of Nomi's bed. Then she shook her sister's shoulder.

Nomi woke slowly, and as she sat up, Serina could see the dried tears that stained her cheeks. She knew Nomi had been awake most of the night; Serina had heard her shifting and sighing. A part of her wanted to hug her sister, to hold her close and tell her everything would be okay. But she was still too angry, her pride too raw.

"We need to clean you up," Serina said briskly. She headed for their small lavatory, returning with a warm, damp cloth to clean her sister's face.

"It wasn't a dream," Nomi said. It wasn't a question, but her wide eyes tracked Serina's face, begging her to contradict it.

Serina shook her head. "No, it wasn't."

Nomi's eyes reddened, as if she were about to cry again.

Serina prodded her toward the washroom. "You have breakfast on the terrace in fifteen minutes, and then a dress fitting."

"I need a minute," Nomi said, rubbing her forehead. "I—I don't think I can eat."

"It's not optional." Serina thrust the floral dress into her sister's hands.

Nomi had always been the one to help Serina into nice dresses, do her makeup, fix her hair. Everything felt alien now. Serina couldn't give herself time to think about it.

Nomi stared at the dress. "I can't wear this. It's practically transparent."

"It's not. It's tasteful." Serina put her hands to her hips. "You're not a servant anymore. You have to dress to entice. You have to—"

"I don't *want* to entice," Nomi countered. "I would never wear this dress."

"Maybe not, but *I* would," Serina stated flatly.

A charged moment passed, and then with a huff, Nomi did as she was told. It was a little big, but Serina wound a length of ribbon around Nomi's waist, up under her breasts, and tied it behind her neck. The makeshift halter accentuated her sister's curves.

"I can hardly breathe," Nomi complained.

"I haven't taken a full breath in years," Serina snapped. "You'll get used to it." She donned her own dress, plain brown with a white apron. The fabric was scratchy and the color hideous.

When she sat Nomi down before the vanity and opened the cosmetics bag, Nomi reached for a stick of kohl. "I'll do it," she said. "You don't know how." For years, Nomi had been the one to do Serina's makeup.

"You'll have to teach me." Serina couldn't help studying her sister's reflection in comparison to her own, wondering what had tipped the scales in Nomi's favor. Her sister's clear amber eyes held more fire than Serina's darker brown ones, but Serina's skin was flawless, her hair shining and thick. Nomi's cheeks had a ruddy tinge, and her lips were pressed tightly together, thinning them. She looked tired and anxious, and so very young.

"Play up your eyes," Serina ordered. "They're your strongest feature." She sat down on the end of the bed. She was probably supposed to make up the sheets, tidy the room, but she watched Nomi do her makeup instead.

When Nomi finished, she made a face at Serina in the mirror. "I look ridiculous in this much makeup."

"You look fine." Serina got up and brushed out Nomi's hair. The ends were dry, and the rest needed a tonic to brighten it. But it was thick, like Serina's. She helped Nomi curl it into a demure bun at the nape of her neck. Then Nomi insisted on braiding Serina's hair.

Now they looked their parts: Serina the handmaiden, Nomi the Grace.

They wore matching, miserable frowns.

"Go," Serina said. "I have to clean up."

Nomi didn't move. "Serina? I am so, so sorry."

Serina's heart cracked at the fear in Nomi's eyes. She knew she should say something reassuring, that she should stop being so cold. But she was dealing with their new reality too.

With a sigh, she said, "I know."

Nomi's gaze fixed on something over Serina's shoulder in the mirror. She turned, blanching. Serina followed her gaze and saw it. The book, sitting on the bedside table, where anyone could see it.

Serina shot Nomi a look as she hurried over and snatched it up. "You need to hide this. Or dump it out the window. It's dangerous, Nomi."

Serina held out the book, but when she saw the cover, she hesitated. Why did it look so familiar? She sank to the bed and ran a hand across the letters. Nomi sat down beside her. "It's the book of legends. Same as Renzo's. I saw it and I couldn't help myself. Everything is so different here, and seeing it . . . I felt like I'd found a piece of home."

Despite herself, Serina softened. She remembered those secret nights when Nomi and Renzo had read to her, their voices bright as candle flames, wards against the dark. Serina opened the book and found the first story. "'The Lovebirds,' right? It was always my favorite."

Nomi smiled. "You had me read it to you so many times, you memorized it."

Serina's face fell as she stared at the words she couldn't read. The past pushed at her, a weight on her heart. "I wonder if I still remember?"

Nomi smiled. "Try."

Serina closed her eyes, sending herself back to the candlelit corner of Renzo's room. "Long before our ancestors' ancestors were born, there was no land here," she murmured, the memory still living in her mind. "Viridia didn't exist, and the ocean washed unceasingly across the wide expanse of nothingness, with no shore to throw itself against, no rocky cliffs to force—"

The bedroom door opened. Serina's eyes flew open, the words still falling from her mouth: "—a break."

"Nomi, you're supposed to be " Ines stopped abruptly, staring at Serina, at the book in her hands. One of the white-clad men stood right behind her. "What are you doing?"

"We were . . ." Serina began, and then faltered. What could she say?

The Superior's man stepped forward.

"Come with me, Serina," Ines said, her face hardening.

Serina slid off the bed, the book dangling from her hand. The man snatched it away.

"Wait," Nomi said frantically. "You don't understand. It's—"

But before Nomi could finish, Serina was torn away, her hands grasping at empty air. As the Superior's man hauled her from the room, she twisted toward Nomi. She fought against the hand on her arm. Fought for one last glimpse of her sister.

Nomi hugged herself as tears streamed down her cheeks. She looked too small in that big room by herself, dwarfed by the huge, curtained bed. Serina realized she'd never seen Nomi without someone by her side—Renzo or Mama, or Serina herself. Nomi had never before been so painfully, inescapably alone.

With a thunderous crash, the bedroom door slammed shut between them.

———

Serina waited for word of her punishment in a small, dim room in the depths of the palace. She thought it unlikely the Superior would let her remain as Nomi's handmaiden. But perhaps, after a probation period of some sort, maybe he'd be willing to reinstate her. Or maybe he'd have her flogged and let her continue her duties.

Serina had never dreamed she'd pray for a flogging.

She hadn't revealed that the book was Nomi's, or that Nomi could read. Ines had already caught Serina in a compromising position. All it would do was bring them both down.

If I'd hidden the book right away—

40

If Nomi hadn't stolen it in the first place—

The pointless ifs circled through her mind, dogging her as she paced the small room.

"Serina Tessaro." A tall man in green unlocked her door. "The Superior will see you now."

Her heart stuttered and lurched.

She followed the man into a part of the palace far from the Graces' chambers, but even so, Serina couldn't help glancing through doorways and around corners for Nomi.

At last, the servant slowed. She expected a receiving room, something imposing. But instead, he led her into a small room lined with bookcases.

The library.

The Superior sat in a leather chair near the window. His face had a grayish tinge, and he was so thin, his bones looked as if they were trying to tear through his skin. But his eyes burned.

"Serina Tessaro," he said, his voice an icy wind. Gooseflesh rose along her arms. "My Head Grace says you can read."

Serina dropped her gaze to the tiled floor. She couldn't move, couldn't respond. Could barely breathe. He'd said nothing threatening—yet—but he watched her like a falcon would. Like she was prey.

"Who taught you?" he asked, a little fire creeping into the ice.

"No one," Serina whispered.

The Superior shifted, and Serina heard the pop and crackle of his bones grinding against each other. She swallowed down bile. "Your father? A cousin?"

Oh, Nomi. What have you done?

Serina shook her head miserably. She had to say something.

She had to lie. She couldn't let him punish her family. "I—I taught myself," she stuttered. "I stole books."

For a moment, the room was silent, the only sound a faint crash of waves from outside the open window.

Leather creaked as the Superior sat back. "Like you stole mine."

Serina hung her head, terrified. In this moment, every breath the Superior took felt like an arrow, and she was the target.

"And your sister? Does she share . . . your proclivities? Sisters often share, I'm told."

Mutely, Serina shook her head. Part of her wanted to say yes, to let Nomi face the consequences of her choices. But she couldn't do that to her sister. It'd only mean they'd both be punished. "She can't read, Your Eminence. She didn't even know I could until today. Please . . . please. She had no part in this."

"Hm." For a few minutes, the Superior said nothing.

Serina couldn't bear to look up, couldn't take the even hiss of his breath, in and out. In and out. She prayed.

A flogging, please, a flogging.

But before the Superior even announced her sentence, instinct told her it would be so much worse.

SIX

NOMI

NOMI PICKED UP her bag and threw it furiously across the room. The sickening thud of it hitting the wall made her cry harder, consumed by fear for herself and her sister. Her empty stomach churned. She climbed onto the bed, into the indentation still left in the cloud-light bedding by Serina's body. She curled up, squeezed her eyes shut tight, and tried to block out every shred of harsh morning light, every thought. Every regret.

But instead, her sister's voice came back to her. *Long before our ancestors' ancestors were born, there was no land here.*

One night a year or two ago, Serina had told the story just for the joy of it. They'd been curled up in one of Mama's quilts on the floor of their small bedroom. Renzo was supposed to be studying his sums, but he was listening too, leaning back on his elbows, legs stretched out so they touched the far wall.

"One evening," Serina had recited from memory, her recent singing lessons coating her voice with honey, "as the sun eased toward the horizon and the moon rose from its slumber, two birds flew along the path made on the water by the setting sun. They dipped and sagged, their battered wings barely holding them aloft. Every now and then, one would falter and fall toward the water, all strength gone. The other would dive and catch the first on its back, carrying its partner for a time.

"The two birds traveled this way for many leagues, until the path of the sun had faded and the moon's silver road appeared. The ocean shimmied and danced beneath the birds, intrigued by their obvious love for each other. The ocean had never loved anything so much, to burden its own back with another's survival. It didn't understand why the birds didn't fend for themselves—the stronger leave the weaker and carry on.

"It took the ocean some time to understand that apart, the birds would never have made it so far," Serina had continued, wrapping an arm around Nomi's shoulders. "That their love, their sacrifice, gave them both strength. When at last, the two little birds, their bright red and green feathers tarnished from their long journey, could no longer hold themselves free of the endless water, the ocean took pity on them. Rewarding their steadfastness, it pushed land up from its depths—huge, lush hills with fresh, clean water, towering cypress trees, and all the fruits and berries and seeds they could ever desire. The lovebirds alighted in the shady, cool branches of an olive tree, their tired wings wrapping around each other, their beaks tucked into each other's feathers. And at last, they were able to rest."

Back then, it had only been a story, but now she felt it in her bones. Serina loved her that much—enough to sacrifice herself for her sister. Serina could have said it wasn't her book. She could have said *Nomi* was the one who could read. But she hadn't. She couldn't have, or they'd have come for Nomi too.

She didn't know what had happened to Serina or if her sister would be back. But Nomi knew Serina had protected her, as she always did. Nomi made the mistakes. Serina cleaned up the mess.

Nomi tightened her arms across her stomach, locked in misery and guilt.

At some point, she fell back asleep, the sheet damp under her cheek from her tears, and dreamt of her sister's arms holding her up.

When she awoke, someone was leaning over her.

"Serina?" she murmured hoarsely.

"It's time to get up," a gentle voice said. "You've slept all day."

Nomi sat up quickly, reality crashing over her.

The girl stepped back to give her space. "I'm sorry," she said. "I didn't mean to startle you." She was about Nomi's age, with a slight frame, lightly tanned skin, and a small, pointed face. Her tawny hair dangled in a braid down her back, and she stood with her hands clasped together at her waist. There was nothing remarkable about her, nothing of note, except that she wasn't Serina.

"I'm Angeline, your new handmaiden," the girl said, bowing slightly. "I've brought you some food. It's well past luncheon." She pointed to a plate of pastries on the dressing table. "The almond spirals are my favorite. Have you ever had one? They're a Bellaquan specialty."

Nomi looked around, disoriented by the late-afternoon sunlight slanting through the room. The clothes from her bag had been folded and neatly placed on an upholstered chair in the corner. A light breeze drifted in the open window. The steady crash of waves hummed in the background.

It all made her sick—the beautiful room, the comfortable bed, even the lovely weather. She felt Serina's absence like the loss of a limb. How would she survive here without her?

"Where's my sister?" she asked.

Angeline shook her head. "I don't know, I'm sorry. . . ."

Nomi surged to her feet, determined to find Ines—or someone who *would* know—but the sudden movement sent a patina of color exploding before her eyes. She swayed.

"You should eat," Angeline said. She tentatively put her hand on Nomi's arm, drawing her toward the dressing table. "Ines said you missed breakfast as well. You must be famished."

Nomi sank into the delicate wrought-iron chair. She wanted to reject the food, the pale pink juice in its chilled crystal glass, but she hadn't eaten since the morning before. Nomi took a bite, the buttery cornetto melting on her tongue. Angeline retired to just outside the half-open bedroom door to give her privacy. For an instant, it felt as if the handmaiden were a guard, and Nomi's room a prison.

The pastry turned to dust in her mouth, and she struggled to swallow it. She needed to find out where they'd taken Serina and what was going to happen to her. Nomi had never heard of a woman being caught reading before; she had no idea what the punishment was. But surely *someone* knew. Serina might be sent to a work camp, or ordered to a factory. Best case, they might let her continue working in the palace in a punishing, menial job. Then at least Nomi could be near her.

She stood slowly, to avoid another dizzy spell, and headed for the door. "Angeline," she said. "I'd like to speak to Ines."

Angeline lowered her gaze. "I'm sorry. I'm to take you to get cleaned up."

Nomi opened her mouth to protest, then closed it again. She couldn't very well storm down corridors demanding to know what had happened to Serina. It wouldn't help her sister to draw attention to herself. She'd have to wait for the right moment.

"Fine," she said.

Angeline led Nomi through several empty sitting areas and along a terrace, eventually entering a large room with a vaulted ceiling made of glass, girded with delicate swirls of metal that glinted in the late-afternoon sunlight. A large pool of gently steaming water was sunk into the slate-tiled floor. In the face of such luxury, all Nomi could think of was the small, stained tub in her home, with its creaky pipes and two minutes of hot water a day. Serina had always bathed first—those two minutes had been hers.

Nomi struggled not to cry.

The two other new Graces sat neck-deep in the water as their handmaidens knelt at the edge of the pool to brush out and wash their long hair. In the corner by the door, one of the Superior's men stood with his back to the room, giving the illusion of privacy.

After Angeline helped remove her wrinkled dress, Nomi lowered herself into the shallow pool, sighing as the warm water enveloped her. While the handmaiden assembled a dizzying array of soaps and lotions, Nomi dunked her hair under the water.

"Ah, our little recluse," Cassia, the blond one, said when Nomi surfaced. "Missing meals and training on our first day? You're not worried the Heir will hear of it?"

"No," Nomi bit out. What did it matter if the Heir was displeased? She had bigger concerns. "My sister, Serina, was taken away this morning. Have you seen her? Or heard anything?"

Cassia affected a concerned frown, her gentian-blue eyes widening. "There were rumors of an . . . incident. Someone said she'd been removed from the palazzo."

Removed.

Had they sent Serina back to Lanos? Nomi imagined her arriving home in disgrace. Their parents would shun her. Her prospects for marriage to a wealthy man would evaporate. She'd probably be contracted to the textile factory. Only Renzo would be there to comfort her, but even he would be powerless to help her.

"Who told you that?" Nomi asked.

Cassia shrugged, sending ripples along the surface of the glowing pool. "One of the Superior's Graces. Rosario seems to know everyone's secrets here."

"Not everyone's," Maris muttered. The girl's black hair was swept back, revealing broad cheekbones, ivory skin, and luminous brown eyes. When she noticed Nomi looking at her, she said, more clearly, "Rosario didn't know if your sister was ill, or if she'd done something wrong. Is she okay?"

A sharp pain slashed through Nomi's stomach. She wished she knew. But at least Maris's concern sounded genuine, unlike

Cassia's. "Serina is not ill," was all Nomi could say. Angeline silently soaped up her hair, her presence a reminder that, wherever Serina was, she wasn't coming back. Not soon, anyway.

"What a relief," Cassia said sweetly. She shook out her silver-blond hair, the droplets stinging Nomi's face, and climbed from the bathing pool. "But then," she added, cocking her head as if she'd just thought of it, "that means she did something wrong, doesn't it?"

Nomi didn't answer, holding her anger in check with an effort. Cassia smiled quite happily as her handmaiden set her robe across her shoulders.

When the girl had left the room, Nomi bent forward, put her face in her wet hands, and groaned. "Why is she so delighted with all of this?"

"She believes she'll gain from your scandal," Maris said. "The Heir will choose a favorite, and Cassia hopes it will be her. She has set her sights on becoming his Head Grace."

"You mean she wants to give birth to the next Heir?" Nomi shuddered. How could that be someone's goal? "She may have him, and welcome."

Maris's dark eyes flashed, but before she could respond, Nomi caught a glimpse of Ines passing by the doorway.

Nomi hurried out of the pool, splashing Maris in her haste. Angeline scrambled after her with a robe.

"Ines, wait!" Nomi's voice echoed too loudly.

Ines paused in the hallway, frowning.

"You have to tell me—" Nomi began.

Ines grabbed Nomi's arm and pulled her down the corridor. Eventually, she stopped in an empty sitting room. The last rays of daylight slanted in through the open windows, which she promptly shut.

"You may *not* challenge me," Ines said sternly. "There will be no shouting after me, no questions. *Especially* where the Superior's men can see. Do you understand?"

"What happened to my sister?" Nomi demanded, undeterred.

"Let it go. You're lucky the Superior didn't punish you too," she said.

Nomi *should* have been the one punished. It was *her* book. Her crime. "The book . . . it wasn't—" she began, tremors snaking through her body.

"Your sister took responsibility for her actions," Ines interrupted. "Nothing you say will change her fate."

"But—"

"*Nothing*. It is done." Ines's eyes filled with an unspoken warning. If Nomi told the truth, Serina would be exposed as a liar, and that held its own punishment. "Now all *you* can do is stop asking questions and follow the rules. This is your life now, whether you like it or not."

Then she disappeared through the doorway, leaving Nomi, shattered, in her wake.

SEVEN

SERINA

THE BOAT PITCHED, slamming Serina and the other prisoners hard against the slippery metal rail. Her body ached from the constant push and pull on her bound wrists, which were fixed to a rusted ring just below the rail. Tears joined the film of seawater on her cheeks as she twisted to watch the glow of Bellaqua shrink behind her.

She'd expected the Superior to punish her; a woman reading was a serious offense. But she hadn't expected *this*.

Nothing felt real, except for the pain in Serina's arms and the cold ocean spray burning her face. All her life, she'd been afraid of what Nomi's rebellion might mean. A broken law, a merciless punishment.

Serina had never imagined, not once, that *she* would be the one led off in chains.

Nomi's crime had cost her everything.

The girl beside Serina was crying so hard, her gasps sounded like choking.

One of the guards paused on his rounds, right behind the sobbing girl. "Shut it, or I'll throw you overboard."

The girl tried to be quiet, but she couldn't quite manage it. The guard reached for her. Serina's shackled hands strained toward the girl, as if somehow she could stop whatever was about to happen.

"What, you can't handle a little crying?" a rough-edged voice called from down the line. "Obviously she's terrified. Isn't that what you want? To scare us? Punish us?"

The guard rushed down the slick deck, growling, "I'll punish *you*."

But as he reached her, he went down, landing hard on his back.

Serina craned around and caught a glimpse of brown skin and a defiant glare.

"Try," the girl said. "You wouldn't be the first. But I didn't back down before, and I won't now." She held her ground, even when the guard stumbled to his feet and backhanded her across the face.

Serina and the rest of the prisoners watched in awe. Women didn't speak like that to men. They didn't stand up for themselves. *Or . . . or they ended up here*, Serina thought, stomach sinking.

The crying girl's sobs rose again, the gagging sounds more pronounced this time. The guard turned to her.

Desperately, Serina bumped the girl's arm. "Hey. What's your name?"

The girl shook her head, wiping her dirty face against her shoulder.

"Talk to me," Serina cajoled, watching the guard from the corner of her eye. "It'll distract you."

"Jacana," the girl said, just loudly enough to be heard over the deafening pulse of the boat's steam engine.

"Pretty name," Serina said. "That's a kind of bird, right?"

The girl nodded, her wild hair whipping against her bone-white cheeks. Her breathing was ragged, but her sobs had subsided.

"I'm Serina."

The girl nodded again, a little color returning to her face.

Something out beyond the ship caught Serina's eye. Faint at first, folded into a blanket of cloud. As they approached, an island emerged, gray and scarred. A black mass rose from its center and disappeared into the pink-tinged haze. A volcano.

Like every other child in Viridia, Serina knew the story of Mount Ruin. Long ago, the island had been called Isola Rossa. Its coasts had been home to expensive retreats for Viridia's wealthy, designed to look like royal buildings that had been destroyed in the Floods. When the volcano had erupted, sending endless waves of lava and fatal gases pouring down upon the lush beachfront buildings, thousands had been caught in the cataclysm. Most had died, buried under lava and ash, choked by the poisonous air, or drowned off the unforgiving coast.

Isola Rossa had become Mount Ruin.

The island had been abandoned, a blackened memorial to the many lives lost, until the current Superior's father had reclaimed it as a prison for women. Serina had always assumed those sent here were the most depraved of Viridia. She'd never, even in a nightmare, dreamed she'd be one of them.

The boat slammed into a chipped stone pier, the impact driving the prisoners to their knees. Jacana cried out. Serina's voice

53

was caught in her chest, trapped between her laboring lungs and pounding heart.

The guards went down the two lines of prisoners, releasing their restraints from the rusted rings. Serina's hands dropped like rocks, still weighted by the shackles.

She stared at her wrists as if they belonged to a stranger. A week ago, she'd been confident that she could charm the Heir, that she could make her mother proud, that she could secure Nomi and herself a future in the palace. Nothing had happened as she'd expected. How many shocks would it take before her heart could bear no more?

"Straight forward, single file," one of the guards barked. The other two shifted several full burlap sacks onto a rusty cart that shrieked as they pushed it onto the pier.

Serina took a wobbly step onto shore and looked up at her surroundings. There was no beach, just jagged cliffs with a treacherous path carved into the rock. On the headland, an ugly stone building stood sentinel, surrounded by barbed wire.

"Move along." One of the guards cuffed Serina on the shoulder, and she stumbled, her feet catching on the uneven ground. Here, the earth was frozen into strange black waves, like the mountain had melted. The building they approached was cut right into the otherworldly rock, with heavy, warped-glass windows and wide iron bars.

Even the wind was different here; instead of sighing, it screamed.

The guard pushed her again, through the door and into a hallway that smelled of urine and stale smoke. In front of her, Jacana slowed to a stop, still weeping. The guard raised his arm to strike her, but Serina gave her a nudge to keep her moving. It was all she could do: Move forward. Pray her heart kept beating.

At last, they shuffled into a windowless room. The guards lined the women up with their backs against the far wall. A collection of rusted tools hung on the right wall; the left was hidden by shelving stacked high with clothes and water-stained crates.

The boat guards handed off their paperwork to a group of black-uniformed prison guards. A tall, muscled man entered, and the boat guards tipped their heads to him, saying, "Good evening, Commander Ricci," in reverential tones as they left.

The Commander's weathered face and massive stature made him look as immoveable as the cliffs outside. He gestured to the line of women. A younger guard hurried forward, his angular face twisted into a frown. One by one, he unlocked their shackles.

Serina sucked in a breath when the heavy metal rings clinked open. She rubbed her sore wrists. Angry marks marred the smooth skin.

When everyone was unbound, Commander Ricci ordered them to strip. "Put your clothes in a pile in front of you. Slippers too."

Serina's hands shook as she unzipped her handmaiden uniform, wrinkled now from the night she'd spent in it, waiting in a small locked room down at the wharf for the prison boat to come in. The dress dropped to the floor.

She'd never been naked in front of a man before. She shivered, her body raw and vulnerable.

The angular-faced guard went down the line again, collecting the clothes as Commander Ricci inspected each prisoner, one by one. Serina had no idea what he was looking for. When it was her turn, he told her to open her mouth, raise her arms, and turn around. But she couldn't move.

He grabbed Serina's arm and jerked her forward, his fingers digging into her flesh. "Are you deaf? Open your mouth, raise your arms, and *turn around.*"

Serina straightened and somehow managed to do as he said. But she couldn't help the tears that silently spilled down her cheeks.

Had her sister guessed the punishment she was courting, when she'd asked Renzo to teach her to read? When she'd stolen that book? Serina didn't think so. Nomi had probably thought she was risking a flogging. Maybe a fine.

She'd been so *stupid.*

By now, most of the other women were crying too. Jacana sidled closer. Serina noticed the girl who'd spoken out on the boat standing a few feet away. She looked a couple years older than Serina and was much thinner, her brown body taut with muscle. The girl kept her gaze pinned to the guards, black eyes blazing. Serina expected someone to reprimand her for her disrespect—or punish her for what she'd done on the boat—but none of the guards paid her any attention. Maybe they didn't notice.

The narrow-faced guard handed out scratchy towels and a handful of clothes to each of the prisoners. Serina donned the underwear, faded blue pants, and threadbare shirt as quickly as she could. It took far less time to get dressed when there weren't corsets, endless rows of buttons, fragile lace, or high heels to contend with.

"I'll call you forward for in-processing," Commander Ricci said, his craggy face revealing little beyond bland indifference.

There was something in his eyes, though, an occasional too-quick move of his head that suggested he was paying close attention.

"Anika Atzo."

The muscular girl stepped up to the scale. The name fit her, all hard edges. This time, she kept her mouth shut.

When it was Serina's turn to be weighed and measured, the guard manning the scale let out a low whistle. "It'll take *you* a while to starve, flower."

Serina stared hard at the floor, arms crossed over her chest. Her mother had gone to great lengths so Serina would grow up soft and curvaceous, as befitted a Grace. Even Renzo and her father's portions of food had been smaller than Serina's.

The man elbowed another guard. "Want to guess how long she'll last? An extra bag of rice crisps says—"

"I don't wager on dead girls," the younger guard interrupted, speaking with a bored conviction that jarred Serina into looking up. He was tan and clear-eyed, with dark hair that curled up along the rim of his hat as if trying to escape. She could sense his cool appraisal without meeting his gaze. "Send her to the Cave," he said. "That'd be interesting."

"Not the Hotel?" the other guard mused.

The young guard shrugged. Serina had no idea what they were talking about, but their words filled her with fear. The guard in charge of the scales checked something off on his paperwork.

"The Cave it is," he said, waving Serina on.

As Serina followed the other women out of the room, the younger guard's deep voice murmured, almost gently, "Welcome to Mount Ruin, Dead Girl."

EIGHT

NOMI

THE DAY AFTER Serina was taken away, Nomi woke long before the sun rose, her sister's absence dogging her dreams. As she lay in the silent dark, she imagined she was home in the bedroom she'd shared with Serina. Their two narrow beds pushed close together, the pipes hissing gently along the ceiling, Serina's dresses looking like shadowy dancers clustered in the corner, where Mama had hung them on a wire because there was no closet. But the illusion faded quickly. The shapes hunched in the darkness of this room were all wrong. And Angeline, sleeping in the cot by the door, didn't hitch an extra breath every few minutes, or shift to her side and sigh the way Serina did. She wouldn't crawl into bed with Nomi when it was cold or comfort her when she woke from a nightmare.

The question of where Serina was, what punishment she'd endured, was a weight on Nomi's heart, heavy as a boulder. With every passing hour, it threatened to crush her. If she knew, Nomi could daydream of escape and reunion with her sister.

Nomi shifted in the bed. Ines had said to stop asking questions, to play by the rules. But Nomi had always asked questions, and she'd *never* wanted to follow the rules. It was why she knew how to read in the first place. It was, presumably, how she'd caught the Heir's eye.

Surely *he* knew what had happened to Serina, she realized with a start. And perhaps, if she found the right moment, she could persuade him to tell her. She'd figure out a way to impress him, to become valuable to him. . . .

She swallowed, panic rising. There was an obvious way. But it was something she couldn't bear the thought of. Serina may have been prepared to *entice* the Heir, but Nomi was not. She'd grown up assuming she would be a factory worker or a handmaiden, bound to a job rather than a master. Not having a choice for her future was bad enough, but being forced to please a man. . . .

She'd made the mistake of thinking she would avoid that fate, at least.

Nomi had resolved to stay as far from the Heir as he let her. Remain unwilling. Force as much distance as she could. Cassia wanted the Heir's attention, his affection, and she was welcome to it. But what if pleasing him meant discovering what had happened to her sister? Could she do it?

The question twisted through Nomi's mind without answer.

When the first threads of sun unraveled across the windowsill, Angeline stirred, and their day began. Nomi let the handmaiden help her into a flowing, lily-patterned dress. She sat quietly while Angeline brushed her hair and twisted it up into a nest of braids and ribbon, accented with several silver butterfly pins. Nomi looked into the mirror and frowned, feeling as if she were facing a stranger.

She'd spent so much time looking at Serina's face, and little time contemplating her own. But now Nomi could see, with brutal clarity, all the ways Serina had been prepared for this life and how she had not. The dullness of her hair compared to Serina's sleek strands. The way her wide, dark-lashed eyes looked combative rather than demure.

She didn't belong here.

When Nomi was as polished as Angeline could make her, the handmaiden led her to a long wicker table on a terrace overlooking the ocean. Maris and Cassia were already seated at one end, picking delicately at their plates, piled high with colorful fruit and soft cheeses. Baskets of cornettos dotted the table.

The Superior's Graces took up the rest of the long table. The Superior didn't seem to have a specific standard of beauty: Some Graces had dark skin, others ghostly white. They had brown hair, blond, black. Curly, straight. The women ranged in age from midforties to a year or two older than Maris and Cassia. The Superior had been collecting his Graces for a long time.

At seventeen, Nomi was easily the youngest here. You had to be eighteen to be considered as a Grace. But those were the Superior's rules—apparently his son could break them.

If only I had the same privilege, she thought mutinously, lowering herself into the empty chair beside Maris. She reached for a pastry without enthusiasm. Cassia was turned toward the girls sitting on her other side, listening avidly as they gossiped about the Superior.

"But the foot massages, Rosario!" one of the younger Graces was saying.

A woman with deep brown skin and tight curls, presumably Rosario, shuddered. "It's like rubbing blocks of ice wrapped in rice paper."

Nomi glanced at the woman with guarded interest. Rosario was the Grace who knew everyone's secrets.

"Is the Superior very sick?" Cassia asked, inserting herself into the conversation.

Rosario shrugged delicately. "He's sick, but he's stubborn. I'd say there's still life in him yet."

"What happens to all of you when he dies?" Maris asked, her voice expressionless.

Rosario shot a look at the girl across from her. "Cheerful, this one."

Nomi glanced at Maris. Maybe it was an odd question, but not an unreasonable one. The last Superior had died before she was born; no one ever talked about what had happened to his Graces.

"Do you know?" Maris asked, not letting it go. "Will you stay in the palace, or be sent home?"

Rosario shrugged, but a shadow passed across her features. "It will be the Heir's choice. When his father dies, he will decide what becomes of us."

Nomi's eyes widened. There was so much about this world she didn't know.

Rosario noticed Nomi's look and nudged the girl on her other side, smirking, her good humor apparently restored. "Did we all look that stunned when we were chosen?"

Embarrassed, Nomi dropped her gaze to her plate. She stabbed at a piece of melon.

"Don't worry, flower," Rosario said, her honeyed voice teasing. "You've got time to get used to it here. It's mostly dress fittings and dance lessons until the Heir's birthday. That's when the fun really begins. I wonder which of you he'll choose to celebrate with?"

"Maybe all three?" someone else suggested, laughing.

Cassia sipped her espresso, a little smirk on her face. Maris looked stony-eyed out to sea.

"Why does the fun begin on his birthday?" Nomi asked.

Cassia arched a brow. "Don't you know? That's when our positions become official. There's a ceremony and everything. The Heir won't consummate"—she said the word with a purr—"his union with us until then. The girl he chooses to entertain him that night is the one to have first chance at becoming Head Grace. Just look at Ines. She was one of the Superior's very first Graces."

Nomi's face flamed. She knew if Serina were in her place, she'd be competing with Cassia to have the Heir's first male child and become his Head Grace. But the thought made Nomi's stomach turn. Still, she saw value in becoming Head Grace. When the Superior died, Ines would have the comfort of knowing her *son* would decide her fate.

Rosario leaned forward. "Ines isn't just the Heir's mother; she's the second-born son's as well. She's a legend."

Cassia's eyes lost focus as she, presumably, imagined a similar life for herself.

"Do Graces raise their own children?" Nomi asked. She

couldn't remember anything from Serina's lessons about it; then again, she'd never paid close attention. She'd always been elbow-deep in laundry water or scalding herself on the stove.

Rosario looked at her like she'd sprouted another head. "Raise children? Do you see any children here?"

Cassia rolled her eyes. "That's what nursemaids are for."

Nomi had never felt a desire to have children, and yet a strange surge of grief still gripped her at the thought that if she *did*, they would be taken from her. Did Ines ever look at her sons across a crowded ballroom and yearn for those lost moments? Those lost years?

"I heard Malachi will be hosting a masquerade ball for his birthday," Rosario shared.

The girl across from her grinned eagerly. "Really? A masquerade? Those are always delicious."

The Graces reminisced about other masquerade balls, other Grace ceremonies, but Nomi stared at her plate of fruit and pastries, lost in thought. Serina filled her mind, every worry and fear leading back to her. Was she okay? Was she hurting? Did she hate Nomi for stealing the book?

Nomi swallowed around the lump in her throat. Of course she did. All of this was Nomi's fault.

Ines stepped out onto the balcony. "Good morning, Graces," she said. Her gold-flecked dress sparkled in the late-morning sunlight. "The Superior has requested the presence of Eva, Aster, and Rosario at luncheon. There's a concert this evening for a delegation from Azura. His Eminence requests only his most senior Graces to attend. Ysabel, you are to play the harp." Down the table, a woman in her thirties with coppery-red hair nodded. Ines turned to Nomi and the other new Graces. "The Heir has requested an audience with each of you today," she said. "While you're waiting your turn, I'd like you to go through your gowns with your handmaidens and set aside the ones that need altering." She eyed each girl in turn, ending with Nomi. "You're first."

Nomi gulped down the piece of bread caught in her throat. "It will be my pleasure," she managed.

She didn't miss Cassia's look of envy as she stood up and followed Ines inside.

Ines took Nomi down a long tile corridor to an ornate wooden door carved with crashing waves and leaping fish. "Don't ask about your sister," she said before opening the door. "It will not please him."

Nomi nodded, but felt a flare of defiance. "So what *should* I do?"

Ines looked at her as if the answer were obvious. "You do whatever he says."

She opened the door and nudged Nomi into Malachi's rooms.

The large sitting area flowed to a wide balcony. Through an open doorway to her right, she caught sight of a massive bed. Heat crept up her cheeks.

"Good afternoon, Nomi," the Heir said, rising from one of two leather chairs arranged in the center of the room. His tall muscled frame filled the space. He wasn't close enough to touch her, and still she felt his presence pushing toward her, stealing all the air from the room.

"Good afternoon, Your Eminence," she echoed, with a

wobbly curtsy. Her hands clenched the fabric of her dress too tightly. Just seeing him brought her fury to the surface. His ancestors were the reason women weren't allowed to read to begin with. His father was the reason Serina wasn't here. He was the reason Nomi *was*.

Malachi said nothing, and Nomi stared at the ankles of his linen pants with a fixed attention so he wouldn't see the hatred in her eyes. How could she hope to please this man, even to find out what had happened to Serina? She could barely look at him.

"I'm sure you didn't expect to be chosen," he said finally.

Nomi swallowed back a bitter laugh. "No, I didn't." She added, "Your Eminence," a beat too late.

"You do not seem pleased with your good fortune," he rebuked her, crossing his arms over his chest. A whisper of fear unfurled in Nomi's belly. She couldn't afford defiance now. She belonged to him; he could do whatever he wanted to her.

He could hurt her.

"I am honored to be your Grace," she said, somehow managing to say the words without grimacing. "I—I only wish my sister could be here. She knows what's expected of a Grace. I—I do not."

At the mention of Serina, Malachi turned away abruptly, stalking to the terrace. After a moment, Nomi followed him uncertainly. Malachi stared over the railing at Bellaqua's stone bridges and gondolas. It was uncanny, the way the Superior's palace perched between the city's canals and the sea, like a great ship, isolated and forbidding.

"I will be riding out to inspect Bellaqua's troops tomorrow,"

Malachi announced. "I will be gone for two days. Shortly after I return, my Graces will attend the Premio Belaria with me. You are behind the others in your training and appearance. I expect you to catch up in time for the event, when you will appear publicly at my side for the first time."

"Of course, Your Eminence," Nomi replied, caught between disappointment and relief. His trip would mean more time without news of Serina, and no opportunity to persuade him to share what he knew. But it also meant time free of his unnerving presence. It meant she would have time to make a plan. Hopefully one she could live with.

"What is the Premio Belaria?" she ventured. If it were some kind of ball, she was doomed. She couldn't learn to dance properly in two days.

"It is a horse race," he said shortly. "The most famous in Viridia."

"Ah," she said faintly. No dancing, at least.

"Do you ride?" he asked.

"Horses?" she asked, surprised.

He nodded.

"I've never had call to, Your Eminence," Nomi replied. *Silly question*, she thought. Only the wealthiest wives and daughters were taught to ride.

The tips of his ears turned pink. "Of course."

"Do *you* enjoy riding?" she asked, for once managing to be polite.

"I do," the Heir replied. His voice softened slightly as he added, "My horse, Bodi, has been with me since he was foaled. I broke him myself."

Nomi didn't know what he meant by that, but the word *broke* sent a thread of ice down her spine. "'A man's worth can be found in the value he places on both man *and* beast.'"

"What did you say?" Malachi shifted toward her, his eyes narrowing.

Nomi's breath caught in her throat. *Stupid*. It was a line from Renzo's book of legends: from the story of a poor farmer who impresses a rich merchant when he sells a precious heirloom not to feed himself but to feed his horse. Malachi must have recognized it. She scrambled to cover her misstep. "It's—it's something my brother used to say a lot, Your Eminence," she said. "Have I displeased you in mentioning it?"

Malachi shook his head. "It's from a book I read a long time ago. That line, in particular, struck me."

Nomi knew that in her place, Serina would turn the conversation back to more superficial topics. But she couldn't seem to hold her tongue. "My brother liked that story. He said it was about valuing all life equally. Man, beast . . . woman." She met his eyes.

"Do you think I value only my own life?" He was so close to her that his breath feathered against her face.

"I wouldn't presume," Nomi replied. She'd tried to make her tone innocuous, but from the way Malachi's eyes narrowed, it was obvious she'd failed.

"You . . ." he said, stepping a little closer. Too close. "You have a good deal to learn."

Nomi shivered under the intensity of his gaze. His eyes were a cinnamon brown, with amber flecks that sparkled in the light. She wished she could break free, run, hide away from the unnamed feelings suddenly coursing through her.

He raised a hand, and she stumbled back a step.

But he didn't strike her, only gestured toward the door. "You may go."

Nomi curtsied and crossed the room on watery legs, still feeling under threat.

NINE

SERINA

INSTEAD OF TAKING the prisoners to cells, as Serina expected, the guards led them outside. Then they opened the prison gates with a tooth-rattling shriek. The sun had fallen to just above the horizon, swollen and sickly red. For the first time since she'd left Lanos, Serina longed for its cold, jagged mountains and smokestacked factories.

She spotted Jacana's small form and headed to her side. "Where are they taking us?"

Jacana wrapped her arms around herself. "One of the guards said this building is just for processing. That we live . . . out there." She nodded toward the desolate rock outside the gate.

"Out *there*?" Serina echoed, horrified. *The Hotel, the Cave* . . . were those other prison buildings? Beyond the fences and barbed wire?

Anika came up beside them. "What'd *you* do to end up here?" Her gaze raked Serina from head to foot. "They'll eat you alive."

Serina knew she looked different from the others—her skin buffed and polished, her body soft. "I stole something," she said calmly, burying her fear so deep it didn't show. "Something from the palace." No one needed to know the truth.

Anika narrowed her eyes.

"What did *you* do?" Serina asked.

"I killed someone," Anika said, her voice hard. But a shadow passed across her face so fleeting Serina almost missed it.

A guard by the gate yelled, "Everyone assigned to the Hotel, come forward."

Anika left the compound with four other women.

Serina watched until the girl was out of sight. "Where'd they put you?" she asked Jacana, who still huddled nearby.

"The Cave," Jacana said to her toes.

"Me too," Serina said, relieved. "At least we'll be in the same place."

Jacana straightened a little. Serina wondered what had brought her here. What crime could this tiny, terrified girl possibly have committed?

"The Southern Cliffs, come forward!" the guard yelled. Another group of women disappeared.

Then, "The Cave!"

They followed two other girls through the tall gate. In whispers, the girls introduced themselves as Gia and Theodora. The guard pointed to a couple of women waiting outside, backlit by the last dregs of the setting sun. "Follow them," he said.

Somehow, Serina found herself leading the way through the gate.

The women watched them approach. The shorter of the two was maybe forty, with a wide plain face, sun-reddened skin, and heavy brows. "I'm Cliff," she said when Serina and the others reached her. "This is Oracle. She's in charge of the Cave."

Serina's breath hitched in her throat. A fellow prisoner was in charge? A *woman*? How was that possible?

Oracle regarded the small group of girls in silence. One of her eyes was brown, the other a strange, filmy white. She was a little younger than Cliff but no less intimidating.

"Follow close. We won't wait for you," Oracle said. Without another word, she turned and led them down a rocky trail along the cliffs. They followed in the footsteps of the other groups, the distant flicker of torchlight guiding them. Oracle hiked quickly, Cliff following with ease.

Serina tripped, her flimsy shoes catching against the rough volcanic rock. "Shouldn't there be a guard with us?" Serina hazarded. "Isn't there—"

Cliff's barking laughter cut her off.

"Please," Gia mumbled, swiping at the sweat coating her forehead, "could we have a sip of water? They didn't give us any food, or—"

"You won't want to eat before," Cliff said. "Probably not after either."

Before? After? What was about to happen?

Serina trudged next to Jacana, her mouth dry with fear. They followed the winking torches, down along the headland to the beaches and behind a broken building with the sprawling memory of grandeur. Lights glowed from glassless windows.

A cracked marble fountain stood in the center of the courtyard, the blind eyes of its female dancers staring toward the volcano.

Cliff nodded toward the building. "Hotel Misery."

A shiver crawled down Serina's spine.

The rumble of voices rose over the roar of waves. Serina could at last see their destination, out beyond the hotel. A massive semicircle of stone, ridged into seats, faced a stage with a tall building behind it. Lava rock spilled over one entire side. A half-destroyed amphitheater.

Serina thought of the hours she'd spent practicing the harp, waiting for the day when she'd perform in front of the Heir. She couldn't guess what was performed on this stage.

More than a hundred women filled the stone benches or sat on the swaths of frozen lava. Serina stared at face after face, but she didn't see a single smile. Her chest tightened.

Oracle led them to a section of seating in the center, where twenty or thirty women clustered. Then she went on alone, gripping a couple of women by the shoulder as she made her way to the stage. Around its edge, ten women gradually assembled. Oracle stood next to a tall woman with a strip of bright red hair down the center of her head, the rest of her skull shaved clean.

Serina stared fixedly at the woman's head. In Lanos, girls were not permitted to wear their hair shorter than their shoulders, but most preferred to keep it waist length or longer, as a point of pride. *Such a stupid thing to think about now.* Serina swallowed.

Guards crowded onto the balcony of the building behind the stage. She couldn't tell how many, as some disappeared into the shadows, but she suspected there were forty or so, far fewer than the women filling the amphitheater.

Cliff eyed Serina and the other new girls, her thick brows drawing low over her eyes. "Whatever happens, don't cry," she ordered. "The guards will watch for weakness. They'll use it to their advantage. Don't give them any power over you. Do you hear me?"

"What exactly is happening?" Serina asked, trying to keep her voice steady. The tension in the air pressed against her, making it hard to breathe.

Cliff stared down at the stage. "The first time, it is better not to be prepared."

Commander Ricci stepped onto the stage. The amphitheater quieted in an instant. The man's body language was relaxed, authoritative, but his hand didn't leave his firearm. All along the balcony above him, guards drew their weapons and pointed them into the crowd.

"Fighters, take your positions," Ricci ordered.

Fighters?

Five women stepped onto the stage, including the woman with the red hair who'd been talking to Oracle. Commander Ricci disappeared into a stairwell that led to the balcony.

No one moved. No one spoke.

Serina watched with wide eyes, uncomprehending.

A few moments later, Ricci reappeared at the edge of the balcony. He was holding a wooden crate. He let it drop as he shouted, "Begin!" When it hit the ground, the wood cracked apart with a sound like an ax hewing firewood. A coil of thick black tubing flopped out. Only . . . it wasn't tubing. It didn't stop moving, slowly uncurling over the shattered scraps of wood. Serina gaped as the snake's head lifted, testing the air.

One of the girls tried to stomp on it, but she missed its head. It twisted and struck her on the ankle. She screamed. Time seemed to slow. One second. Two seconds. She crumpled, her leg swollen, as the rest of her twitched sickeningly. Another woman grabbed the tail of the snake and swung its head down against the hard floor, again and again, until it hung limp and unmoving from her hands. The other women met in the center of the stage, their fists and knees and elbows flying.

Serina's heart went into freefall. Women didn't fight. Ever. Not against men, not against each other. Violence always earned the strictest punishment. Serina knew stories of women who'd tried to defend themselves—a distant cousin who'd fought back against an abusive husband, a girl in the textile factory who'd slapped a man when he tried to kiss her. Those women had been severely punished. Flogged, imprisoned. Sent to Mount Ruin or a prison like it. How was this allowed in the very place that was meant to contain such behavior?

Another woman groaned as someone kicked her in the knee. Serina closed her eyes. She covered her ears. She curled into herself. This couldn't be happening. This couldn't be real.

The thuds and shouts were muffled, the darkness behind her closed eyes absolute. For a few minutes, she let herself recede. She lived in the thud of her heartbeat and shush of her breath.

Then a sharp, pain-filled scream carved a hole into the black, rising from beyond her cocoon. Serina's breath froze. The sound slid into an agonized moan and petered out. For a second, there was silence. Then she heard the unmistakable, horrifying sound of applause.

TEN

NOMI

IN THE HALLWAY outside the Heir's chambers, Nomi leaned back against the heavy door, the curve of a leaping fish digging into her spine. His expression as she'd left the room haunted her. She tried to steady her breathing.

Ines hadn't waited for her. Nomi turned down the hall in the direction she'd come, but somehow she never found the short flight of stairs they'd ascended. She kept walking, the impulse to get away overwhelming, even though she had no idea how to return to the Graces' chambers.

The hallway eventually ended at a wall of glass, some partitions pulled back to reveal a wide terrace overlooking the ocean. A cool breeze slipped into the hallway, caressing Nomi's cheeks. Drawn forward by the soothing wind, she approached the marble balustrade, gripped the hard stone in her cold hands, and closed her eyes.

Homesickness ate her hollow. She missed her mother's soft voice, her father's gruff pride. Renzo's mischievous support of her little rebellions. For years, she'd been his shadow, and he'd been her voice of hope. But most of all, she missed Serina. Nomi had always known she'd have to say goodbye to her parents and her brother someday. But she and Serina were supposed to stay together.

"You look like you need some time to yourself," a young man's voice said, "so I am loathe to interrupt, but I suspect you are lost."

Nomi's eyes snapped open. Mortified, she stepped back from the railing, the world of the palazzo rushing over her, the glare of late-afternoon sunlight bleaching out the soft glow of memory.

In a cushioned chaise a few feet away, the Heir's younger brother lounged. Her eyes immediately went to the book in his hands, navy leather with the title, *The Feasts and Follies of War*, embossed in gold. Curiosity flared through her, until she realized Asa was waiting for her to speak.

Flustered, she backed away, curtsying awkwardly as she went. "I'm s-sorry to disturb you, Your Eminence," she stuttered. "I did get a bit turned around. I'll leave immediately."

Asa stood up and followed her, the book still cradled in his hand. "Wait, wait," he said, reaching out his other hand. "I'll help you find your way."

"Please don't trouble yourself, Your Eminence. I'm sure I can "

"It's no trouble at all," he interrupted with a smile.

With bowed head, Nomi followed him into the hallway. The Superior's second son was as tall as his brother but not as muscular, and his shaggy hair gave him a more relaxed air, very different from his brother's brooding intensity. The back of his neck was tanned, as if he spent a lot of time outdoors.

"You're one of the new Graces, aren't you?" he asked as they walked.

"Yes, Your Eminence. My name is Nomi Tessaro."

"Ah, Nomi. Of course," Asa said, shooting a look over his shoulder at her. She couldn't be sure, but there seemed to be a new interest in his expression. A sharpening. "You came to the palazzo as a handmaiden, right?"

She stiffened, expecting derision. "I did, Your Eminence."

"This must be very different for you," he said kindly. Her tense muscles eased a fraction. "Where are you from?"

"I'm from Lanos."

He slowed until they were walking side by side down the gilded hall. She lowered her gaze to the marble floor. "I remember visiting the mountains north of Lanos as a child," he said, his voice softening. "It was the first time I ever saw snow."

"I've always loved the way snow can transform things," Nomi said. "Old, broken buildings, dirty streets—the world can become bright and pristine in the space of an afternoon."

Asa's voice turned rueful. "I admit, I was more interested in making snowballs than admiring the scenery. Though in my defense, I was seven."

Nomi smiled at her feet. "Completely understandable, Your Eminence."

"And how are you adjusting to life here?" he asked. "Are you satisfied with your new role?"

Her face fell, and the fleeting moment of connection was broken. She wondered if these questions were a test, like everything else here seemed to be. "The palazzo is beautiful, and I am very happy to be here," she said dutifully, even as her cheeks flushed with anger.

He glanced at her again. "It must be difficult, with your sister gone."

Nomi's breath froze at the mention of Serina. Her feet froze too, tripping on the hem of her flowing dress. Automatically, she reached out to steady herself, and gripped Asa's arm. He turned to face her, steadying her. For an instant, they stood still in the middle of the hallway, holding each other.

Nomi let go of his arm and stepped back, face hot. "Pardon me."

Asa cleared his throat. "I apologize. I shouldn't have brought up your sister. I didn't mean to upset you."

He looked so much like his brother, but the features that looked hard on Malachi were softened on Asa. Nomi leaned a breath closer. Maybe she could ask him—

A door ahead of them swung open, and Ines emerged.

Asa turned to face the Head Grace. Nomi's question died in her throat.

Ines curtsied, her eyes narrowing as she noticed Nomi standing beside Asa. "Hello, Your Eminence."

"I found your wayward Grace," Asa said cheerfully, erasing any tension lingering in the hall. He stepped out of Nomi's way.

"I'm sorry," Nomi said, keeping her head down. "I got lost."

Ines nodded and ushered Nomi inside. But Nomi slowed, glanced over her shoulder, watching until Asa rounded the corner and disappeared from view. She ignored Ines's stern look as she headed for her room, deep in her own thoughts.

Maybe the Heir wasn't the only way to find out about Serina. As she thought of Asa again, the hint of a smile curled her lips.

ELEVEN

SERINA

THE RED-HAIRED WOMAN from Oracle's crew won the fight. When Serina finally opened her eyes, the women around her were pumping their fists in the air, and the rest were standing silently as their leaders dragged the fallen fighters from the amphitheater.

"Are they—are they dead?" Serina whispered.

Jacana swallowed, her small face ghostly pale in the torch-light. "Most of them."

Cliff came to collect the new girls, leading them out of the amphitheater with the others. She held a flickering torch aloft to light their way.

"What *was* that?" Serina hissed as they walked. Her hands shook, and her teeth chattered. What she'd just seen, what she'd heard . . .

Cliff shot her a glance. "There isn't enough food for everyone. The Superior doesn't care if we live or die." She spit into the darkness. "So we fight."

Jacana whimpered.

"Fight? For food?" Serina asked, her voice cracking. "Why do the guards allow it?"

"Allow it? They're the ones who started it. The guards watch and cheer, even bet on who will win." She bared her teeth, her voice bitter. "We are their *sport*."

Serina remembered the Superior's dignitaries passing her around on the dance floor. Not caring who she was or what she said as long as she smiled. It hadn't bothered her then. "But this—"

"There are five camps on this island. Whenever a boat comes in, each camp must choose someone to send to the ring. Only the winner's crew gets rations." Cliff climbed over a broken boulder. "Tonight, our champion won. That means we eat well tomorrow. The rest of the crews will have to scavenge the island for whatever they can find until the next haul of prisoners arrives."

Serina swallowed back a wave of revulsion. "How do the guards decide who wins?"

Cliff raised a brow, as if the answer were obvious. "Didn't you see? The winner is the one who lives."

"We have to kill each other?" Jacana's voice broke in, a high, terrified squeak.

Cliff didn't spare her a glance. "Cowards can submit. Be exiled from their crews. But most of those who fight and lose prefer death. It's quicker than starving."

Serina's eyes burned with unshed tears. When she had opened Nomi's book, she'd done it so innocently. A quick peek at a part of her childhood, a memory of her brother to stave off homesickness and grief. A tiny moment, before she hid the book and lectured her sister on her recklessness. Serina had never imagined what she risked. What *Nomi* risked by learning to read. As Serina stumbled up the path, the screams of dying women echoing in her ears, she had never wanted anything more than to see that book of legends burn.

Cliff and the new prisoners followed Oracle's crew up a twisting, rocky trail that led through the scorched remains of a forest. The occasional gnarled cypress pushed its way out of the ruined earth, and tenacious ivy snaked across chunks of stone from what might have once been a road. The only other plant to find purchase was a hardy grass that sprouted in little clumps across the black volcanic rock, rustling mournfully in the wind.

"Where are we going?" Gia asked. She kept twisting her hair in her hands, as if desperate for something to hold on to.

Serina tried to catch her breath, her legs flaming.

Cliff didn't slow her pace. "We live in a cave. Well, a lava tube. The outer layers cooled while the lava still flowed, leaving an empty space behind."

"That doesn't sound safe." Gia grimaced. Her deeply tanned skin and sun-bleached hair suggested she came from a southern city, or maybe one of the nomadic fishing families that lived on boats along the western coast.

"It isn't," Cliff snapped.

"Then why do you live there?" Serina asked.

"Oracle doesn't want us to be safe." Cliff shot a glare over her shoulder. "She wants us to be tough. The tube is a terrible place to live, which is exactly the point. No more questions. Get moving."

The dark pressed in around them. Cliff's flickering torch only illuminated so much, and Serina frequently stumbled. Jacana, for all her timidity, tore up the path quickly.

Eventually, they reached a gaping mouth of stone. The crew disappeared into the cave. The new prisoners hesitated at the entrance, sagging with exhaustion. The air smelled like a burnt match. A red glow seeped into the sky from the hills in the center of the island.

Theodora stared at the tunnel and shook her head, eyes wide with horror. "I don't think I can do this."

Gia yanked on her arm. "You want to stay out here alone all night?"

"It's harder without a torch," Cliff said over her shoulder. She didn't wait.

As Serina entered the cave, bitter dust coated her tongue. The torchlight flashed madly against the walls. Even so, it was too dark to see more than the pale form of Jacana in front of her.

At last, a brighter flicker of firelight appeared to guide their way. The tunnel ballooned up and outward, creating a natural room. Women sat on rusted chairs in the center or sprawled on pallets lining the curved walls. At the far end, a fire had been lit beneath a large, ragged hole.

There were no guards. No men at all. Serina had never seen so many women in one place in her entire life.

Oracle walked over to the new girls. When she stood before them, she crossed her hands over her chest. The noise in the cave echoed to nothing. "Everyone has a moment here," the leader said, her voice carrying, "when they stand at the edge of a cliff and wonder if it will be easier to jump." She stared at each of the new prisoners, one after another. "Let me save you the internal debate. It *is* easier."

For a long moment, the words hung in the air, depressing and inescapable. Serina swallowed down the lump forming in her throat.

"Here on Mount Ruin, we have to earn our rations," Oracle continued. "And *everyone* is hungry. So jump if you have to, but don't expect to be fed unless you work. Unless you fight. The guards control the island, but *you* control your own survival. Listen, learn, and remember this one thing: Every rule you were ever taught in Viridia—about being quiet, modest, humble, weak—won't help you here. *Here*, strength is the only currency."

Serina had been trained to be soft. Pliant. Her grace had been her greatest strength. Now it was useless. *She* was useless. No one needed her harp playing, or dancing, or embroidery here.

Oracle's gaze found her, that strange milky eye seemingly reading every terrified thought. Almost as if she spoke straight to Serina, Oracle added, "You must be as strong as this prison, as strong as the stone and ocean that hems you in. You are brick and barbed wire. You are iron."

On another day, Serina might have wept. But she had no tears left, no energy for sorrow. This was her life now. Somehow, she would have to learn how to survive.

Serina woke, stiff with panic. A phantom weight pressed down on her, heavy as the rocks above her head. She sat up and tore at her shirt, trying to free her lungs from their cage.

84

A hand clamped onto her shoulder. "It's a dream. Relax. You're fine."

The strange voice shattered the haze of sleep that still clung to her. Suddenly, with a great gasp, she could breathe again.

Torches had been left burning at intervals throughout the main cavern, breaking up the darkness into waxy orange blocks of light and shadow. Serina tried to get her bearings in the low light.

"The tunnel makes some people claustrophobic. Me, I like it." The raspy voice belonged to the woman on the pallet beside Serina's. "I spent ten years living in the windowless basement of a powerful man's house, dreading the sound of his key turning in the lock. I've become accustomed to the dark."

"How did you end up here?" Serina asked shakily as she tried to ground herself in the here and now.

"The man took my child." The woman's gnomish face turned grim, her eyes dark holes the dim light didn't touch. She held her hands up, fingers curved into claws. "So I took his eyes."

Serina gripped the edges of her mat, trying to keep her expression neutral. "Oh."

"They call me Claw," the woman said, holding out a hand. "Here, we earn our names."

"Serina." As she shook hands, her stomach balked, and sweat broke out along the back of her neck. She suddenly couldn't bear the weight of the rock above her head, the press of so many strangers. She had to get out. "Where's the privy?" she asked hoarsely.

"Out the tunnel, beyond the steam vents to the left." Claw nodded her head toward the opening on the other side of the banked fire.

Serina scrambled to her feet and crossed the length of the cavern on shaky legs.

The tunnel wasn't lit, except for a faint gleam of dawn that filtered through several small openings where the tunnel had collapsed—a fact Serina tried not to dwell on. She stuck close to one wall, running her hand along the ridged rock to keep herself steady. The ground was uneven and snagged at her useless slippers, igniting fire in her blistered feet. She'd noticed a few of the women wearing boots and wondered what they'd done to procure them.

Away from the others, she thought she'd have more space to breathe, but the lava tube still hemmed her in, filled with the memories of so many women who'd come here frightened and alone, just like her. Who'd come here and fought and died.

Eventually, the tunnel opened up, its rock floor crumbling into grassy, vine-threaded gravel. Squat red-edged aloe plants broke through the rocky ground, and scrubby citrus trees lined a small patch of woods. Serina was pretty sure this was how they'd entered the cave the night before, but it'd been too dark to notice any of the details.

To her left, steam billowed from the ground, turning silver-gray in the morning light. Heavy, humid air replaced the cool damp of the cave. She picked her way over the rocky ground. She'd never relieved herself outside before. It was certainly a change from the creaky pipes of their house in Lanos, or the airy, marble-tiled bathrooms of the palazzo.

When Serina was finished, she clambered back over the rocks.

A squeak and rattle broke the quiet of the morning. Serina

retreated to the mouth of the cave as a guard came into view pushing a rusty cart. He stopped in the clearing between the rows of citrus trees, took off his hat, and wiped sweat from his forehead. It was the young guard who'd suggested she be placed in the Cave.

Serina looked around for Oracle, for someone else who might know what was happening, what to do, but no one materialized from the shadows of the lava tube. Automatically, she ran a hand along her greasy, tangled hair and tried to straighten her shirt.

"Ah, Dead Girl," the guard said, noticing her. Serina chafed under the callous nickname. She couldn't bring herself to meet his gaze, instead staring at the dark, unruly hair curling up along the edges of his cap. He leaned back against his cart and crossed his arms, his gray shirt streaked with sweat. "How are you settling in?"

It would have been a polite question demanding a polite answer, if they were in the palazzo. But Serina wasn't in the palazzo, and last night she'd watched girls fight to the death while guards like this one cheered. Nomi wouldn't smile and be polite. So Serina didn't either.

"How *does* one settle into hell, I wonder?" she asked, venom coating her voice. "And why should I? As you've made quite clear, I'll be dead and gone soon enough."

He nodded with something like appreciation. "You've got a little of your fire back. That's good."

Thrown off balance, Serina snapped, "What do you mean?"

He shrugged. "A lot of the girls who come here are already angry, ready to fight. But others need help. I figured if you had any chance at all, it'd be with the Cave. And here you are, a day in, already standing up for yourself."

"So, I'm rude to you and now you think I'm ready to fight?" Serina put her hands on her hips. The morning sun beat down on her, scalding the exposed skin of her arms.

The guard laughed as he turned back toward his loaded cart. "You're *definitely* not ready. But Oracle will get you there, if anyone can. She knows how to rein in the mad ones and toughen up the scared ones. Her crew wins the ration fights more than any of the others. She'll be good for you."

Confused, Serina stuttered, "Wait, so, you—you were trying to help me?"

With a grunt, he hauled a bulging burlap sack onto his shoulder. "I try to help all the girls, put them where they might last the longest. You looked especially needy."

"Well, thanks," she said bitingly. But she found she was actually grateful. She wasn't like Anika, all hard edges and defiance. Serina didn't fit in this terrifying new world.

The guard carried his sack over to the entrance of the cave and deposited it against the rock wall. Then he headed back for another.

The rations, Serina guessed. Her stomach rumbled painfully at the thought.

"So, Dead Girl," the guard said as he passed her the third time. "What's your real name?"

"Serina." She was about to ask his name, when a cluster of women appeared from the shadows of the cave.

Oracle strode toward the guard. They shook hands, and

Oracle's hard frown relaxed a fraction. Until she looked at the heap of bags. "That's three fewer than last time," she said.

Lowering his voice, the guard said, "Commander Ricci kept more for himself again. I snuck out an extra bag, but couldn't get the rest without suspicion."

"Thank you." Oracle squeezed his shoulder. "Any of the other crews at critical levels?"

He shook his head. "Southern Cliffs is close, but they've had some luck fishing. They'll last another month if they have to."

A hand gripped Serina's arm tightly, making her jump. She whirled to find Cliff frowning at her.

"There you are," the woman said. "I was looking for you."

Serina let out a breath. "Sorry. I—I woke up early and had to use the privy. I was just—"

"Ogling Valentino?" Cliff asked, jerking her chin toward the guard.

Serina's cheeks reddened. "He showed up when I was on my way back in."

"Oh, I'm teasing." A grin split Cliff's broad, plain face. "We all like Val. He's the youngest guard, so he gets to deliver rations. Sometimes he offers a tip or two, lets us know when the Commander's in a mood."

Serina opened her mouth to ask what that meant, but Cliff's smile vanished. "Stay away from the rest of the guards. Val's the exception, you understand? The others make promises to the girls sometimes. . . ." Cliff shook her head. "It never ends well."

Serina didn't understand, but she nodded mutely.

"Come on," the older woman said. "Time for breakfast."

Inside, everyone had gathered around the fire. Serina noticed Jacana sitting by herself, outside the ring of women. She dropped to the ground next to the girl.

"Did you get some sleep?" she asked quietly.

Jacana nodded but didn't look up.

Someone handed them a couple small lumps of gritty bread, leathery strips of dried meat, and several sections of an orange. Serina hunched over her portion, gulping everything down. The food tasted delicious after going for so long without. Jacana took tiny bites, like a bird, but her food disappeared just as fast.

Neither Cliff nor Oracle introduced the four new girls to the group, and no one made any attempt to talk to them. When Serina had finished her meal and could begin to think beyond the gnawing hollowness of her stomach, she lifted her head and surveyed her fellow inmates. There were about thirty women here, the youngest around fifteen or sixteen, the oldest woman a wizened crone who reclined on a pallet near the fire and chewed her bread with toothless gums. The majority of the women had the same look: young with narrow, hungry faces, hair cut short or pulled severely back, uniforms patched and stained, dark circles under their eyes.

All around Serina, the women told one another stories and jokes as they shared their meager meal. The cavern was filled, shockingly, with laughter. And not the quiet titters of the women at the Superior's ball. These women laughed with abandon.

Serina wondered who the mad ones were, and who the scared.

"I dreamt last night that Oracle threw me off a cliff," Jacana mumbled.

"Did you wake up happy or disappointed that it wasn't true?" Serina asked with a wry smile.

Jacana looked at her in surprise. And for the first time, she laughed. "I'm not sure. The hell doesn't really end either way, does it?"

Serina noted Jacana's small nose, dirty hair, and haunted green eyes. The girl was pretty, but she carried the toll of a hard life in the tiny premature wrinkles at the corners of her eyes and the permanent furrow between her brows.

"How did you end up here?" Serina asked, curious.

Jacana looked down at her empty hands. They were coated with fine volcanic dust, her nails ragged. "I was a thief. I got caught."

Serina could see it, almost. Jacana was small and fast. But she was so timid. "What did you steal?"

"Anything I could." Jacana shrugged. "My parents died when I was seven, so I was on my own. I stayed away from the orphanage. Didn't want to be contracted as someone's wife. They wouldn't have asked my permission."

"Where are you from?" Serina asked. "I'm from Lanos City."

Jacana shot her a surprised look, the fear falling from her face momentarily. "You don't look like you're from Lanos," she said. "I would have guessed Golden Isle."

Serina smiled at the compliment, despite herself. It wasn't as if her looks did her any good here.

"I was born in Bellaqua," Jacana said. "But I've lived all over. Cities mostly—I spent a lot of time in Ressida and Diamond

City." She leaned forward, her frail arms hugging her knees. "I was good at hiding my tracks. But a friend betrayed me." She seemed to shrink into herself. "And now I'm going to die here."

Serina stared at her empty hands, her stomach still growling. The truth weighed as heavily as the rocks above them, inescapable.

We are all *going to die here.*

TWELVE

NOMI

OVER THE NEXT few days, Nomi watched for Asa whenever she left the Graces' chambers, which happened only twice. She imagined and discarded several terrible schemes for seeking him out. She fought against the sinking sense that she'd pinned her hopes on a circumstance that would never arise. She couldn't ask Asa about Serina's whereabouts if she never saw him again.

Now Nomi dragged her feet on the way to the seamstress, studying each Grace and handmaiden who passed her, wondering if any of them knew of her sister's fate. She'd asked Rosario, but she had only heard what Cassia had repeated—that Serina had been removed from the palace under mysterious circumstances.

"I think they're doing the black dress today," Angeline said as she plodded along beside Nomi. "That one isn't as structured. It shouldn't be too much of a chore."

"Thanks," Nomi said. Her handmaiden knew how much she loathed the fittings.

"I think you should wear that one for the race," Angeline said thoughtfully. "It will sparkle in the moonlight."

"Have you ever seen it? The race, I mean?" Nomi asked.

"Papa let me watch from the upstairs window once. It was mad. A horse race through city streets . . . It's so famous people come from all over the world to watch. And you'll get one of the best views in all of Bellaqua. The Superior and his entourage always watch from the Bell Tower, near the finish line."

They reached the door just as someone pushed it open from the inside. Nomi took a hasty step back to avoid a collision.

Maris stopped abruptly, nearly treading on Nomi's toes. "I'm sorry," she said. "I didn't realize you were right there."

Nomi waved her off. "It's fine. No harm done."

Maris brushed her curtain of black hair behind her ear. She was the tallest of the new Graces by a good margin; Nomi suspected she was almost as tall as the Heir himself. At the moment, she seemed even more imposing, in a statuesque green gown covered in tiny, spiky silver studs.

"That dress looks lethal," Nomi commented as Maris shifted and the silver hardware caught the light. Angeline stared at it with an appreciative look.

"Better suited for dinner parties than balls," Maris agreed. "It's my favorite. Gives me the illusion I can maintain some distance."

The response surprised Nomi. Wasn't trying to get *closer* to the Heir the whole point?

Maris's handmaiden chose that moment to approach. "It's time for your harp practice."

Maris nodded and, with a little shrug at Nomi, followed the handmaiden down the hall.

"You've got a dance lesson after," Angeline said. "I'll come get you when it's time."

Nomi nodded her thanks, but her stomach churned. *Dance lesson.* This would be her first. At least it wouldn't be with the Heir; he had not yet returned to the palazzo.

As soon as Nomi stepped into the dressmaker's room, a handful of seamstresses swarmed her. Her clothes disappeared within moments. Nomi was placed on a raised dais in the center of the dim room, shivering in her shift, as the women whirled around her.

"Tsk, tsk. So thin," the dressmaker muttered as she dropped the black gown over Nomi's head. She sniffed down her nose at the way the drape of the dress enveloped Nomi's slight frame. "This dress wasn't designed for a *handmaiden's* figure."

Over the past few fittings, the seamstresses had made it clear that they didn't approve of her lowly origins. But the woman was right about the gown.

It would have fit Serina perfectly.

"More pins!" the dressmaker yelled.

Nomi kept her spine rigid and her face blank. She'd have preferred to rip the dress off and throw it at the dressmaker's feet, especially when the woman had "accidentally" pricked her with a pin. But Serina would have kept calm in this situation, and for her sake, Nomi was determined to do the same.

Another pin jabbed into Nomi's thigh, drawing blood. She winced, but she didn't give the seamstress the satisfaction of making a sound. The gown Serina had chosen for her was a deep silvery black, like a star-studded sky, and Nomi might have actually liked it, if the neckline didn't dip nearly to her navel and the waist didn't cinch so tight.

"There," the dressmaker said. "That'll do." She stepped back and surveyed the hemming and tucking. Her narrowed eyes saw nothing but the form of the dress. Nomi could have as easily been a straw mannequin in the back of a shop.

Ines stepped into the room as Nomi undressed. "Wait, leave it on," she said. "You're due for your dance lesson. A long dress and some well-placed pins will help you learn."

Nomi nodded calmly, but inside her heart was spitting flame.

Ines didn't wait for Angeline, instead leading Nomi out of the Graces' chambers herself. Nomi had almost unraveled the Graces' labyrinth, but the rest of the palace was still a mystery— probably because she paid more attention to the servants than her surroundings. Despite what Rosario had said, she still fantasized that Serina was living in the palace in some punishing, menial role, and that someday, if Nomi were patient, their paths would cross. But so far, Nomi had seen no hint of her sister.

She followed Ines through corridor after corridor, her dress whispering against the tile. Eventually, they found themselves in a small music room.

The walls shone with rose-threaded wallpaper and were hung with a vast array of instruments. Skylights brightened the room. A piano sat in one corner with a woman in muted orange bent over its keys, coaxing out a melody. The furniture had been cleared, and in the center of the room, Cassia twirled in Asa's arms. A dance instructor stood to one side, calling out frequent instructions.

Asa? They were practicing with *Asa?*

Nomi slammed to a stop in the doorway, shock running through her.

Asa caught sight of her and faltered. Cassia hissed when he tread on her foot. A blush crept up Nomi's cheeks.

"My apologies," Asa murmured, his attention returning to his dance partner.

Cassia bowed her head. "It was nothing, Your Eminence."

"That'll be all," Ines said, and the woman playing the piano ended the piece with a little flourish. Asa relinquished Cassia's hands.

"Thank you for the dance," he said, bowing.

Cassia dipped into a graceful curtsy, her long, loose hair falling in a shimmering curtain to hide her face. "It was my pleasure, Your Eminence," she purred.

Nomi moved aside so Cassia could leave, but her mind was still sluggish. Her gaze never left Asa, who was waiting in the center of the room, scuffing a foot on the floor. In all her fruitless scheming, she'd never imagined he'd be at her dance lesson. But could she risk asking him about Serina here? Did she dare?

The instructor, wraith-thin with graceful hands, clapped twice.

Nomi jumped. Awkwardly, she stepped forward. She had never learned how to dance. Serina had always practiced with Renzo, and no one had thought to include her in the lessons. The instructor would have to do more than give her pointers to refine her style. He would have to teach Nomi every step, every turn.

97

"Stop frowning," Ines ordered. "A Grace never frowns."

Nomi straightened her shoulders. If she was going to survive here, if she was going to find out what happened to Serina, she had to control her frustration. She had to *learn* these things. She couldn't risk displeasing anyone.

She stood before Asa and dropped into a curtsy. At least practice had helped in that regard. The sunlight picked out the silver in her dress as she moved, making it sparkle like starlight.

"I must apologize, Your Eminence," she said. "I've little experience with dancing."

His warm hands enveloped hers. Her fingers trembled. He guided her left hand to his shoulder and held on to the other. The first glittering notes of a song filled the room as he drew her closer, close enough to whisper, "Neither do I. That's why Father makes me do the lessons with the Graces."

He smelled of espresso and warm sand. Without quite realizing it, Nomi swayed a breath closer. A hidden pin pricked against her thigh.

The instructor counted out the beats. "One, two, three, four. Step back, step left, step forward, and back."

Nomi tried to focus, but the question she wanted to ask him drowned everything else out. Did she dare? She risked impertinence, and Ines was there, watching. She'd *told* Nomi not to ask questions. If she heard Nomi . . .

Asa stepped forward, right onto Nomi's foot.

She jerked back and tripped on the edge of her pinned-up gown, wobbling. Asa's arms tightened. He stepped to his left as she stepped to *her* left, and their arms strained, pulling them back together.

The instructor cleared his throat. "Your Eminence, please forgive me for creating confusion. My instructions were for Nomi."

Asa made a strange noise in his throat, like he was swallowing a laugh. "Of course."

The music started again. Asa stepped forward, Nomi stepped back, and somehow they found a bit of rhythm. They did several revolutions around the room before Ines said, "Nomi, lift your chin. You're looking at your feet as if you're afraid they'll walk off without you."

Nomi lifted her gaze in time to see Asa bite back a smile.

He leaned a little closer. "I never trust my own feet when dancing," he said. "They have a habit—" He stomped on her dress, jerking her against his chest and more pins into her waist. She struggled not to wince as his laughter rumbled up. "Well, of that," he finished.

She stepped to the left. He might be a little wooden, but she wasn't helping. Neither were the pins. "And I'm a poor partner. I'm sorry."

His hand tightened on hers. "You are not the awkward one here. Not in that dress, with all the heavens embracing you."

Nomi had never been paid such an extravagant compliment in her life. Cheeks flaming, she looked down, and the dress winked back at her, little glitters flashing against the black.

"I feel like a stranger," she confessed. "Not like myself at all."

"Your whole life's been upended." He shrugged. "Of course it's unsettling. Everything's different and unexpected. . . . This wasn't *your* choice."

99

Nomi glanced up in surprise. No one else seemed to understand that. Everyone acted as if she should be thrilled, or else they denigrated her for being a lowly servant elevated without cause. She darted a look at Ines, whose attention was caught by something outside the window. Perhaps this was her chance.

"I wanted to ask—" she began.

"Try a spin," the instructor interjected.

Asa took an exaggerated breath. "Here we go. . . ."

He spun Nomi out, hard enough that she had to grip his hand lest she sail across the room. And then, suddenly, they *were* sailing, twirling in impulsive circles better suited to a faster, wilder song than the pianist played.

Nomi's hair blew back from her face and she couldn't help it—she laughed outright. Asa spun her out and back against his firm chest, and they teetered a little.

He smiled down at her, and his eyes were a deep coffee brown, turned up at the corners.

They took off around the room again, galloping through a pattern of steps Asa may have made up, for all she knew. But she didn't care, nor did she feel a single pinprick. For the first time in nearly a week, her nervous muscles loosened, her worry faded, and her head didn't ache with questions and regret.

It was a gift to spend one moment spinning like a child, pretending she was free.

Ines cleared her throat, loudly and pointedly. The piano music stopped. "That will do," she announced.

With a chuckle, Asa sent Nomi into a last spin and ended the dance with a bow. He smiled, his cheeks as flushed as hers felt. They both were breathing quickly.

Nomi cast her gaze to the floor. Part of her hem had come unpinned and dragged over her silver shoes.

"I'm sorry. I seem to have forgotten myself," Asa said, not sounding sorry at all. "Thank you for the practice."

"Thank *you*, Your Eminence." Nomi curtsied, her heart falling. Their dance was over, and with it, any opportunity to ask about Serina.

Nomi followed Angeline back to the Graces' chambers in silence, wondering if she'd get another chance. *Praying* she would.

When Nomi reached her bedroom, Angeline made short work of the shimmery black dress, now a little bedraggled. "Don't worry," the handmaiden said cheerfully. "I'll have it cleaned and sewn up straightaway so it's ready for the Premio Belaria."

Then she helped Nomi into a soft cream tunic and flowing pants.

"Thank you, Angeline," Nomi said. "May I have a few minutes to myself, please?"

The girl bowed. "Of course. I'll wait outside."

As soon as she was alone, Nomi slumped into a chair, elbows on the dressing table, and put her head in her hands. Over and over, the dance lesson played through her mind. She *should* have found a way to ask Asa about Serina.

Nomi's frustration bubbled to the surface. She'd hoped to rest for a bit, but she couldn't lie down. Not while she was thinking of Serina. She stood, clumsily, and knocked a small pot of lip shimmer to the floor. She sighed and picked it up, opening the dressing table's top drawer to put it away.

As she opened the drawer, she gasped. A book sat half-hidden under a silk scarf and two sticks of kohl.

Nomi slammed the drawer shut, looking around her room in wide-eyed panic. When she was sure no one was watching—the room's curtains had been drawn and Angeline remained outside—she opened the drawer again slowly.

It was still there. Her fingers caressed the smooth leather, and a tremor passed through her as she drew it out.

A Brief History of Viridia.

Nomi wrapped her arms around herself. A book was a dangerous thing to have—Serina's removal proved that. So where had it come from?

Before she could stop to think about what she was doing, Nomi stuffed the small volume between her mattress and frame, deep enough that it wouldn't be disturbed when Angeline changed the sheet. Nomi's heart pounded madly. She slid to the floor and leaned against the bed.

She felt suddenly like an acrobat balanced on a swaying rope, the world dangerously far below. Someone was playing with her, and she didn't know the game.

THIRTEEN

SERINA

"ORACLE WANTS TO see the freshies. Come on." Cliff crossed her arms over her chest and loomed. Serina finished the last bit of bread from her meager lunch and scrambled to her feet. Cliff seemed to be the official handler for new prisoners. She was always the one telling Serina and the others what to do.

Jacana, Gia, and Theodora climbed to their feet after Serina and followed Cliff out of the lava tube. Many of the other women were working—some were collecting oranges and lemons, while others scrounged through the small patch of woods. Cliff caught Serina studying one of the girls, her arms laden with citrus and other plants.

"We'd die without that little bit of extra food," Cliff said. "There are also a few berries that won't kill you, though they taste like acid, and boars that roam the island. Won't be for too much longer, though," she added, pushing the girls toward a path through the foliage. "They can't breed and birth fast enough before we hunt them. Anyone with a chance at fresh meat takes it."

"Do you fish?" Gia asked. It turned out the blond girl was from a boat family. She'd been caught dressing as a boy to sell her family's fish in the market when her father had taken ill.

Cliff rubbed the sunburned skin at the back of her neck. "Beach Camp and Southern Cliffs do. Everywhere else, the currents keep fish from getting close enough to shore. Jungle Camp catches a few in a bit of fresh water near where they live, but it isn't much. They're as hungry as anyone else," she ended grimly.

Serina's brow furrowed. "What happens if a crew loses the fights time after time?"

"They find enough food on their own. Or they starve," Cliff said with a tone of finality.

They emerged from the patch of trees to another lava field. A grunt and the smack of skin against skin drew Serina's attention. A few yards to their right, on a wide stretch of grassy earth the lava had missed, several women faced off. Oracle and the woman with the red strip of hair down her shaved skull stood off to the side, watching.

Jacana shuffled to a halt. Serina froze too.

Cliff nodded toward the fighters. "This is where we train. Ember leads most of the training, but if Oracle gives you advice, listen."

Serina gasped as one of the women punched the other in the stomach. Their whirls and dodges looked like a strange kind of dance; the heat and brilliance of the sun made their movements dizzying.

Ember hiked over to where the little group stood, watching.

Cliff raised a brow. "Oracle wanted to see the freshies?"

Ember surveyed the new girls. Serina noticed a nasty scar just under her chin, shiny white and puckered. It looked like someone had tried to slash her throat.

"Pull back your hair," the woman ordered.

Cliff dug several pieces of twine from her pocket and handed them out. Serina cringed as she tied her oily hair up.

"Let's see what you've got," Ember said, starting toward the field.

Gia made a noise in her throat. "You've got to be joking," she said, voicing Serina's own disbelief. Surely, *they* didn't have to train . . . not yet.

Ember paused to level a glare on the girl. "Everyone fights for rations eventually. The sooner you start training, the less likely you are to die."

Theodora swallowed. She was the tallest of the freshies, with arms that moved loosely at the joints, like a marionette. Her long, thin fingers picked at the hem of her shirt, a nervous habit Serina had noticed before.

Ember gestured to the makeshift ring. "Now get in there."

No one else protested. Serina took a place next to Jacana, her heart pounding a frantic rhythm. She'd been told that other women were her competition all her life. Her mother had pounded the message into her: *Never trust another woman. Never trust that she won't try to take your place as a Grace, or your chance for a husband. You must always be the most beautiful, most poised woman in the room.*

But the only thing she knew how to fight for was attention.

"Petrel, Mirror, work with them," Ember said, pointing to Serina and Jacana. The other two fighters faced off with Gia and Theodora. Ember joined Oracle and Cliff, standing at the edge of the clearing.

One of the fighters shot Serina a grin. She had straight, shoulder-length hair and pierced ears, marking her as a former resident of Sola. "I'm Petrel," the girl said. "Don't let us scare you too much."

"Too late," Serina muttered before she could stop herself.

To her surprise, Petrel laughed. The other girl, Mirror, grinned. Freckles covered every inch of her exposed skin, and her black hair was cropped close to her skull. Her gaze caught everything.

"Everyone has cut their hair," Jacana said quietly.

Petrel nodded. "Yes, most of us have. It's easier to manage, and the rules here are not so defined. Or, well—" She broke off, as if considering. "Maybe it's just that they are different." The lightness in her voice dimmed a little. "Everywhere has rules, right?"

So far, Serina couldn't grasp what the rules were here. And that was more terrifying, she found, than living in a society where everything was forbidden. If she didn't know the rules, how would she know if she'd broken them?

"Get on with it," Ember shouted, ending the introductions.

Petrel raised her hands, curling them into fists. "Keep your hands loose, like this. Raise them chest level, arms ready but not tense. You understand?"

Serina didn't, but she lifted her hands and made an effort. Beside her, Jacana did the same.

Suddenly, a fist shot toward Serina's face. She landed on her back in the grass, pain exploding along her jaw. For an instant, she stared at the hazy blue sky, rimmed with cloud. Then she struggled to her feet, rubbing her mouth.

"Petrel, work on her footwork." Oracle's voice fed the panic thudding in Serina's chest. "She knows how to dance. Start there."

Serina's gaze snapped to Oracle's face in surprise. How did Oracle know she could dance?

Petrel's fist connected with Serina's stomach, and she fell again.

"Sorry," Petrel said cheerfully as Serina picked herself back up. "Stand with your legs farther apart. Bend your knees more. Keep loose."

The training lasted all morning. First Petrel knocked Serina down, again and again, the whole time spouting nonsense about Serina's stance and response times. Then the other fighters took a turn. And then the freshies fought each other. All the other girls knocked Serina down too. Even Jacana did; she was small and timid but, as Serina had noted before, surprisingly fast. It made sense now, given her history.

Serina's knuckles cracked. The blisters on her feet bled. The taste of blood filled her mouth from a split lip. The only thing she could manage was to pull herself up and stand, swaying, ready for her next beating. The girls she fought were knives; she was dough—a soft, pliant body, useless as anything but a punching bag.

If Nomi had followed the rules, Serina would never have been sent here. The thought sent a bolt of anger coursing through her. Serina thrust her fist at Mirror's face, only to have the girl block the blow and send her to the ground again.

When the training ended, Serina could do little more than stand on wobbling legs, bruised fists loose at her sides, as the other girls dusted themselves off and headed back to the cave. Petrel swung an arm around Serina's shoulders and dragged her along.

"Come on. Let's get you some food. First time's always a beast. Oracle has us go hard on the freshies to see what you're made of," she said. "It'll get easier."

"I doubt that," Serina rasped, her voice as sore and halting as the rest of her. She didn't share Val's newfound optimism over her prospects. He'd been right the first time. She *was* a dead girl.

And it's Nomi's fault.

Serina shook her head, trying to dislodge the thought. It felt like a betrayal.

"When you've recovered, walk," Petrel suggested. "Stay away from the guard stations and the other crews. Everywhere else is okay. Walk as much as you can, run when you feel ready. Climb with your hands and feet bare . . . the volcanic rock will help you form calluses. You need to toughen up."

Serina laughed. What an understatement.

Petrel smiled again. "What's your name?"

"Let's call her Softie," one of the other fighters yelled from the front of the line.

Her companion laughed.

"No. How about Wallop, since we walloped her."

Serina couldn't bring herself, in that moment, to care what they chose for her name. She *was* soft. Defeated. Weak.

Ahead the line slowed to a stop. Oracle waited for them to catch up. She glanced around the small group, all sweat-stained and sagging in the heat, Serina the most disheveled of them all. In her whole life, she'd never spent a day without clean, brushed hair, nice clothes, and a perfect smile. What she must look like now, her mouth swollen, jaw bruised, and hair a wild tangle.

Oracle leveled her with a stare that seemed to see everything, seemed to understand all of Serina's hopes, dreams, desires . . . and all her failures. As she spun away, Oracle shouted over her shoulder, "Call her Grace."

FOURTEEN

NOMI

THE BOOK WAS burning a hole through Nomi's bed. She could feel its sharp corners keeping her awake at night, tempting her as Angeline slept. In the dark, Nomi's heartbeat spoke in black ink and silken paper, her mind filled with a craving that grew more painful the longer she resisted. She wanted so much to steal a moment, steal a glance, but she left it where it was. It wasn't worth the risk. She never forgot Serina's face as she pretended to read the book of legends, or the sound of her scream as they dragged her away.

Nomi shook her head a little, trying to put the book from her mind. The trouble was, if she wasn't thinking about the book, she was thinking about Asa. Did he help with all of the dance lessons, or just when the Heir was away? Would he be at the big horse race coming up? When would she see him again? She was determined to find a way to speak to him about Serina. She couldn't afford to waste any more chances.

At that moment, she and the other new Graces were

ensconced in one of the more private sitting rooms, with dim light and ceramic bowls of warm water set in front of the upholstered chairs. The new Graces were supposed to be learning how to give foot massages by practicing on one another.

With a firm grip, Nomi slid her thumbs, slicked with oil, up the center of Cassia's foot.

"I can't believe I'm saying this, but I think you might actually be getting better," Cassia said, letting out a little sigh as she dropped her head back against the seat.

Nomi fought the urge to rake her fingernails down the girl's foot. But she smiled wryly and said, "It's about time I got something right," as if she actually cared about such things.

Maris made a noise in the back of her throat. "I hate feet." She was practicing on her handmaiden, who kept giggling because Maris wasn't pressing hard enough. "I can't believe we're expected to do this. It's disgusting."

The handmaiden's foot jerked as Maris hit another sensitive spot. "Sorry," she muttered.

Cassia lowered her feet into the bowl of water. "I think it's sensual."

Nomi wiped off her hands, her own level of disgust somewhere in between the other girls'.

"My turn," Cassia said. She patted Nomi on the head like a dog as she stood up. They switched places. Nomi sank into the soft chair and set her bare feet on the toweled footstool.

But before Cassia could start, Ines's shadow filled the doorway. "The Heir has returned," she announced. Nomi's heart jolted.

"He'd like to see you, Cassia," Ines added.

Nomi let out a breath. Thank the stars she wasn't first this time.

Cassia swept toward the door, throwing a smug grin over her shoulder. Maris made a scoffing noise in her throat as Cassia left.

Nomi leaned forward to stretch out her spine before collapsing back into the cushioned chair. She closed her eyes and tried to block out thoughts of Serina, Asa, Malachi's return . . . everything. She'd had so few opportunities growing up to just sit in a comfortable chair and breathe. Her parents both worked at the textile factory and Renzo was in school, so it had fallen to her to keep the house clean, go to the market for food, prepare their meals, and wash up afterward.

Maris's handmaiden giggled again. Maris threw down her pumice stone in disgust. The man by the door shifted his weight.

"Are you okay?" Nomi asked quietly. She glanced at the pale, white-clad man at the door briefly, wondering what he thought of them.

Maris used a towel to mop up the oil on her hands. "I wish we could walk on the beach, or swim," she grumbled. "I feel like I'm waiting for a storm that's hovering just offshore, and it never gets any closer."

Nomi smoothed her hands over the tops of her own feet, trying to rub the remnants of oil from her fingers. She said, "The Heir's birthday is only a few weeks away. After that . . ."

After that, they'd be required to fulfill their full duties as Graces. Nomi shivered.

They sat in silence for a long time, neither of them eager to move on to the next task. Nomi had almost drifted to sleep, exhausted by her own thoughts, when Maris stood up with a jerk.

"I'm *covered* in this oil, and the smell is making me sick. I'm going to take a bath."

"I should probably wash up too," Nomi said. The trade winds had died the night before, and her skin was sticky from the warm, humid air, her mind thick with fears of Malachi's birthday and what she'd be expected to do.

Nomi and Maris strolled through the quiet, opulent rooms, their handmaidens following silently. Even Angeline was quiet when they were in the common areas. The Superior's men dotted each room, part of the furniture and yet not—Nomi could never forget that they reported everything to the Superior.

When they reached the pool, Nomi and Maris removed their clothes with the help of their handmaidens. At Nomi's nod, Angeline slipped outside, with Maris's handmaiden following suit. Even the male servant stepped outside the room, though he lingered just beyond the doorway. Maris plopped into the water with a little groan, sending ripples across its surface. Nomi joined her.

"Do you like it here?" Maris asked. Her black hair shone against the surface of the water like an oil slick.

Nomi hugged herself, the movement causing ripples to fan out across the bathing pool's surface. She watched them hit the curved marble edge until the last one died. If Cassia had asked, Nomi would have said yes. But for some reason, with Maris, she felt safe telling the truth. "I hate it," she whispered so the man outside wouldn't hear her. "I miss my sister, my family. . . . My brother and I were born minutes apart. We'd *never* spent more than a day without each other in seventeen years. And my sister—" Her voice broke. She couldn't talk about Serina.

Maris stared for a long time at the shadow of the man in the doorway. "My mother used to tell me that raging against a life you can't change only hurts you." Her voice hitched. "But she was lucky. She died young."

"I'm so sorry," Nomi said. Something about Maris's fixed glare made her heart beat too fast. Nomi realized she was scared. Scared Maris would say something she shouldn't. Scared she herself might too.

Maris's voice flowed across the water, inexorable. "I *could* have been happy here. But my father, he . . . he ruined everything." Her mouth snapped shut.

Before Nomi could ask what she meant, a handful of the Superior's Graces entered the bathing room. Maris pasted a smile on her face, and it was as if the girl she'd been only a moment before had evaporated.

Nomi wasn't the only one with a secret here, she realized. Maris had one too.

FIFTEEN

SERINA

SERINA SPENT EVERY day for a week sparring with Petrel. She was getting better at keeping her feet and faster at avoiding the fists and elbows, but her arms were still weak, her punches ineffectual. Her body didn't feel like her own when Ember ordered her into the makeshift ring, over and over again. Her muscles screamed as angrily as the gulls that screeched overhead.

"You're coming along just fine," Petrel said cheerfully, patting Serina on the shoulder.

Serina bent over, hands on her knees, and tried to catch her breath.

Petrel laughed. "Go take a walk. It'll stretch out your legs, keep them from cramping." She headed over to watch Mirror spar with Jacana.

"What do you want, Grace?" Oracle asked when Serina approached her. The crew chief was sitting just outside the cave entrance, sharpening sticks into spears for boar hunting.

Serina bristled. She hated the name she'd *earned*. She'd never even been a Grace.

Serina certainly didn't look like one anymore. She hadn't cut her hair, but she'd have to soon; it hung in a limp, dirty braid down her back and was constantly getting in her way. Her hands were coated with fine black volcanic dust. No matter how many times she scrubbed them, they never seemed to come clean. And her once-luminous olive skin was now red and chapped by the sun.

"The volcano," she said, glancing up at the cloud of smoke that hung above the hills behind Oracle. "What if it erupts? Why do you stay so close? Isn't it dangerous?"

Oracle paused, hands poised over her spear. "If the volcano wakes again, everyone on this island will die. Would you prefer to go first, and quickly, or have time to panic and pray?"

"I don't think I'd accept death so easily," Serina shot back.

"Death comes, whether you accept it or not," Oracle stated. She bent over her work again, an obvious dismissal.

"Can I go for a hike?" Serina addressed the top of the woman's head.

Oracle laughed but didn't bother looking up. "Why are you asking me? Do what you like. Just stay away from the guards."

Serina stomped away. Was it so strange that she had asked? She was in a *prison*.

She hiked north, around the rim of the caldera. The ragged terrain tore at her flimsy shoes. A narrow guard tower loomed in the distance; as she approached it, she noted the one silent guard standing watch, his hand on his firearm. She walked faster until he was out of sight.

Eventually, she reached the far rim of the massive crater, the gray and white rock smoking in places. No plants grew here, not even the hardy golden grass. Her head ached from sun glare and dehydration.

Panting, she scaled a large rock fall and collapsed on the top. She brushed grit from her sore, blistered hands. No calluses yet. Before her, stretching to the horizon, the ocean glinted. Behind her, the caldera smoked.

There wasn't another person in sight, not in any direction. Even the guard tower had disappeared, hidden by a fold in the land. Out here, she might as well be the only person on the island. The only person in the world.

Do what you like.

Oracle's words pounded in her head. No one had ever said that to her before. Her life had been ruled by duty. And no one, not even the people she loved, had let her forget it.

She'd hoped that becoming a Grace would be her reward. But Nomi had been given the life Serina had always imagined for herself: a series of balls and concerts and delectable meals. *Nomi* was primped and pampered. *Nomi* slept in a soft bed in her own room. *Nomi* didn't fear for her life every day.

Sometimes Serina wished Nomi had been the one caught with the book, that she'd been forced to pay for her own crime. On those days, Serina felt like the worst sister in the world. Who could wish a place like this on anyone, let alone someone you loved?

Today, all Serina could think about was Nomi's bed, and how her sister had wanted Serina to sleep with her that first night in the palazzo. Serina's only night in the palazzo. Nomi had needed her, and Serina had turned the other way. She thought about the morning after, when she could have given Nomi a hug or words of encouragement, and she hadn't.

Serina was going to die here, one way or another. She would never see Nomi again. She could have told her little sister she loved her, that she was proud of her. And now she'd never have the chance.

With a sigh, Serina climbed down from the rock and started the slow trek back to the lava tube. The setting sun paced her, hovering just above the horizon, staining the edges of the guard tower red.

Serina heard a clatter of stones, just as a figure appeared from the scrub beside the path. The guard stepped in front of her, blocking her way, his narrow face cocked to the side.

"New or banished, I wonder," he said, appraising her from head to toe. "No other excuse for you to be out here on your own."

Serina didn't like the calculation in his eyes. She lowered her gaze and crossed her arms protectively over her chest. A scratch on her forearm burned when the skin pulled taut.

"Excuse me," she said, and moved to go around him, her heart trip-hammering in her chest.

He blocked her, stepping into her space. He wasn't particularly tall, but he didn't need bulk to frighten her. All it took was his hand on his firearm, and the way he moved so close, so fast. Like he was used to intimidating the prisoners here.

He leaned into her and murmured in her ear, "Your shoes are falling apart. Let me find you a pair of boots."

One hand stayed on his firearm. The other rose to her shoulder, his fingers splaying against the side of her neck.

Every breath Serina took felt like a scream. What was she supposed to do? It was obvious what this man wanted in exchange for boots, and she didn't want to give it to him.

She was unwilling.

But when had that ever mattered before?

It wouldn't have mattered if she'd been chosen as a Grace.

For the first time, Serina really understood what Nomi had meant that night in the palazzo, when she'd said it wasn't a choice if you weren't allowed to say no. Serina had chosen to be willing, to *want* the Heir. But it wouldn't have mattered if she hadn't.

And it didn't matter now.

"I—I don't want any boots," she stuttered, unable to force her voice out louder than a whisper. She tried to take a step back, but he held her fast, his hand on the curve of her throat.

"Yes," he said, his fingers digging into her skin. "You do."

Serina closed her eyes. Her breath came in gasps.

"She doesn't want the boots, Bruno," a voice rang out. There was a grunt and a thud. Free from the guard's hand, Serina stumbled backward.

She opened her eyes. Bruno was on the ground, legs akimbo. Petrel stood over him. "She's Cave crew," she said, staring him down. "And she said *no*."

Bruno scrambled to his feet, his narrow face reddening. "You better watch yourself," he growled, but Petrel laughed in his face.

"You know where Oracle draws the line," she said.

He spit at her feet before heading back into the scrub, toward the guard tower.

Petrel turned back to Serina. "Are you okay?"

Serina nodded, mutely, even though she wasn't. Her heart still pounded in her chest, and a headache filled her skull with flames. Petrel had *hit* that guard. She had stopped him. "What is Oracle's line?" Serina asked, her voice still faint and shaky.

Petrel swung an arm around Serina's shoulders and drew her along the path. "The system is delicate here. In the ring, the guards have all the power. But out here, split up in their patrols and towers . . . out here we can sometimes fight back. Oracle doesn't tolerate the guards forcing themselves on us." Petrel smiled reassuringly. "Most of the guards leave us alone now. Bruno's stupid. He won't last long here."

Serina's hands shook. She stared down at her feet, scrambling along the rough path. "I didn't know what to do."

Petrel squeezed her shoulder before letting her arm fall to her side. "You fight back. Always."

When they reached the cave, Petrel kept walking. No one was loitering in the entrance, even though it was nearly dinnertime.

"Where are we going?" Serina asked. Her headache blurred the edges of her vision, giving the twilight a surreal quality.

"It's time for another fight." Petrel brushed her shoulder-length hair behind her ears. "Oracle sent me to collect you. She knew I wanted a few moments to myself before I headed for the ring."

Serina's head snapped up. "Another boat came in? Already?"

Petrel nodded. "New rations. New prisoners."

Serina swallowed, her throat dry. "Who did Oracle choose to fight?"

Petrel didn't answer. She navigated the rugged trail with ease, even in the near dark. Serina stumbled after her. A deep, sickening unease spread through her. There was only one reason why Petrel would need time alone before the fight. "Petrel . . ."

"Don't worry," Petrel replied at last, her voice deceptively light. "I've won two fights already."

By the time they reached the ruined amphitheater, most of their crew had already arrived. With a last squeeze of Serina's arm, Petrel headed to the edge of the stage, where Oracle stood. Serina found a spot to sit next to Jacana and Gia. Cliff climbed down to them with a bedraggled, terrified older woman in tow.

"Sit here," she told the woman. "And don't cry. The guards will see your weakness, and they'll use it. Don't let them." It was the same speech she'd given the last time. Serina wondered how many times she'd said the words.

"Where were you?" Jacana whispered, nudging Serina's arm.

The ghost of Bruno's hand pressed into her throat. Serina glanced up at the balcony but didn't see him. "I was walking," was all she said.

Serina shifted her gaze to Petrel. Oracle stood next to her, their heads bent close together.

"Cliff, what's she saying?" Serina asked, pointing.

Cliff followed her gaze. "Oracle can tell someone's fighting style, their strengths and weaknesses, almost immediately. One, two moves and she knows exactly what they're going to do before they do it. It's how she got her name. She's watched all these women fight before. She's telling Petrel how to beat them."

"Those are the other camp leaders, with their champions?" Serina watched the women at the edge of the stage. Sized them up. Were the fighters good this week? Could Petrel beat them?

Cliff cocked her head to the pair at the far left. One woman towered over the other, her arms and legs thin and straight as iron bars. "The tall one's Twig, leader of the Beach. They live on a stretch of shoreline along the north coast."

"Is she called Twig because she's tall and thin?" Serina tried to focus. She tried to breathe.

Cliff shot her a glare. "People call her Twig because she likes to break bones when she fights. Snaps 'em like twigs."

Serina's stomach rolled.

Cliff pointed to the next pair. "Slash, leader of Hotel Misery. She's the one with spiky hair. She makes knives." The girl next to Slash was bouncing on the balls of her feet, her cloud of dark hair bobbing in time.

"The guards let you have weapons in the fights?" Gia asked, her eyes wide.

Cliff snorted. "No. The guards take them from her and her crew, but they always seem to find material to make more. We're not exactly the kind of women who follow rules, are we?"

"Why do people call you Cliff?" Jacana asked.

Cliff gave her a long look. "Because after I watched my first fight, I almost jumped off a cliff."

Commander Ricci called the fighters onto the stage, like last time, and then headed up onto the balcony. The only sound was the rumble of male voices as the guards placed their bets.

Ricci hefted a crate above his head.

"What are the crates?" Serina whispered to Cliff, whose full attention was focused on stage.

"He likes to make the fights interesting," the woman replied. "The crates are filled with different things each fight. Once,

122

he dropped a crate of rope, and the girls all strangled one another."

Commander Ricci released the box and shouted, "Begin!" When the crate splintered against the ground, a cloud of wasps erupted from the broken nest inside. The women in the first few rows scrambled away from the stage.

Jungle Camp's champion kicked the nest toward one of the other girls and went after Petrel. She thrust a fist at her face, but Petrel ducked and, with one quick, brutal movement, wrapped the girl's head tightly in her arms and twisted.

The girl crumpled, her neck bent at a strange angle.

Above the fighting, the guards cheered. Serina stifled a sob. She couldn't block it out this time, couldn't close her eyes. Couldn't believe she'd have to do this too. She'd never survive when it was her turn to fight.

A scream sliced the air—one of the women was backing away from the others, writhing in agony. The wasps had swarmed her. She clawed at her face. A tall girl—the champion from the northern beaches—kicked out the girl's knees. She fell to the ground, writhing, and howled, "I submit! I submit!"

No one pulled her away or helped her with the wasps. A few seconds later, while the three remaining fighters wove and parried, the girl stopped crying. Stopped moving. Stopped breathing. Her face was swollen and purple, like she'd been strangled.

Every muscle, every atom of Serina's body ached to pull her up off the rough stone bench, up out of the arena, away from the horrors unfolding in the ring.

With a sickening crunch, the girl from Hotel Misery dispatched the champion from the northern beaches. While she still stood above the body, Petrel hit the Misery girl hard and fast. They were the only two left.

The girl fell, but before Petrel could slam her again, she swept a leg and brought Petrel down too. Instead of grappling on the floor, Petrel sprang to her feet and retreated a couple steps.

For a moment, the two girls sized each other up, bodies littered around them. Petrel's adversary was the same height, with a brown puff of hair and a narrow face. From Serina's vantage, it wasn't clear who would be stronger.

Punch, thrust, parry.

Petrel dodged each of Misery's moves, almost as if she knew exactly what to expect. The girl's easy manner and sweet smile had disappeared beneath a cold calculation Serina would never have imagined her capable of.

Petrel connected with Misery's jaw again, and the girl let out a scream of frustration. Petrel pressed her advantage, delivering another punishing blow. Misery stepped back. Petrel advanced. She pounded at Misery's face and stomach, each punch driving forward with all her force behind it. They were blows to break bones.

No one cheered or booed, not even the guards. No one made a sound.

Misery's face was bloody and swollen. Her cloud of hair sagged, weighted with sweat and blood. She was standing at the edge of the stage, hands up to protect herself, not even trying to fight back. Petrel spun sideways and thrust her foot into Misery's knee. With a hollow scream, the girl crumpled. She curled into herself, around the injured leg, and bowed her head. Petrel paused, and Serina realized she was waiting. She wanted Misery to submit.

The girl didn't say a word.

Petrel clenched her fists for an instant, her face twisting. Then she reached down with both hands, to choke her or break her neck.

Bile rose in Serina's throat. She couldn't watch. She couldn't watch *another* girl die. It was so deliberate this time, without the heat of multiple battles, the struggle to survive. Petrel was no longer defending herself. She was committing murder.

Suddenly, the press of bodies was too much, the heat, the electric silence as they all laid witness to Misery's final moments. Serina couldn't stand it. She dropped her head into her hands, just as a collective gasp rose around her. She glanced back up in time to see a flash, something catching the light.

Petrel's mouth opened.

Her hands dropped from Misery's throat . . . and grasped her own.

Petrel's fingers turned black. No. Red. She was trying to stanch the blood. The blood pouring out of her, pouring from her neck.

She made a strange gurgling sound. As she drifted slowly to her knees, Misery rose, favoring her injured leg. In her hand, something glinted. A knife.

"Cheater," someone shouted angrily. Whispers of outrage rippled through the amphitheater.

The gurgling stopped. Petrel fell to her side, eyes still open.

Serina couldn't breathe, and the world faded in and out, as if she were the one lying there, dying in a pool of her own blood. She couldn't get her brain to work. She couldn't accept—

Hotel Misery's champion thrust a bloody fist into the air.

Her crew cheered.

There was a flurry of movement near the stage; Oracle and Ember leapt up and collected Petrel's body. As they carried her away, blood dripped to mark their path. Serina stared at the slash of red against the pale stone. So much blood had been spilled here. How could so much death not leave a stain?

SIXTEEN

NOMI

NOMI STOOD ON the roof of the tallest building in Bellaqua, her black-and-silver gown billowing in the howling wind. Angeline had been beside herself all day, regaling Nomi with stories of the Premio Belaria, *the most famous horse race in the world. The only one ever to be run through city streets. The most difficult race in history.* Nomi had heard, in detail, about all the most famous runners, some of whom had won, and some of whom had died.

"His Eminence Asa ran it two years ago," Angeline had said, practically swooning. "He was the youngest ever to run it, and he *won*. It was a brutal year too. Many racers died."

Nomi had never been remotely interested in horse racing. But as she stood there, high above the streets below, she found herself awash in reluctant anticipation.

In almost every window and on every roof in view, she could see the silhouettes of other spectators. But the lamp-lit streets and canals below were eerily empty.

"The city is holding its breath," Maris murmured. She was wearing her studded green gown. With her unbound hair whipping in the wind and the torchlight flickering across her face, there was something dangerous about her.

Behind them, a turret rose into the darkness; the narrow walkway that encircled it was full of people: the Superior and his Graces, and the Heir and his. There were a few dignitaries and servants, and several soldiers standing at attention on either side of the doorway that led back inside to the stairwell. And somewhere, there was Asa. She'd spent the evening looking for him, wondering if there would be a moment to speak with him alone.

Nomi had seen him briefly when she'd stepped out of the twisting stairs, her feet sore from climbing in her impractical shoes. She looked again now, but he had disappeared.

"This is so exciting," Cassia said, appearing at the rail beside Nomi. "We've no horse racing in Sola."

Maris shook her head. "I still don't understand how the horses don't kill themselves, racing along cobbled streets and over all those narrow bridges."

"Many of them do," Malachi said, coming up behind them. "Sometimes the riders too. The Premio Baleria is a brutal race. Blind corners, narrow streets, uneven footing, even some swimming—it takes skill, luck, and a superior horse to win."

"How dangerous." Cassia turned and leaned back on the rail, which accentuated her voluptuous figure. Her purple dress glittered in the lamplight. "Have you ever raced in it, Your Eminence?"

A muscle in Malachi's jaw jumped. "I haven't," he said. "But my brother has."

Nomi couldn't read his expression, but there was a hum of tension beneath the words. She stared back down at the city; the race route was well lit, the rest cloaked in darkness. The finish line was marked by two large red flags hung high above the street from the base of the building where she stood.

One of the Superior's emissaries would signal the start of the race, and then, when it concluded, the Superior himself would bestow the prize on the winner. His Eminence was standing not far away, his skeletal hands gripping the rail. He looked frail and gaunt, but he stood ramrod straight. As she watched, he nodded to someone, and a soldier peeled away from the wall and disappeared into the stairway.

Nomi turned back to Malachi. "I heard your brother won the race, Your Eminence." Nomi had been trying all day to imagine Asa competing in such a race, but all she saw in her mind was his wry, gentle smile.

"Yes," Malachi said flatly. "He did."

Nomi raised a brow. Was the Heir jealous of his younger brother's accomplishments?

Suddenly, a piercing shriek cut the air.

Nomi's ears rang in the silence that followed. There wasn't a view of the start of the race from this vantage point, but she could hear a sound that resembled distant thunder, and a horse screamed.

Cassia squealed with excitement. Maris leaned over the rail, craning to catch a glimpse of the runners. The crowd shifted to the other side of the turret to get a better view. Malachi offered his arm, and Cassia took it, quickly, before Nomi or Maris had the chance. They followed the gaggle of spectators. Maris trailed behind. Nomi turned to follow, but she caught sight of Asa leaning against the rail a few yards away, on his own. There were only a few people left on this side of the tower. Nomi hesitated.

Malachi didn't look back. He disappeared around the curve of the building, Cassia and Maris in tow. With a last flutter of uncertainty, Nomi headed the other way.

Distant cheers rang out, and the thunder of hooves grew louder. Nomi wandered to an empty spot along the rail next to Asa, hoping she wasn't being too obvious.

He smiled when he noticed her. "Not much of a view here. Are you not a horse racing fan?" There was something infectious and irreverent about him, so different from Malachi and his narrow-eyed brooding.

"I've never seen a race, so I can't say," Nomi answered. "But I'm not fond of crowds."

Asa leaned over the rail, trying to see the horses as they approached the home stretch. The sound was building: the roar of spectators, the screams of the horses, the percussive throb of hoofbeats.

Nomi wanted to pull him back, away from the edge. It made her nervous, the way he hung himself over the rail, more of his body suspended in the air than fixed to the ground. "*You* are a fan of horse racing, I hear. Word is you won this race once, the youngest man ever to do so," Nomi said.

He glanced back at her with a devilish gleam in his eye. "I did," he said. "Premio Belaria champion. I have a great golden cup. Sometimes I drink wine from it to remind myself of how incomparably talented and accomplished I am."

"And modest?" Nomi added, laughing.

Asa affected an innocent, wide-eyed expression. "Supreme

130

master of all things, at your service," he said, bowing. "I apologize, but supreme masters are not at all modest."

Nomi rolled her eyes at him, but she couldn't stop smiling.

The first of the horses careened around the corner and down the street directly below them. They still had to make a loop through the main piazza, up a small bridge and through a canal before arcing back to the finish line, but from this vantage, the rest of the race would be visible. Already, the rail was filling with people again.

"Are supreme masters all-knowing?" Nomi asked, shooting Asa a look.

"Of course," he said. "In fact, I can tell you that the horse in yellow, with the blood-streaked jockey, will be our winner." The horse and jockey in question were not the only ones showing signs of battle. Nomi saw another horse with a gash in his shoulder, and another whose jockey had sagged low over his neck and seemed on the verge of tumbling off.

"When I raced, I was covered in blood by halfway through," Asa continued conversationally. "Gashed my forehead on the underside of a bridge going through a canal. Take it from the all-knowing supreme master—it's a wild, wild race."

Nomi's heart hammered in her ears. She glanced around. Malachi was nowhere near, and no one else was paying attention. This was her chance. "With all that all knowingness," she ventured, staring at the race because she couldn't bear to look Asa in the eye, "does the supreme master have any idea what happened to a lowly Grace's sister?"

One of the leading horses suddenly buckled, its hooves slipping off the walkway and into the canal. The horse sputtered and screamed.

131

Nomi held her breath. Someone jostled her—an older man with heavy jowls and overgrown eyebrows. Asa put a light hand at her elbow, drawing her a step closer to him, away from the man. His voice, when he spoke, had lost its teasing edge. Gently, he said, "The supreme master does, but I fear it will not be the answer you seek."

Nomi's stomach twisted. She closed her eyes. "What happened to her?" she whispered, bracing herself.

"She was sent to Mount Ruin," Asa murmured. "I'm so sorry."

The words fell like stones against Nomi's chest, crushing her. *Mount Ruin* . . . "For how long?"

"I'm sorry," he said again. "No one leaves Mount Ruin."

Nomi covered her face with her hands as her heart broke open. She couldn't bear it.

This is my fault.

The cheers of the crowd exploded all around them as the winning horse clattered across the finish line. Nomi opened her eyes to catch a flash of yellow before the rest of the riders thundered past. She wiped the tears from her cheeks, remembering herself. She couldn't break down here, now, in the center of this maelstrom.

Spectators hung from every doorway and window, waving white towels above the streets. One by one, the towels floated down onto the competitors, who sagged and limped now that the race was over.

Asa's hand touched her arm again, startling her. "I can try to find out more," he said quietly. "The conditions, if she's comfortable . . . something."

Nomi's throat closed. Women were never put to death in Viridia. The harshest punishment was prison, and Mount Ruin was the worst of them all. It was where they sent the murderers, traitors, and thieves.

Serina had only held a book in her hands. How had this happened?

"Do you remember the terrace where we first spoke? Do you think you could find your way back there?" Asa asked, urgency creeping into his voice.

She nodded mutely.

Asa squeezed her arm encouragingly. "Meet me in three days, when the moon is high and everyone is asleep. I should know more by then."

"Thank you." The words came out hoarse and strange.

Out of the corner of her eye, she caught sight of Malachi heading her way, with Cassia and Maris on either side.

Desperately, Nomi tried to calm the emotions playing across her face.

Asa glanced up himself, noticing his brother as well. He shot her a cheeky grin. "I'm off to collect my winnings. The supreme master of all things picked the right horse."

He disappeared into the crowd just as Malachi and his entourage reached her. "There you are," the Heir said. "Did you enjoy the race?"

Nomi nodded. "It was even more exciting than I expected, Your Eminence."

And devastating.

She joined the celebration, a wooden smile fixed to her face, but inside, she was a wasteland, everything burning to ash.

SEVENTEEN

SERINA

ORACLE AND EMBER carried Petrel's body back to the cave. They placed it with care on an old wooden table with scorched legs that sat in the back corner, away from the sleeping pallets. Two women lit torches near Petrel's head and feet. Another brought water to wash away the blood.

Serina sat with the others, arms hugging her knees to her chest, and watched. No one talked or readied themselves for sleep, even though it was well past midnight.

Serina's eyes burned.

Oracle wrapped Petrel in a white sheet, smoothing the threadbare material over the girl's cheek and down her arm. Ember and two other women approached, and between the four, they raised Petrel's body onto their shoulders.

Serina joined the procession back out of the cave and into the night. She didn't know where they were going. She was only aware of the darkness pressing close, Petrel's white sheet leading the way.

They walked for what felt like hours. At some point, a reddish glow subsumed the light of torches. The path steepened, narrowed. When at last the line of women stopped, dry sulfuric heat pulsed against Serina's cheeks.

Another caldera extended into the darkness, but this one was alive.

Below them, the skin of the earth had burst, exposing a small pool of lava, bright enough to stain Serina's vision red.

Oracle's voice rose into the night. One by one, the other women joined, and a song flowed out above the restless snap and crackle of the lava. Serina didn't know the words, but the eerie cadence dug inside her chest and soon she was singing too.

Fire, breathe
Water, burn
Terror, wane
Your reign is over.
Fire, breathe
Water, burn
Stars, lead the way
Your sister is here.

With a great cry, Oracle and the other three raised Petrel's body high above their heads. Then everyone else screamed too, their voices swooping out into the night like a flock of hunting birds. The white sheet glowed red as Petrel's body dove into the volcano. Sparks flew high, fluttering right up to the stars.

The women stood vigil until the last of the sparks died, and the night was silent again.

Serina swallowed against the grittiness in her throat, sore from yelling. Her hands balled into fists at her sides, and her cheeks were wet. She followed the line of women back down the side of Mount Ruin, down into the jungle, but when she reached the entrance to the cave, she kept going, desperate to be alone.

A narrow path led toward the coast. The moonlight guided her through the trees, out to another massive lava field, where the whorls and waves of rock shone silver. The quiet of the night was absolute. But out of the corner of her eye, far away, lights twinkled.

She picked her way across the wasteland toward them. It wasn't until her feet skidded to the edge of the cliff and the screaming wind and crashing waves pounded against her ears that she realized that the glittering beacons were the lights of Bellaqua. In daylight, the city was invisible, but the faintest sparkle now shone from out of the black.

Her heart twisted. Somewhere out of sight, in a palazzo girded with gold and glass, Nomi was probably dancing with the Heir. Serina knew her sister hadn't meant for any of this to happen. But with every cell of her body, she wished that Nomi had, for once, behaved as a woman of Viridia should.

Serina stared down at the white morass below. Could she jump? She could try to swim, escape the pull of the island and let the currents take her to Bellaqua. Or maybe she would sink, and find her own sanctuary to follow all the despair.

"It's not the best cliff for jumping."

Serina staggered back, away from the ledge, terror shooting through her. But it wasn't Bruno. Instead, Valentino stood next to her, his dark hair ruffled by the wind. With the roar of the waves, Serina hadn't heard him approach.

Looking down at the roiling surf below, he added, "There

are currents here that'll bob you along for a fair distance before they suck you under. The best cliffs for jumping are the ones with lots of rocks below. You're more likely to die on impact that way. Quick. Maybe painless, if you hit it right. Some girls don't. They break their backs or their legs, and then they scream as they drown. The southern cliffs are best. They have the hardest landings."

Serina wrapped her arms around herself. It would almost be worth it, to wash the blood from her mind, to silence the nightmares.

"Don't jump," Val said, his voice stolen by the wind.

Serina glanced at him. In the darkness, she couldn't read his expression. "You just told me how."

"That's because it's your choice. And you should make an informed one." He stared out at the distant lights. "But I hope you don't jump."

"Why?" Serina asked. He wasn't forcing some power play on her, like Bruno. And it wasn't possible that he could be forming a romantic interest in her. In her threadbare prison uniform, her face sunburned and her hair dirty, she was a far cry from the elegant prospect who had ascended the stairs of the Superior's palazzo two weeks ago.

So why did he care if she lived or died?

He shrugged, his gaze never leaving the star-touched ocean. "Somebody I cared about was sent here. Before I came. She jumped."

Serina's breath caught, a tightness spreading across her chest. "I'm sorry, Valentino."

"Val," he corrected. "I think about her a lot. Mostly I

wonder what would have happened if someone had stood by her, like I'm standing by you." He removed his hat and ran a hand through his unruly hair. "Maybe she'd still be alive."

"So you try to talk down the jumpers," she said. But he was still a guard. He still stayed here, playing his part in this cruelty. Like Bruno. Serina stared at his profile, clear in the moonlight. Her voice hardened. "What about the fighters? Does it bother you to watch women kill each other? Or do you cheer, like all the other guards?"

"Bother me?" He turned fully toward her, a muscle working in his jaw. His voice vibrated with emotion as he said, "Every night, every time I close my eyes, I see them. Always, always they're in pain. I carry them with me, and I will until I die."

Serina stared at him, shocked. It was the last thing she had expected him to say.

"Please," he said, and now he was pleading, barely audible over the screaming wind. "I'd rather you didn't haunt me too."

Serina stared at him, softening despite herself. She was sure the words weren't meant as a comfort, but nevertheless they reassured her. If she died here, at least one person would remember her.

He turned back toward the cliff, and something about the way he stood, the pain she'd heard in his voice, made her ask, "Do *you* ever find yourself on the ledge?"

Val glanced at her, and the shadows in his eyes were deep and unfathomable. "All the time."

Sometimes Serina wondered what Nomi would do if she were here. Maybe Nomi would be a strong fighter, or like Oracle, smart enough to strategize and help the others. Maybe she'd try to work a way around the rules, like she did at home. It was impossible to predict, but there was one thing she *did* know. If Nomi were here, she would never give up. It had always been one of her most frustrating qualities.

Tears built behind Serina's eyes.

Nomi wouldn't want Serina to give up either. Serina would have to live with Petrel's memory, with the blood and the nightmares. She'd have to keep fighting. Even Petrel had told her to. *You fight back*, she'd said. *Always*.

The steady, screaming wind cut through Serina's thin shirt. She turned away from the cold, distant sparkle of Bellaqua and back toward the path. On impulse, she reached out and squeezed Val's wrist.

"Don't jump," she said.

EIGHTEEN

NOMI

IT BEGAN AS a dream, not a nightmare. Nomi and Serina were huddled with Renzo as he read "The Lovebirds" to them.

The small dark room of Nomi's memory split apart and became the sky, wide open and rushing, and Nomi and Serina became birds, their faces feathered by the wind. Nomi rode on Serina's back, just like in the story.

Her sister flew far, far, far out to sea. Soon Serina tired, dipping closer and closer to the rolling water. Nomi flapped her wings and flew free of her sister and let Serina settle onto her own back.

But Serina was too heavy, Nomi too weak. Nomi looked for the land to push up from the ocean, waited for their salvation to come, but instead the sky darkened. The waves savaged each other. The wind scoured her face.

Nomi couldn't hold on. Her wings dropped, heavy as lead.

And Serina fell, screaming, to be swallowed by the sea.

Nomi woke in a sea of sweat, her heart pounding. For a split second, she thought she was home, in the room she shared with Serina. But this bed was too soft. Too big. And her sister wasn't brushing her hair back from her damp forehead, comforting the nightmare away. Across the room, on the small cot by the door, Angeline shifted and sighed in her sleep.

No. This was not home.

Outside the window, Nomi could see the fading stars, the slow, creeping glow of dawn. Was Serina looking out at this same sky? Was she all right?

I let her fall.

Nomi couldn't shake off the despair of her dream. Serina was in Mount Ruin, living an actual nightmare, because of *her*.

Even as guilt left her ragged, the siren song of the mysterious book called to her. Someone had left it for her. Why? Was it a trap? A message?

Behind her, Angeline shifted again. Nomi climbed out of bed and grabbed a sundress from the armoire.

She was the first to the terrace for breakfast. She chose a wicker chair near the railing so she could watch the sparkle of the ocean. White puffs of cloud slowly crept up from the horizon. Several servants appeared with bowls of fresh-cut fruit and yogurt. Another carried a basket of warm, flaky rolls.

Behind them, Maris slipped out onto the balcony and claimed the chair next to Nomi.

"Good morning," she murmured, yawning.

Nomi picked at a small bowl of yogurt topped with a scoop of the colorful fruit, the ache of Serina's absence gnawing at her.

"Did you enjoy the race?" she asked, glancing at the other girl.

"It was too bloody." Maris stared at her plate, her expression twisted with disgust. "Those poor horses."

Cassia glided onto the terrace. "I've never seen anything so exciting. Did you see the horse that *leapt* from the top of the bridge into the canal? I thought for sure he would drown."

Nomi was happy she'd missed most of the race. She'd heard the men talking about it afterward: how many horses died, how many would need to be killed because of broken legs. A jockey had died too.

"And where did you sneak off to?" Cassia added, wiggling her fingers at Nomi. "Malachi didn't like having to look for you."

Nomi's stomach tightened. "I wanted to stay by the finish line to see who won."

Cassia rolled her eyes. "You really don't understand how this works, do you? You need to please the Heir, Nomi, not frustrate him."

Nomi shrugged. It wasn't that she didn't understand how to please him. It was that she didn't want to.

When all the Graces had arrived, Ines gave them the day's announcement. "There are no evening activities today, so rest up. We've a boat party next week to honor a delegation from Gault. The Superior has requested several harpists and one vocalist. I'll let you know who he's chosen in the next few days. Please make sure to select your gowns and secure my approval *before* the end of the week." She turned her attention to the Heir's Graces. Nomi tried not to fidget in her chair. "The Superior was not impressed with your appearances last night. Your handmaidens need more practice with your cosmetics. After breakfast, I'd like you all to work on this problem together. Your handmaidens can learn from each other."

Nomi bit back a sigh.

Maris shook her head, muttering, "I hate makeup."

They gathered in a dressing area near the bathing room. Delicate tables with gilded mirrors lined the wall, with backless stools to accommodate their wide-skirted gowns.

Angeline appeared with a brush and makeup kit in her hand. Nomi sat down at the vanity next to Maris's. Maris was staring at herself in the mirror as her handmaiden brushed out her hair. Grief darkened her eyes.

"Those poor horses," she whispered again.

Angeline placed Nomi's makeup kit on the vanity and turned to give Maris a sympathetic look. "I've always been fascinated by the race, but it's certainly not without risk." She put a hand to her heart. "When I was a child, I would lie in bed, the vibrations of hooves pounding in my chest, and pray that the horses would live. I didn't care so much about the jockeys back then." She smiled.

Maris smiled back, her face relaxing. "I was more concerned for the horses myself."

Nomi turned her attention to her own reflection. The dim light and twisted filigree surrounding the mirror gave her skin a golden cast. Before coming to the palace, she'd never had the time or desire to look at herself; now it seemed to be all she did. She wondered if her eyes would always appear so haunted.

The handmaidens tried different techniques on their Graces, until Nomi's skin felt tight and her eyelids heavy. As soon as Ines approved of Angeline's work, Nomi stood up.

"Angeline, I'm still tired from last night," she murmured. "I think I'll go lie down."

"Of course," Angeline said. "Enjoy the rest."

Nomi headed for her room. She closed the door and leaned against it, staring at the stark white sheets of her bed, the small cot Serina had slept on that first night, precious now in Nomi's memory. Outside, the fluffy white clouds had grown thick and dark, obscuring the blue of the sky.

How long did she have before Ines sought her out for more training? Before Angeline returned?

Did she dare?

Nomi slid her hand under the mattress, reaching until her fingers touched a hard corner. She drew the book out and sprawled on the bed. She cradled the soft leather in her hands.

A Brief History of Viridia.

She already knew the history of Viridia. A king had ruled the country before the Floods wiped out most of the land. When the waters receded, much of the population had perished, along with the royal family. A new government had to rise. The first Superior had been one of the king's closest advisors. He took over and rebuilt Viridia.

Nomi opened the book anyway.

Viridia's past is long and storied, from the moment the first settlers arrived in ancient times. . . .

Nomi relished the words, rolling them in her mouth without voicing them, letting them quiet the questions in her head. If she was reading, she wasn't thinking about Serina.

She was living in the language set black and stark against the page. She flipped page after page.

The settlers gave way to the rise of a religious government, led by Cardinal Bellaqua. Renzo had learned a lot about Bellaqua at school. He was seen as a heroic but tragic figure, overthrown by the mercenary King Vaccaro.

Cardinal Bellaqua's long and illustrious reign came to a stunning end when he was seduced—seduced? Nomi's brow furrowed—*and poisoned by a female warrior from Azura. Claiming the throne for herself, the warrior became Queen Vaccaro, holding the country by force—*

Nomi's whole body tensed. *Queen* Vaccaro? This wasn't the history she knew. The world tipped sickeningly on its axis.

—despite attempts to overthrow her, for nearly thirty years. She clung to power, and her daughter and granddaughter after her, but the resistance grew.

Nomi read faster and faster, disbelieving. But there it was. All the history she thought she knew of her country was recast.

And in a last shock, the book laid out the root of the Floods— Nomi had always been told the Floods were a natural disaster, affecting the whole world. But *A Brief History of Viridia* stated that in fact, infrastructure throughout the country was tampered with, expressly to cause a disaster that would threaten the monarchy. The orchestrators? The queen's senior advisors, who then rose to power in the aftermath.

The heroes of Viridia, the historian claimed.

The first Superior took the queen and her two daughters as his first Graces and limited the rights and activities of women in the country, for fear of a threat to his rule similar to that which Cardinal Bellaqua suffered. The powerful approach was successful, ensuring the Superior and his Heirs kept a secure and

145

unquestioned grip on the country. Today, the tradition of the Graces is the most revered in all of Viridia.

The first Superior's Grace was *the queen*. All the laws in this country, all the ways women were kept ignorant and powerless . . . it was because the new rulers didn't want history to repeat itself.

The Superior's great-great-great-grandfather destroyed Viridia, Nomi realized. *On purpose.*

Nomi stared out the window at a bank of clouds building along the horizon. Fury filled her up, heavy and hot and enduring. The kind she wouldn't be able to will away.

In Viridia, women were oppressed because men were *afraid* of them.

Women had ruled this country. And history had denigrated them. Erased them. Nomi was *certain* this wasn't what Renzo had been taught. He would have told her.

But the Superior knew. Whoever had given her this book knew.

And now she did too.

NINETEEN

SERINA

SERINA HANDED JACANA half of a hard roll. After Petrel's loss, there wasn't enough bread left for everyone to have her own piece. A boar roasted on a spit over the fire, dripping fat that popped and hissed in the flames. The scent of fresh meat made Serina's mouth water. But it was only lunchtime—the boar wouldn't be ready until dinner.

A few feet away, Tremor, one of the women from the hunting party, groaned. A deep gash ran the length of her forearm, courtesy of the boar's sharp tusk. Each crew had a small stash of medical supplies bandages, a salve to stave off infection, needle and thread—but they were limited in what they could heal without doctors. Mirror was trying to sew up the injured woman's arm, but Tremor kept flinching each time the needle punctured skin, and the stitches were clumsy and uneven.

Tremor groaned again, and Mirror's face blanched beneath her blanket of freckles. Serina couldn't stop staring. The stitches were so spread out that parts of the wound were still open. It would likely get infected. The salve could only do so much.

She couldn't handle it any longer.

Serina handed the rest of the bread to Jacana and stepped through the group to reach the injured woman's side. "Give me the needle," she said, crouching by Mirror. "You're messing up her arm."

Mirror looked up, eyes wide. "Excuse me? I'm doing fine."

Serina pulled the needle from her fingers. "You're not. Now move over. I can do better."

At least, she thought she could. If it were a length of fabric and embroidery yarn, she would be certain. She'd never tried to sew up skin before.

Serina looked into the injured woman's ashen face. "Okay, Tremor," she said, trying to sound calm and reassuring. "I'm going to fix up your arm, okay?"

"Fine," she growled. "Just get it done."

Serina nodded. Mirror moved out of the way, mouth pinched into a frown. Serina focused on the wound. It had been cleaned but was still oozing blood. About a third of the gash had been stitched. She began at that end, adding tiny stitches to fill the places where the skin still gapped. After the first, she forgot everything but the movement of her hands, the snick and pinch of needle, the quick tie-off of thread. Skin became fabric, thread became embroidery yarn, and in minutes, Tremor had a line of tiny, neat stitches closing her wound. Serina tied off the last and then picked up the pot of salve and covered the ridge of thread.

"There," she said. "All done."

The woman looked down at her arm. "You were so fast," she said wonderingly.

148

Ember bumped Serina in the shoulder. Her strip of red hair had been freshly cut, making her look especially fierce. "Good work, Grace."

Mirror squeezed Serina's arm. Some of her color had come back. "You were right. Your stitches are better. Next time, I'll come get you."

Serina stood up and, for the first time, noticed the blood coating her hands. Sweat beaded on the back of her neck, and her fingers trembled. She rushed for the tunnel. Outside, the heat of the afternoon pressed down on her. She plunged her hands into the trickle of stream that fed the orange trees. Then she scrubbed, over and over, long after all vestiges of blood were gone.

She'd pierced skin, sewn someone up with barely a thought. What was this place turning her into?

A little later, she heard footsteps from within the cave. Jacana came up beside her. "Ember said we should be training."

Mutely, Serina followed the smaller girl down through the trees. When they reached the training grounds, Gia, Oracle, and a handful of others were already fighting. The new freshie still looked blank with terror. Serina had only been here a few weeks, but somehow she was adapting. All that training she did to become a Grace, the endless lessons and forced neglect of her own needs, served her well here. Instead of dancing, she fought. Instead of playing the harp, she foraged for food. Instead of embroidering a pillow, she sewed up skin. And instead of pleasing the Heir, she tried to please her crew.

If Serina thought about it like that, if she focused on her purpose, she didn't mourn so much the things she might have wanted for her life. Or the people she missed.

"Grace, you're up!" Oracle shouted from within the circle.

Serina steeled herself and headed for the older women. She was getting better at fighting, but she still hated it.

When she'd reached a clear space in the trampled grass, Oracle faced off with her. Serina's eyes widened. She glanced at Gia, who was facing the freshie. "I thought I'd be fighting—" she started.

"You'll be fighting me," Oracle interjected. Her mismatched eyes zeroed in on Serina, who suddenly felt horribly exposed. If it was true that Oracle could tell what you were thinking, where you were going to move, just by looking at you, she had to know Serina wished she could run.

But Serina had learned already that running wasn't an option. Not here.

She raised her fists.

Oracle jabbed her in the stomach before she was even aware they'd begun. Serina grunted. She sidestepped Oracle's next jab, weight focused on the balls of her feet. She ducked and swerved, throwing her own punch. She didn't connect, but at least it had a little force behind it. Oracle dropped and twisted, trying to sweep Serina's legs, but she managed to leap out of the way. Spinning, she used her momentum to push forward and shove Oracle. It was an ugly move, and for once, Oracle didn't anticipate her. The woman rocked back a few steps, though she didn't fall.

Serina pushed her advantage, getting in one good punch to Oracle's stomach. Then she shoved her again. Oracle ran into one of the other girls and tripped over her leg. She fell, but before Serina could reach her, she'd already heaved herself to her feet and rushed forward, catching Serina around the belly. They both went tumbling to the ground, inches from scraping their heads against the rough volcanic rock surrounding the training field.

Serina stared at the sky, gasping, as she waited for the air to return to her lungs. Oracle sat up, rubbing her forearm. "Not bad, Grace," she said, sounding more sad than impressed. "Shoving can be good for the element of surprise, but don't do it too often. It leaves your head and the back of your neck exposed."

Serina sat up slowly, wisps of air finally finding their way to her lungs. It was another minute before she could respond. "I'll remember that."

"Keep practicing your footwork. Your dancing skills help, but you're still moving too slow. Work on your speed, your reaction time." Her attention turned to the other fighters.

"Why do we do this?" Serina asked. It was a question that had dogged her since her first night on the island. "Why do we let the guards make us fight? If we all just said no, wouldn't they be forced to feed us instead?" She understood that the rations were limited, but surely it would be better to share what food they had rather than this system.

Oracle's gaze shifted back to Serina, and without a word, she pulled her to her feet. "Come on," she ordered, drawing her away from the other fighters.

They walked in silence for a few minutes, until they reached a stand of scrubby trees out of sight and hearing of the others. Then Oracle rounded on Serina. "Don't ever talk about refusing to fight, do you hear me? Never."

Serina's eyes widened. "I don't understand."

Oracle's brow furrowed, deep frown lines appearing around her mouth. Her pale, milky eye, a complete contrast to the other, brown one, almost seemed to glow. For a long time, she stared at Serina in silence.

"When I first arrived," she said at last, "some of the women protested. The champions stood on the stage and refused to fight. They knew no one would get the rations that week. But none of them wanted to be the guards' pawns any longer."

Serina took a ragged breath.

"The guards shot them all," Oracle said, voice flat. "Sprayed bullets into the audience too. Fifteen women died. The guards wouldn't allow the bodies to be moved. The next week's champions had to fight around the rotting corpses. That was the week I won for the first time."

The horror unfolded in Serina's mind, inescapable.

"We fight because we have to. Got me, Grace?" She started back up the hill.

"The name you gave me," Serina said, while she had the chance. "I'm not a Grace."

Oracle stopped. Turned. "But you were trained to become one. I can tell."

"How?" Serina was covered in filth, as aching and sunburned as the rest of the girls.

"The training, the poise. It's unmistakable." Oracle's hands clenched into fists. "I always knew another Grace would make her way here someday."

"Another . . . ?" Serina froze, realization dawning.

Oracle dropped into a slow, graceful curtsy, her hands

clasping delicately at invisible skirts. The sun bleached out the brown hair at the crown of her head.

Serina was shocked into silence. She'd seen Oracle fight, delivering nearly surgical blows that left her training opponents on their knees, panting. She'd seen her carry a woman's body miles up a mountain to commit it to a volcano. Oracle's sudden grace, her courtliness, was the last thing Serina had *ever* expected. "How did you end up *here?*" she asked finally.

Oracle lifted her chin. "I spent my whole life training to be a Grace. I was perfect. But that's not why the Superior chose me. He chose me because I was *smart*." She paused, gathering herself. "And he knew that breaking a willful girl would be more satisfying."

"Breaking you?" Suddenly, Serina saw Nomi's defiant glare in her mind.

"He can have anything he wants," Oracle said. "But he's not interested in things that are easily given. It's a game to him."

Serina remembered the ice in the Superior's voice when he'd delivered her sentence. The way he'd asked about Nomi.

Oracle continued, unguarded emotion flashing across her face. "When I could no longer bear it, I fought back. I knew he would kill me, as he had killed other girls. I knew death was my only escape."

Serina couldn't erase the images flashing through her mind.

"But I couldn't die. I saw the blows coming. I'd learned his patterns. I avoided the killing blows. It was his guard who knocked me out—it was his fist to my eye that did this." Oracle pointed to her blind eye. "If he hadn't stopped me, I would have killed the Superior."

"So they sent you here," Serina whispered. Treason, attempted murder. Nothing so inconsequential as reading a book. Did the Superior consider reading as dangerous as attempted murder? Or were the requirements for being sent to Mount Ruin subject to the fickle whims of the magistrates handing down punishment?

"So they sent me here. I'm happy you didn't suffer as I did," Oracle said, her eyes boring into Serina. "A life in this prison, for all its dangers, is preferable to the Superior's hell."

"My sister . . . my sister was chosen, instead of me," Serina said. She shivered, thinking of the Superior's icy stare. "But she's a Grace for the Heir. Surely, he'll be different; he won't be as bad as his father. . . ." Her voice petered out at Oracle's look.

The woman stared at her, her pity clear. "In my experience, sons are worse. Pray your sister is easily broken. It's the defiant ones who suffer the most."

With a sickening jolt, Serina thought of Nomi and her secret knowledge, her lack of obedience. Why else would Malachi want her, if not to crush her spirit? Serina had been too docile, too *obedient*. Just as she'd been raised to be.

Fury and fear the likes of which she'd never felt before rushed through her with the force of a tidal wave.

She gazed out toward the ocean, its distant sparkle just visible through the trees. Her sister was a captive in silk and lace, suffering at the hands of the Heir. Unwilling.

Then and there, Serina made her choice. Mount Ruin couldn't have her. And sure as the fire eating this island from the inside out, she wouldn't let the Heir have Nomi either. She would escape. *Somehow* she would escape. And she would save her sister.

TWENTY

NOMI

NOMI LISTENED TO Angeline's steady breathing with her eyes closed, the darkness pressing down on her with an almost physical weight. Asa had said to meet when the moon was high, but tonight the clouds that had lingered for days sulked in the sky and hid every scrap of moonlight. Nomi feigned sleep until she was sure her heart would burst. Until she'd counted one hundred of Angeline's inhales and exhales. And then she counted a hundred more.

At last, she rose and slipped a silk dressing gown over her nightdress. She didn't bother with shoes. Angeline's breathing never changed, even as the door snicked open. Nomi peeked into the hall. Hastily, she closed the door, resting her forehead against the cool wood.

The Superior's man was still there, at the end of the corridor.

She waited one minute. Two.

Peeked again. His sturdy form had disappeared.

Nomi took a deep breath, held it, and slipped from the room.

She leaned against the door, the carved doe pressing into her back, and listened.

For the past two days, she'd stayed up later than usual, feigning insomnia. In truth, she'd been watching the men who roamed the Graces' chambers. Most of them left when the Graces went to bed, but two remained at their posts all through the night, pacing the corridors, inspecting the terraces, stomping through the empty dining hall and ballroom. Their circuit took about five minutes. Sometimes the men walked together. Sometimes one took an alternate route.

Nomi prayed tonight they stayed together.

She clasped her dressing gown closer to her body. If she were caught, she'd say she was sleepwalking. She'd act confused. Frightened.

The last wouldn't be too hard.

She tiptoed to the end of the hall. The men usually inspected the terraces first. She should have time to sneak the other way. It wouldn't do to wonder what would happen if her luck didn't hold.

She'd almost made it to the circular receiving room when she heard the thud of a shoe behind her. She ducked inside the doorway and froze, breath held.

Thud. Thud. Thud.

Suddenly, she couldn't remember which direction the guards went after the terraces. Were they coming here or heading down the corridor to the baths? Her pulse clamored in her ears, so loud she couldn't be sure she was hearing footsteps and not the pounding of her own heart.

She made a choice and bolted for the door on the opposite side of the room, the door that led beyond the Graces' chambers.

Her hand touched the knob. No one raised the alarm. Another second, and she was on the other side. The hallway outside was dim, lit at long intervals by flickering lamps. She hurried around the corner and down to the wall of glass.

All the partitions were closed. The darkness beyond was absolute. She couldn't tell if Asa waited for her. With trembling fingers, she slid the glass open just wide enough to slide through.

A gust of wind blew through the gap, sending the hem of her dressing gown fluttering behind her. A hand gripped her wrist and pulled her outside.

She drew in a breath to scream.

"Hush." Another hand covered her mouth in the dark. "It's only me."

Nomi sagged with relief at the familiar voice.

Asa reached around and shut the glass partition. "I'm sorry I startled you," he murmured. "I was afraid someone would see you."

Nomi tried to calm her racing heart, but it was difficult with the wind and the night and his body so close.

She took a step back to give herself space to breathe.

"What would happen if we were caught, Your Eminence?" she asked. Her eyes were adjusting to the dark. She could make out the shadow of his face now, turning toward the glow of the hallway beyond the glass.

"I don't know," he replied. "I've never done this before."

"If a person can be sent to Mount Ruin for reading . . ." Her voice trembled.

"No, Nomi. I would not let that happen to you," he said earnestly. He bent toward her. "I promise."

157

All the frustration, guilt, and grief she'd been holding inside, in silence, threatened to spill out. "I can't stand this. Serina shouldn't be there," Nomi said, the words tumbling over themselves. "It isn't fair."

"You're right—it's *not* fair." Asa led her over to the railing, farther from the light filtering through the glass. "Nothing about Viridia is fair."

"What can I do? Surely there's some way to persuade the Superior to free her?" Nomi knew she was grasping at straws. But she couldn't let Serina suffer for her. Not anymore. Not if she could do something, *anything*. "Maybe, if I said I was the one who took the book, if I was the one who could read . . ."

She hesitated. Would he realize she was confessing? She *wanted* to confess. She wanted everyone to know her sister was innocent, that she didn't deserve to be punished. *Imprisoned.*

But Asa shook his head. "Absolutely not. Father would just punish you both. He and Malachi . . ." She felt his shudder through his hands, still joined with hers. "The slightest infraction can be deadly. Father is always merciless, but Malachi is worse. . . . He's volatile. One day, he offers mercy. The next, agony. I fear what he'll do as Superior. His unpredictability could endanger all of Viridia."

Nomi's stomach twisted. She remembered that first day in the hallway, when Malachi had cornered her against the wall, so angry, only to choose her as a Grace not two hours later. Volatile, yes. And this was the man to whom her life was forever chained.

"So there's nothing we can do?" Nomi felt the burn of tears. For Serina. And for herself.

His grip on her hands tightened. "I'm so sorry, Nomi. I wish I had more power. *Any*, really. There's so much I would do." His gaze lost focus, turning inward. "But there is *one* thing, at least," he continued, his voice a mere murmur, so soft she had to lean closer to hear. The wind blew at her back, urging her, the hem of her nightgown fluttering toward him like reaching hands. "I can help you escape."

"What?" Shock reverberated through her. "Why would you do that?"

Asa ran a hand through his hair. "I see you, Nomi. You were never meant to be a Grace, never wanted to be one, and he chose you anyway."

"Why did he?" Nomi still had no idea. Malachi didn't seem particularly interested in her, certainly not more so than the others. She didn't understand why she would have appealed so much more than all the beautiful prospects who *wanted* to be chosen, who'd been groomed for this life.

Asa didn't answer for so long, she thought maybe he wouldn't tell her, or he didn't know. But, at last, he said softly, "I think he did it to punish you. He could tell you weren't cowed by him. You had power when you stood there that day, telling him where the lavatory was. He will try to break your spirit, like one of his horses."

Hearing it laid out so plainly was horrifying, but Nomi found that she wasn't entirely surprised. It made sense, really. The Heir had been angry. He'd wanted to hurt her. For Nomi, being chosen as a Grace was like being sent to prison. She'd spend the rest of her life serving a man she hated.

Asa gripped the railing with both hands and stared out into

the cloud-dark night. "No one should be made to feel broken or powerless. Not you, not me. Not anyone."

Nomi had never heard anyone talk like this before, not even Renzo.

"Where would I go?" she whispered.

"Wherever you want."

Her mind balked at the vastness of the prospect. *Wherever you want.*

He was talking about freedom.

"It wasn't always like this," he muttered. "Before the Floods . . ."

Before the Floods.

Nomi's breath caught. Had it been Asa who'd left the book? She didn't dare ask, didn't dare confirm that she had a book in her possession. Or that she could read it.

"What happened before the Floods?" she asked carefully.

He shrugged. "I just . . . I think we could do so much *more*, so much better than we're doing now. If my father could see what this country really needs, if we had a visionary leading us, instead of a merciless old man . . . or my brother . . ."

"What do you think this country needs? If *you* were the Heir, what would you change?"

Asa leaned against the railing and sighed. "Honestly? Everything. I would choose no Graces. I would let women read." His glanced at her, his face softening. "I would free Serina."

The answer tasted like chocolate and burned like fire. It was sweet. Seductive.

Dangerous.

He chuckled wryly and shook his head. "I talked to my father about it once. Made my case for me to be the Heir instead

160

of Malachi. Tried to convince him I would be the better son for Viridia."

"He wasn't convinced?"

Asa smiled sadly. "No, he was not convinced."

"I wish you could be the Heir," Nomi said wistfully, staring down at the black-and-silver waves.

Asa laughed. "Me too. But unless something happens to Malachi, we're stuck with him when Father dies."

Nomi thought about Queen Vaccaro, who'd overthrown Cardinal Bellaqua with nothing but her smile and her poison perfume. The history book had made it sound like the worst kind of treachery, but to Nomi . . .

To Nomi it was hope. Women had once been powerful in this country. Maybe they could be again. Her mind spun, teasing out delicate, dangerous strands of possibility. Guilt drove her, and grief. But beneath that, always burning, the fury. Women were *not* lesser beings.

"What if something *did* happen to Malachi?" she asked, so softly the wind stole the words.

Asa shot her a calculating look. "I won't have my brother killed."

"No, not killed." Within her mind, the threads tightened, the possibilities knitting themselves into a crooked pattern that might be a plan. *Scandal. Subterfuge.* Just like Queen Vaccaro, save for the murder. "If he was framed for a crime, maybe . . ."

"He would be punished for something he didn't do," Asa replied, but he sounded thoughtful, not outraged.

"You said there are things he *has* done. He is not innocent," Nomi said.

161

Asa put his hands on her shoulders and turned her gently to face him. "A plan like that takes time. There's uncertainty. Risk. A *lot* of risk." He brushed a strand of her hair off her cheek and suddenly, Nomi was aware of their two bodies so close in the darkness. There was risk in *that*.

"You could just escape," he said. "I could help you leave the palace, find a place for you to live. A new identity. A contract to a factory or a job as servant. Whatever you prefer. You could choose."

"If I did that," she said softly, "nothing would ever change." And it wouldn't save Serina.

He bent nearer. Even in the dark, Nomi could see the spark in his eyes. "So what do we do?"

———

Nomi and Asa spent half the night fine-tuning their scheme.

"The crime has to be something that directly impacts the Superior," Asa said with a touch of bitterness. "Or else my father won't care. He'd probably celebrate."

"Maybe Malachi could plot a war?" she wondered.

"Too many moving parts. Hard to feign. We'd have to really start a war to make it convincing."

"An assassination attempt?"

"Of the Superior? That might work. Father is very ill, but he's got fight left in him. Maybe Malachi's impatient to lead, so he decides to help Nature along."

She thought of the first queen's perfume. "Would he use poison?"

They now sat on one of the chaises, huddled together as the cool wind buffeted them. "Poison is difficult to procure, and no one would believe the threat without the real thing. What if he were to hire someone to do physical violence?"

"And you thwart the attempt at just the right moment, exposing the plot and saving your father." To Nomi, it sounded like a fairy tale.

All the anger seething through her blood had brightened into joy. She was going to change things. She and Asa would give Viridia back its heritage. They would make it into the country it was meant to be.

And they would free Serina.

"It can't be a real assassin," Asa mused. "I won't have my father actually killed. That's important. It has to be someone who understands the subtleties, who knows we need a performance, not an actual threat."

"So, someone we trust. Someone we can protect from punishment."

"Yes," Asa agreed. "Without immunity, why would they help us?"

"Do you know such a man?" Nomi asked.

"There are several palace guards I believe to be loyal to me," he said. "But all are recognizable within the palace. Everyone knows them as my personal guard and couldn't fail to make the connection."

"I don't know anyone at all, except my family." Her heart stuttered. *Renzo.*

No. She couldn't involve him. The risk was too great.

"How would we protect our false assassin?" she asked. "It would not be enough to urge your father to be lenient. You said he is merciless."

"You're right. We'd have to engineer an escape, maybe a disguise. . . ."

Nomi sat up straighter. "The Heir's birthday. The Graces have been talking about it. Someone said it's to be a masquerade." It would be the night the Heir could demand her in his chambers if he so chose.

Not if the Heir is arrested.

"It is. That's perfect." Asa sounded excited. "A disguise *and* means of escape. Our conspirator can remain unknown. Slip in, perform our deception, and then disappear. No danger, no way of getting caught."

No danger.

She turned to study him. The clouds had finally cleared, and a sliver of moonlight now shone on Asa's boyish face. "You can think of no one to help us?" she asked again, praying.

But after a long moment, Asa shook his head. "The only people I know are guards and courtiers. With a disguise, perhaps a guard could do it, but they'd be working during the ball. It would be difficult to avoid exposure. And there isn't a single courtier I trust. But don't despair. I'll keep thinking."

Nomi shook her head. "No. I know someone who can do it. Someone I trust implicitly. My—" She broke off abruptly. "My cousin."

She had to be smart, safe about this. This was Renzo's life.

"A cousin is good," Asa said. His hand lightly rubbed her arm; she wasn't sure he was even aware he was doing it. But she liked the soft touch, the contact. "Where does he live? How do we reach him?"

"I can reach him," Nomi said. She didn't want to tell him more about Renzo than she had to.

"How? Does he live in Bellaqua?"

"I—" She paused. How *could* she reach Renzo without telling Asa who he really was? Where he lived?

Did it matter?

She had already trusted Asa with so much. He could have her sent to prison based on this conversation alone. Still. She would risk herself, not Renzo. She took a deep breath. "I will write to him."

Asa went still. "So you *can* read and write."

Nomi turned to him, suddenly desperate that he understand. "Yes. *I'm* the one who taught myself. *I'm* the one who stole the book. Not Serina. Ines saw her with the book in her hands, but it was mine. I don't know why she didn't tell the truth. But you see? She *shouldn't* be in Mount Ruin. *I* should."

"Nomi, no one should be imprisoned for reading. Not you or your sister." Asa covered her hand with his and gave it a gentle squeeze. "We are going to free her. Together, we are going to change everything."

Nomi balanced on a precipice, as wind-blown and perilous as a real cliff. There was a difference between defiance and outright rebellion. Could she do this? Could she jump over the ledge?

Maybe not for herself. But for Serina, yes.

TWENTY-ONE

SERINA

RESOLVING TO LEAVE Mount Ruin was easy; actually escaping would be much more difficult.

"It's steep here," Jacana said, picking her way across a ribbon of lava rock.

Serina clambered as close to the cliff's edge as she dared and studied the narrow curve of beach far below. "*Too* steep. The guards and other prisoners don't come here, but it'd be almost impossible to get down there ourselves."

"Maybe somewhere farther south?" Jacana sat down on the rock and dusted off her hands before wiping the sweat from her forehead. They'd been hiking all morning.

Serina was glad to have Jacana's company. Every time they passed a tower or a guard on patrol, Serina's muscles tensed and her stomach turned sour. She'd seen Bruno once, from a distance, but he hadn't approached. Apparently Petrel's warning had been effective.

Serina was haunted by the knowledge that if Petrel hadn't

appeared, she would have done whatever Bruno said. She'd been raised her whole life to be submissive. To defer to men. She'd only been learning to fight for a few weeks.

"The best wood is down south," Serina said, pushing thoughts of Bruno—and Petrel—from her mind. "It would save us having to carry our supplies across the island." She settled down beside Jacana. "But Va—" She cut herself off. She hadn't told anyone about her conversation with Val, not even Jacana. "Uh, various people have told me the rocks are very dangerous down there. It would make getting the raft away from the island difficult."

Jacana glanced over her shoulder at the guard tower in the distance. "I think it's going to be difficult either way."

Serina took a deep breath of humid, salt-soaked air. "It's going to be almost impossible, and take time, but I know we can do this."

Jacana pulled on the end of her braid. The crease between her brows deepened. "I'm more worried about building the raft. I've never built anything in my life. And we have no tools, no materials. . . ."

Serina rubbed her dirty, callused palms together. "Between my sweet manners and your thieving, we can get tools. And when we're ready to start building, we'll tell Gia. She lived her whole life on a boat. She'll be able to help. If there's room for two, there'll be room for three."

Jacana stared at the glittering ocean. "We'll be caught. Or we'll get out there, the raft will fall apart, and we'll drown."

"Maybe." At Jacana's look, Serina amended. "Probably."

She climbed back to her feet. There was no denying it was

a dangerous, foolish plan. Find a hiding spot on the beach and build a raft out of timber and vines? Absurd.

But Serina had been over and over it. There was no other possibility. Doing something, *anything*, was better than nothing. Nomi needed her, and the longer Serina stayed here, the more likely it was she'd have to fight. And if she fought, she'd die. No matter how she looked at it, a clock was counting down, with Nomi's fate and her own sliding ever closer to disaster.

"At some point we'll have to fight," she said, her hands clenching into fists. "Would you rather die playing the Commander's sick game or trying to escape?"

"I'd rather not die at all," Jacana said faintly. Suddenly, her shoulders stiffened. "There's a guard coming this way."

Serina's stomach dropped. She turned to look, but the man moving toward them didn't keep his hand on his gun, didn't gaze at them with suspicion. His dark hair clambered out from under his hat, and his bright, dark eyes watched them curiously.

"Got reports from the tower that we had some jumpers," Val said. He raised a brow at Serina.

"We're not here to jump," she assured him. "We were, ah . . . looking for a place we could get in the water and cool off."

Jacana sat on the rough rock, still as a statue. Frozen in fear, maybe. Serina understood. If it had been anyone other than Val . . .

He squinted in the bright, hot sun. "There are some beaches on the east side where you can get in the water without worrying about the undertow," he offered. "But stay on the coast, away from Jungle Camp, and don't go too far north, or you'll run into Twig and her crew."

Serina brushed her hands on her pants and said casually, "We were hoping to find a place with some shade, a few good sturdy trees, you know. And private . . . don't need the guards gawking."

Val rubbed the back of his neck, which was burnt brown by the sun. "Some trees, private . . ." he said, considering. "Yeah, the east side's your best bet. There are a few beaches like that. You might have to dodge some of the other girls."

"Thank you." Serina smiled, eager to check it out. She looked over at Jacana, who was still frozen. "Up for a little more hiking?"

Jacana nodded and slowly got to her feet, still eyeing Val warily.

With a last friendly glance at Serina, he said, "More patrolling to do. You girls be careful. There's a lot of rough ground to cover. Probably take you a few hours." And then he headed south, along the cliffs.

Serina set out toward the center of the island.

"You trust that guard?" Jacana asked, coming up beside her.

Serina thought about that. *Did* she trust Val? "I trust him not to willingly hurt me," she said at last. "And I trust what he said about the east beach." She picked her way across thick tree roots curling over a thin ribbon of lava rock. "But I wouldn't trust him with my life," she added. "He's still a guard, bound by Commander Ricci's orders."

Jacana picked up her pace, practically leaping over the uneven ground. Like she was running from something. "I've heard stories about the guards. When I saw him coming toward us, I just froze."

Unwanted memories of Bruno rose in Serina's mind. Striving to ease Jacana's, Serina told the girl what Petrel had said. "Being in Oracle's crew gives us protection. We're safe, Jacana."

The girl laughed unexpectedly. "Safe? I felt safer in an abandoned warehouse in Sola with the authorities breaking down the door, and I knew I had stolen goods inside. This island, every bit of it, is worse than the worst nightmare I've ever had."

They hiked up into the hills, into the shade of the scrubby forest. Serina looked around at the lush greenery that had somehow missed the volcano's wrath. Here, among the trees, she could almost imagine she was out for a pleasant walk. "Do you know that before I came here, I'd never been on a walk by myself? Or even with my sister, or a friend. Maybe—"

"Maybe it's not so bad? The guards, the fights, the starving, the *volcano*." Jacana dragged a hand through her messy hair and shook her head. "There is no maybe. It *is* bad. It is hell."

Serina had never heard her sound so bitter. Gently, she said, "I was going to say maybe that's part of the nightmare, having *just* enough freedom thrown at you to tempt you, knowing it's an illusion. Knowing that Mount Ruin will kill you, somehow, no matter what you do."

Jacana paused for a moment to catch her breath, her hand on a wind-bent tree. "Unless we build our raft."

Serina smiled. "We will. We're going to find a way off this island."

Jacana didn't look particularly hopeful, but she started walking again. As Serina wove through the forest, she kept her eyes peeled for fruit or anything else they could eat. They'd only had a few bites of bread for breakfast, and already she was so slug-gish it felt as if she wore skirts of lead.

Serina and Jacana hiked through most of the afternoon, skirting Jungle Camp and stopping to drink some water from a trickle of stream that ran uncomfortably close to a guard tower. When at last they made it to the east coast, it took them some time to find a place that would suit their purposes. But even so, Serina was encouraged. They were isolated here, a good hour from Jungle Camp and even farther from Hotel Misery down south. There was little reason for the other crews to venture this far.

At last, they found a spot boasting a soft, easily accessible beach with gentle waves, several cypress trees scrabbling up from the sandy shore, and a bit of a cave as the rocks pushed up into cliffs further down the beach.

Wood for their raft, a place to hide it, and calm waters for its launch.

It was perfect.

"Now all we need are some makeshift tools and the time to work." Serina gave Jacana a quick hug. "We can do this."

Jacana's timid face eased into a grin. "Maybe we can."

TWENTY-TWO

NOMI

THE MORNING AFTER she met with Asa, Nomi bent over the scrap of paper on her dressing table and took up her stick of kohl. Asa had offered her writing materials, but she was afraid Angeline would find them. The deep black eyeliner stood out starkly on a blank page torn reluctantly from the back of the history book. The more she thought about it, the more convinced she was that he'd been the one to leave it for her. He hadn't seemed surprised when she said she could find her own means of writing the letter.

It took her a long time to figure out how to code her message. Hopefully Renzo would understand the words woven into one of their favorite legends, of the brothers and the mysterious tattooed woman.

The story was about a kind brother who falls in love with a scullery maid with a secret: Her father, a pirate, has left her a fortune. She tattooed the treasure map into her skin so she would never forget its location, and plans to find it with the kind brother's help. But the cruel younger brother thwarts their plans, killing them both when the woman refuses to reveal the map. He finds the map and treasure, but the ghosts of his brother and the mysterious woman appear, terrifying him so much his heart seizes and he dies, the treasure lost forever.

It was quite a bloodthirsty tale. Nomi's version altered it to give Renzo clues.

The older brother was the cruel one.

The younger knew how to stop him.

The woman chose to help instead of refusing to share her secret.

And in Nomi's version, the woman's sister was in grave danger. Nomi was as explicit as she dared. She asked him to come to Bellaqua as soon as he could, and to send word when he arrived. She told him it was dangerous.

Even with a mask, even with a plan, it was dangerous.

She signed it with a simple N so Renzo's best friend, Luca, wouldn't know whom it was from. She ripped another page out of the book, folded it around the letter like an envelope, and wrote Luca's address on it. She couldn't get the letter out of the city, but Asa could. She knew Luca would pass the message to Renzo. He wouldn't understand it, but he'd pass it along. She dripped some candle wax to seal it.

Tonight, at the boat party, Nomi would try to slip the letter to Asa. It would be difficult to steal a private moment, but they both decided it was less dangerous than attempting another clandestine meeting so soon.

A quiet knock galvanized her. "Just a minute!" she called. She rushed to hide the note deep under the mattress, with the book.

Angeline shuffled into the room, her arms overflowing with a cloud of red fabric.

"What is that?" Nomi asked, looking askance at the pile.

Her handmaiden heaved it onto the bed. "Your gown for the party tonight. The dressmaker *finally* finished it. Yours was the last one she finished. She cut it close this time."

Surprise, Nomi thought. Her relationship with the seamstresses remained strained.

"I forgot how massive it is." She'd been unable to breathe during the fitting, and she remembered thinking the dress made her look like a stranger.

Unbidden, Nomi found herself wondering what Asa would think of its full skirt and structured, low-cut bodice.

"It's red." Angeline smiled. "Malachi's favorite color."

Nomi's stomach twisted. She tried to return her handmaiden's smile. "It's lovely."

Angeline continued her chatter. "You know his horse is a blood bay?"

Nomi looked at her blankly.

"Red," Angeline clarified. "A great hulking beast with a long black mane. The other day I was cleaning the terrace and saw him riding. Gorgeous thing. The horse, I mean. I've always thought the Heir was quite terrifying, to be honest. Is he always so serious? But handsome, of course, don't you think?"

"I—I don't know," Nomi replied. Suddenly, she wanted to be anywhere but in that room. She had no desire to gossip about the Heir. What would Angeline think if Nomi confessed the Heir terrified her too?

"It's hours 'til the party. I think I'll work on my embroidery.

Get a little air." Nomi collected her materials and scurried into the hall. As she walked through the ornate sitting rooms, all oppressively silent, Nomi wished she could escape outside, take a walk somewhere, feel the air on her face. The best she could do was make her way to one of the terraces.

"Oh! Excuse me," Nomi said, noticing Maris in a wicker chair by the railing. She was staring out at the ocean through the gaps of the twisting iron flowers.

Maris waved a hand at the chair beside her. "I don't mind."

Nomi settled onto the seat and pulled out her embroidery hoop.

One of the Superior's men stepped into the doorway and stood for a few moments, watching them. Eventually he left, his white shoes silent on the tile. Nomi wondered if it was one of the men she'd dodged the night before. Returning to her room had been a little less nerve-racking than sneaking out; Asa had given her directions to the servants' entrance, which wasn't on the men's rounds.

Maris's gaze flicked to the empty doorway. "I hate the way they loom in corners, listening," she murmured. "Yesterday the Superior disciplined Eva for something she said when one of his *guards* was watching."

"Do you know what she said?" Nomi asked.

Maris shook her head. "I didn't hear. But she was scared when Ines told her the Superior had summoned her. And Rosario told me that the Heir is taking us on an excursion tomorrow in place of the Superior and his Graces as punishment for Eva's impertinence. Ines is to announce it at lunch."

"So we're to leave the palace?" Nomi asked. The thought

of the Superior punishing Eva made her shiver, but she couldn't deny she was eager to leave the walls of the palazzo. "Do you know where we're going?"

Maris nodded. "A perfumery. That's what Rosario said. I don't care *where* we go, as long as it's away from here."

Nomi eyed Maris. It sounded like Nomi wasn't the only one who felt trapped. With a sigh, she turned back to her stitches and tried not to stab her finger with the needle.

Maris gestured to Nomi's embroidery. "That's fine work. You're talented."

Nomi studied the frame in her hands, with its cityscape of Bellaqua half-complete. She'd been trying to finish Serina's work, but her stitches were inelegant compared to her sister's, and she couldn't help thinking she was making it worse.

Up until last night, she'd felt like she was making *everything* worse. But now she had a plan. She ran her fingers over Serina's delicate stitches. The absence of her sister was a hole in her chest, growing larger and larger the longer they spent apart. She *had* to save Serina. If she didn't, there'd be nothing of her left.

"My sister did most of it," Nomi said softly. "She's the one with the skill. I'm fine with darning socks and sewing patches, but this is a challenge for me." She made a noise in the back of her throat. "Like everything here."

"Did you ever find out what happened to her?" Maris brushed her ink-black hair off her shoulder.

Nomi stabbed her needle through the fabric. "The Superior sent her away. Rosario was right."

"Home?"

Nomi swallowed. "No."

Maris turned her attention back to the ocean. "It's hard to be separated from the people we love."

"Is that why you're not happy here?" Nomi asked softly. "Do you miss your family too?"

Maris's face hardened. "I have no family. My mother is dead and my father is dead to me."

Nomi glanced toward the doorway. Still empty. No looming shadows. "You said you would have been happy here, if not for your father. What did you mean?"

Maris leaned forward and put her head in her hands.

"Never mind. I'm sorry for asking," Nomi said, contrite. She hadn't meant to upset Maris.

"No," Maris said, through her hands. "It's just that . . . I've never been able to talk about it before. And it's killing me." She took a deep breath.

Nomi kept watching the doorway; she had a feeling this wasn't a conversation Maris would want the Superior to have knowledge of.

In a rush, Maris said, "My father paid off the magistrate of our province to choose me." Her face reddened. "He found me kissing . . . my, ah . . ." She couldn't seem to continue.

Nomi asked softly, "You were in love with someone unsuitable?"

Maris lifted her head to stare out at the horizon. "Her name was Helena," she said in a whisper.

Nomi bit back a gasp. A woman loving another woman was forbidden in Viridia.

"We had a plan. . . . She was going to be my handmaiden. We would have been together. But Father caught us. He threatened me," Maris said louder, anger coating the words. "Make the Heir choose me as one of his Graces, without Helena as my handmaiden, or he'd inform the authorities and I would be sent away." Her mouth snapped shut. She turned her head to meet Nomi's eyes. "So I did."

Nomi couldn't look away. She couldn't move. If Maris hadn't been chosen, and her father had followed through on his threat—she would have been sent to prison, just like Serina.

The greater cruelty: Either way, Maris would forever be separated from the person she loved.

Nomi wondered what her own parents would have done if they'd found out that she could read. Would they have reported her, as Maris's father had threatened? Would they have tried to protect her? Was Maris's father a monster . . . or just a citizen of Viridia, doing what anyone in the country would do?

"What happened to Helena?" Nomi asked.

After a long moment, Maris answered. "I don't know."

"I'm so sorry," Nomi said, at a loss. Did the Heir know two of his three Graces were unwilling? Would *always* be unwilling? Maybe that was why he'd chosen them, out of some sadistic desire to make them suffer. Maybe *that* was what pleased him.

"In all the stories, women give up everything," Maris said, her voice tight. "We are *always* supposed to give. We are never supposed to fight. Why do you think that is?"

Nomi thought of Queen Vaccaro and her daughters, betrayed by their male advisors and erased from history.

She thought of the letter hidden in her room.

Voice low, knowing she was walking on a knife's edge, she murmured, "Because they're afraid of what will happen if we do."

TWENTY-THREE

SERINA

JUST BEFORE LUNCH, a new boat of prisoners arrived on Mount Ruin.

Cave camp roiled. Whom would Oracle choose to fight?

Serina chewed on her tasteless bread, trying to imagine it was Nomi's cinnamon-clove shortbread. Even with strict rationing and the boar meat, supplies were dwindling.

"If they choose me, I'll die," Jacana said softly, staring at her small, empty hands.

"You're so fast, Jacana." Serina squeezed her shoulder. Jacana had "earned" the nickname Mouse, but Serina refused to call her that. For all her slight frame and frightened eyes, the girl often proved quick and resourceful. She had more potential than she gave herself credit for. "I don't think you need to worry, but if . . . if Oracle thinks you're ready, trust her."

Petrel's cheerful face passed through Serina's mind.

"Timely advice," Gia said, her voice tight. She nodded toward Oracle, who was making her way over to them.

Jacana grasped at Serina's hands. On her other side, Theodora hissed in a breath. Her long, loose arms wound around her knees, drawing herself together as if she could make herself small, less obvious.

Serina whispered, "It's okay. Don't worry."

She wasn't sure if she was trying to reassure them or herself. Her heart jumped to her throat and fluttered like a mad thing, desperate to escape.

She remembered how much she'd wished the Heir would single her out. Choose her. The glittering gowns, the golden filigree, the fine music . . . Now she prayed to be invisible.

Please not Jacana or Gia or—

"Serina, I'd like to speak with you outside." Oracle towered over her.

No. The cave shrank around her. For an instant, she thought about refusing. But the eyes of the entire crew were on her. Jacana released her hands.

Serina stood up on watery legs. She followed Oracle down the length of the tunnel, through columns of sunlight and deep trenches of shadow, close and cold as a grave. By the time they reached the entrance, the back of Serina's neck was sticky with sweat and her hands trembled.

Oracle stopped and squinted into the sun.

"I'm not ready," Serina said before the other woman could speak. It was too surreal. *This is a nightmare.* "The crew needs the food, and I—"

Oracle broke in. "The first fight after a win, we always pick a freshie. It's the safest time to test new fighters—the safest time to lose." She looked toward the distant ocean. "I was going to

180

choose you. You were the best of the freshies, but I didn't think you'd win."

Serina made a sound. Oracle had planned to sacrifice her?

The woman held up a hand. "Petrel told me not to. She said with just a little more training, you *could* win. She'd never seen anyone improve as quickly as you." Oracle met Serina's eyes at last. "She volunteered to fight in your place."

Serina's heart seized. "I—I—"

I never asked her to.

"Petrel wanted me to give you more time, and I have," Oracle went on. "You're a thoughtful fighter—some girls use instinct, but you use smarts." She sighed, and for the first time, Serina saw a crack in the woman's armor. "No one knows how you fight yet, which will give you an edge. If you're *smart*, Grace, you can win."

Serina couldn't draw a full breath. She wanted to beg Oracle to reconsider. But who would be chosen instead? Jacana? Gia? Someone more experienced, another like Petrel, sent to die in her place? There was nothing Serina could say. Begging for her own life meant sacrificing someone else.

She'd told Jacana to trust Oracle's judgment. She'd have to take her own advice.

Oracle seemed to understand her turmoil. She gave Serina's shoulder a brief squeeze. "Take some time to yourself. It'll be a couple hours before we head to the ring."

The woman disappeared into the cave. Serina stood still for a moment, bands of fear tightening across her chest. Then she headed for the cliffs.

She didn't stop until she could see the horizon, weighed down by a heavy bank of cloud. She'd promised herself she would escape. That she'd save Nomi.

But there hadn't been enough time.

Serina stared straight toward where she'd seen the lights of Bellaqua, so far away, and shouted into the screaming wind.

Eventually, her voice gave out.

"Feel better?"

Serina didn't turn around. "Hi, Val."

With a little grunt, she sat down and dangled her legs over the cliff's edge.

"You spend a lot of time at the edge of cliffs. You sure you're not thinking of jumping again?" he asked.

"Why do you always show up when I'm here?" she asked, staring into the white froth below her feet.

"I've been making the rounds." Val sat down beside her. "My orders are to let the crews know there's a fight in two hours."

Serina wiped her dirty palms on her pants. "Oracle already knows."

"I'm sure they all do." Val scooped up a handful of gravel and tossed it off the cliff into the waves. "But I have my orders."

Despite her best efforts, tears skated down Serina's cheeks. "It's my day to fight," she whispered, her throat thick.

Beside her, Val went still. "Already?"

Serina nodded. She stared at the waves dying beneath her, destroyed one after another against the cliff. "You were right about me," she added, her determination failing her. "I *am* a dead girl."

"Go for the crate," Val said quickly, almost desperately.

"Excuse me?"

"The Commander's throwing weapons into the ring today. Knives or bricks—he hasn't decided yet. But whatever it is, it won't be a threat. Not like the snake and the wasps." He turned to her and put his hand on her chin, tipping her head up. He wouldn't let go until she met his eyes.

"Don't avoid the crate, do you hear me?" he said. "Get yourself a weapon. Go in hard and fast with every girl. Don't think about what you're doing. Don't stop until you get the job done."

Serina took in every detail of his face—the dark brows, the small cluster of freckles on his left cheek, the urgency of his expression. He really did seem to care whether she won or died.

"Serina? Are you listening?"

He was handsome, very handsome. She'd thought that before, but without staring him full in the face, the opinion had been based on fleeting impressions: a curl of his hair, a quirk of his lips, the muscles of his arms. Now she could see clearly, for the first time, how well his sun-browned cheeks complemented his wide, expressive mouth. How bright and discerning his eyes were. How concerned he looked.

Serina had never broken the law before. She was in prison for a crime that wasn't her own. She had never rebelled. Never railed against her world, not like Nomi. And she was about to fight to the death. Probably *her* death.

Why follow *any* of the rules?

Serina touched Val's face, her rough palm meeting the smooth skin of his cheek. He stopped talking. She leaned forward slowly, until their foreheads touched. He didn't move away.

The warmth of his breath feathered against her lips. Her hand slid back into his hair, drawing him that last bit closer. An electric current flowed through her blood. Her skin tingled. Her heart pulsed in her throat.

Their lips met, soft and yielding.

He reached for her.

She pulled away.

His hands dropped to the gravel between them as she scrambled to her feet.

"Wait." He grabbed her ankle gently, not as if he truly meant to restrain her. She broke the hold easily.

"I'm sorry," she said, although she wasn't. Not really. She'd always wondered what kissing felt like. She'd been prepared for the mechanics of it, but not the tingle in her blood or the heat in her belly when his mouth moved against hers.

"Wait! Serina!" he said again, scrambling to his feet.

Serina had imagined her first kiss as the start of something, not the end.

She shouted over her shoulder as she ran, "They call me Grace now."

TWENTY-FOUR

NOMI

NOMI STEPPED ONTO the boat, the belled skirt of her brilliant red dress fanning out in the brisk sea air. A thick gold belt cinched tight around her waist and matched her golden sandals and the long, dangling earrings Angeline had procured for her.

The handmaiden had dusted her cheeks with golden powder and stained her lips red. It was a dramatic look, more striking than she usually wore, and for the first time, Nomi felt like she looked the part of a Grace.

But she would always be a rebel.

The note to Renzo burned against the skin of her breast. She'd tucked it into her bodice while Angeline was in the washroom. Asa had a contact outside the palazzo he would give it to; now she needed to figure out how to steal a private moment with him on a boat filled with revelers and the Superior's men.

Nomi glided toward an empty spot along the rail, searching the crowd for Asa. The Superior's ship was unlike any she'd seen before. It was moored on the ocean side of the palazzo, as it was much too large for the narrow canals of the city. Its wide deck was strung with lights and little tinkling bells. The railings were polished wood, intricately carved with mermaids and leaping fish.

The top deck was open, with fluttering swaths of white silk strung above. Near the stern, two wrought-iron lifts transported guests to and from the level beneath. Men in white livery operated the ropes and pulleys, ensuring each guest a smooth ride. Other servants wove through the crowd holding trays of fluted glasses and finger foods. In the center of the deck, a small group of musicians played, and around them the Superior's Graces danced with men he'd chosen to reward or curry favor with. The delegation from Azura was dressed in light blue.

Nomi reached the open stretch of rail and leaned against it, turning her attention out to sea. The sun had just set, and fingers of light still clung to the edge of the world. Above, stars were winking to life.

When she turned around, she noticed Asa on the other side of the boat. His eyes caught hers immediately. Warmth spread from her cheeks to her stomach.

A man sidled up beside him and said something. Asa's mouth moved in answer, but he didn't stop looking at Nomi.

A figure blocked her line of sight, and a whisper of a voice blew ice into her veins. "Good evening, Nomi."

The Superior.

Nomi's lungs froze. She curtsied, and suddenly, all her former awkwardness came roaring back. She was a lowly handmaiden again, out of place and ungainly in the glittering assemblage. With a treasonous note stuffed down her dress.

"Ines tells me your training is progressing," the Superior said. He took her hand and held it tightly, his bony fingers like iron bars. He pulled her arm up and indicated that he wanted her to spin. She turned slowly, her hand twisting in his grasp, making her feel even more at his mercy.

His scent—orange oil and antiseptic—choked her. The disease that was slowly killing him had thinned his face and grayed his hair, but it hadn't extinguished the icy flames of his eyes.

"I suppose I can see what my son finds intriguing about you." He pulled her closer, cornering her. Nomi's throat tightened. Her fingers tingled in his grip. His nails bit into her skin. "You've a spirit begging to be broken."

She couldn't stand it. She yanked her hand free.

The Superior's eyes widened. His hand slid around her waist, and for the first time she was happy for her corset because it felt like armor, a barrier between them. His other hand encircled her wrist, so tightly she couldn't pull free. It didn't matter if Malachi wanted to tame her or not; the Superior did. And he would, whenever he chose.

Even if she belonged to his son.

After a short, excruciating dance, the Superior released her and inclined his head. Nomi gave a shaky curtsy. It wasn't the boat's rocking that made her legs suddenly unsteady.

"Dance with Signor Flavia," he ordered. Another set of hands gripped her. A barrel-chested man twirled her across the deck. His sweat-damp chest pressed against hers, and his wine-soaked breath clogged her lungs.

"Excuse me," a deep voice said over her shoulder. For a split second, she thought it was Asa. But it was his brother.

Signor Flavia stopped spinning her. "Your Eminence," he said, bowing.

Another set of hands drew Nomi away, as if she were a pipe passed between friends. But the Heir didn't dance with her. He led her to the railing, where the sea breeze swept across her heated cheeks.

Malachi was so much larger than Asa. Muscled, where Asa was wiry. Imposing, where Asa was friendly. "You're shaking. Does the boat unsettle you?" Malachi asked.

Nomi was afraid to look him in the eye. What if he could see her deception? Her hatred?

"I am overheated from dancing, Your Eminence," she said.

"Your hands are cold."

She pulled them from his, galvanized into looking at him. "Are they?" she said, her voice tight.

His short brown hair was freshly cut. He wore a navy suit with thin lines of gold thread running through it. The sharp planes of his face, his dark eyes, told her nothing.

Did he enjoy her discomfort? Did he revel in the knowledge that she was at his mercy?

He was quiet for so long, she said, "What are you thinking?" just to break the silence. She expected him to tell her it was none of her concern.

But he cocked his head, still studying her, and said, "I think you would have been better suited to another time."

Nomi huffed out a breath. "What does *that* mean?"

Impertinent. Why could she never hold her tongue?

He eyed her narrowly, almost as if he were gauging her reaction. Then his gaze focused suddenly on her arm. He grabbed her hand again, raising it to reveal the purple half-moons on her wrist where the Superior's fingernails had dug into her skin. He stared at it for a long time. "Did my father do that?" he asked at last.

"Are you surprised?" Nomi looked at the sky, now hung with stars, bright as a million crystal chandeliers, and wished she could be up there, far away.

"You are not his to touch."

Nomi's eyes widened at the undercurrent of anger beneath Malachi's words. But of course. She understood.

It was a question of property.

Her fury rising, she said, "Because I am *yours* to touch, you mean."

His gaze dropped from her face for a second. If she didn't know better, she'd think she'd shamed him. Then his brows rose. "You have something. . . ." he said instead, and then faltered. He pointed toward her bosom.

Nomi glanced down and lost her breath. A corner of the letter was peeking out of her bodice.

Her face flamed. Her heart stopped. Her brain scrambled. She covered the paper with her hand. "A—a part of my dress, Your Eminence. So embarrassing." She curtsied and excused herself.

She hurried to the lift, weaving around the circle of dancers, her head down. Once in the lift, she turned, just as the ornate metalwork closed. She looked out at the graceful dancers, twirling around the musicians in the center. A flash of green flew past—Maris in the arms of an older, portly gentleman with red lips and a sheen of sweat along his brow. Her eyes were blank

189

and unfocused, her movements precise and controlled. She was smiling, but there was misery in every line of her body.

If Malachi cared so much about the Superior touching his Graces, why didn't it bother him that other men did too?

With a whoosh, the lift dropped, obscuring Nomi's view.

Hurriedly, she stuffed the edge of the letter out of sight. How could she have been so careless?

The small metal box stopped, and the door slid open. There were fewer torches here. More shadows. It was quieter, the music and laughter from above muffled. The narrow passage, paneled with wood, closed in around her.

The other lift swished down. Its doors opened, revealing a palace guard, wide and weathered as a mountain. She stepped back, head down, to give him room. Down here, the gentle rock of the boat was more pronounced. Her stomach tumbled into her throat.

The guard didn't walk past.

"Follow me," he said gruffly. She'd become accustomed to the silence of the men in the Graces' chambers. His voice sent panic through her. She followed him, even as every muscle strained to pull her the other way. Her heart pounded, *escape, escape*, through her blood.

They passed one servant. She could hear laughter and the thud of feet from the deck above, but saw no one else.

Bats exploded in Nomi's belly when the guard opened a door and gestured her into a tiny room. He left her there, alone, in the dark.

Nomi fought back tears. Malachi had seen the letter. And now he would punish her for it.

TWENTY-FIVE

SERINA

SERINA STOOD AT the edge of the stage with Oracle. Somewhere behind her, Jacana was sitting with Gia and Theodora, Cliff was ordering the new girls not to cry, and Ember was standing near the crew, arms crossed over her chest. And above it all, the guards bet on which fighter would win. Serina wondered if Val had bet on her.

She couldn't look for him; she couldn't look at anything but the empty stage in front of her. In a few minutes, that pale stone would run with blood.

"Jungle Camp's putting Venom in," Oracle said, glancing to their left. "They must be desperate for the rations."

"Why?" Serina asked, the word scratching her throat. Her hands tingled and her pulse pounded in her temples. The air held an electric charge, the heavy calm before the storm.

"She's their best fighter. Stay away from her if you can," Oracle said. "She likes to bite—coats her teeth in poison. No one knows how she withstands it herself."

Venom caught them looking and smiled, exposing teeth filed to points. Serina thought she might vomit.

Oracle grabbed her arm to get her attention. "Pearl is fighting for the Southern Cliffs. She's strong, with a wicked gut punch, but her knees are weak. Go for her knees."

Swallowing, Serina nodded. She snuck a glance at the woman. With broad shoulders and narrow hips, Pearl towered over the leader of her crew. Even in the midst of her efforts to keep breathing, Serina had to ask, "How'd she get the name Pearl?"

Pearls were supposed to be small and delicate, weren't they?

Oracle continued her inspection of the day's champions. "She comes from a family of pearl divers. She was sent here when the authorities discovered she'd been working for the family business, even though women aren't permitted to dive." Oracle nodded toward a girl on the other side. "The Beach's fighter isn't their strongest. She's favoring her left side, probably a training injury. Take advantage of the weakness."

Serina wiped her damp hands on her thighs. She wondered what the other crew chiefs were saying about *her*. Commander Ricci strode onto the stage, and another rush of adrenaline flooded her system.

"Fighters, take your places," he announced before heading for the staircase leading to the balcony.

Serina couldn't seem to move her legs. The last of the daylight was fading, and a sickening thought stole through her. Had she seen the sun for the last time?

"Hotel Misery won last week, so they're testing a new fighter. Watch her," Oracle said. "She doesn't look as scared as she should."

Somehow, Serina knew Oracle was talking about Anika, the girl from in-processing with the defiant glare, even before she watched Anika take her place onstage. She was the first of the champions to do so. She'd ripped the sleeves off of her shirt, revealing her wiry, muscled arms, and pulled her hair into rows of tight braids. Hadn't Anika said she'd been sent here for killing someone?

"I can't do this," Serina whispered, terror breaking over her in a wave. It wasn't just fear for her own life. It was fear of taking someone else's. She may have trained in the logistics of fighting, but her heart—her resolve to take a life—was entirely untested. Again, miserably, she whispered, "I can't."

"Petrel thought you could," Oracle said firmly. "And I do too. It's like being chosen as a Grace—only *you* get to decide who wins. And you get to be angry about it." She gave Serina a push. "Get angry, Grace."

Serina stepped onto the stage. And somehow, as she stared at the other fighters and at the scared, hungry women watching them, Oracle's words sank in. And Serina's anger rose.

Oracle was right. Every aspect of their world, down to Viridia's prisons, pitted women against each other while men watched.

"Begin!" Commander Ricci shouted, dropping a crate into the center of the ring.

Go for the crate, Val had said.

Serina lunged for it, praying she could trust him. Behind her, one of the fighters screamed. Serina reached the broken crate and wedged it open, revealing a handful of knives. She grabbed one and threw the rest off the edge of the stage, just as someone kneed her in the spine. She went down, gasping, but if there was one thing Serina was good at, it was getting back up.

She surged to her feet, slashing outward with the knife. Pearl dodged the blow, barely, rocking back on her heels. Serina rushed her, aiming for her knees, and shoved as hard as she could. The larger woman stumbled back. Serina swept her legs while she was still unbalanced.

The woman fell, arms pinwheeling, and cracked her head against the first row of stone seating. Her body collapsed, boneless, and her eyes rolled back in her head. She was still breathing, but she didn't get up.

Bile churned in Serina's throat.

She whirled in time to see Venom take the Beach fighter down. The girl's face had turned purple, and there were deep, bleeding wounds on her shoulder. Venom stepped back as her victim crumpled, and locked eyes with Serina. When the woman smiled, her spiked teeth were red. She started for Serina.

Every muscle in Serina's body yearned to run.

A knife flew through the air, burying itself in Venom's chest. The woman staggered but didn't fall. Another blade found Pearl's throat, killing her before she ever opened her eyes. Serina gasped. Anika stepped back into the ring, more knives in each hand. She must have taken advantage of the other fights to retrieve them.

Serina braced for one of the knives to find her. But Anika lunged at Venom and slashed her throat.

Spots danced before Serina's eyes. A guard cheered. The rest of the audience watched in silence.

Three bodies lay where they'd fallen.

Don't think. Don't stop. Val's voice filled her mind.

Only one more fighter. Then this would be over.

Anika turned toward Serina, brandishing a knife in each hand. Her determined frown sent ice down Serina's spine. The wavering torchlight threw grotesque shadows across the stage, moving like ghosts.

When Anika rushed her, Serina spun away, dodging the deadly arc of her knives. At the same time, she flung her leg out. For a split second, it *did* feel like dancing. Then Anika went down and Serina kicked one of the girl's hands as hard as she could. The knife went skittering across the floor with a hollow clank.

Anika let out a frustrated scream. Serina stomped on her other hand, but Anika was ready this time. She heaved her shoulder up and into Serina's stomach. Serina staggered back a step, slipping on the slick stone. Anika slashed Serina's arm, opening a long gash.

Fiery pain spilled out with the blood. Serina gasped. Anika lunged forward, trying to push her advantage. But Serina danced out of the way at the last second, and Anika's momentum sent her lurching. Serina twirled and kicked the back of her knee. The girl fell hard. As Anika rolled, trying to get her feet under her, Serina kicked at her hand, sending the second knife flying.

Serina was scared Anika might have another knife hidden somewhere. She couldn't take the chance. She dropped onto Anika's chest, thrust her knife up against the girl's throat, and dug her knees into her shoulders, putting pressure on the joints.

Anika struggled, but she couldn't dislodge Serina. As she'd so helpfully pointed out when they'd first met, Serina wasn't like the other hungry girls. Her added weight gave her an advantage now.

"Submit," Serina growled, pressing the knife harder into Anika's throat, hard enough to draw blood.

Anika spit in her face. *"No."*

Time slowed. Serina stared at the girl. Anika wasn't fighting to get up anymore. But her expression was still defiant, her mouth twisted and her eyes fever bright.

Serina was going to have to kill her.

All she had to do was press the knife a little harder, put her weight behind it, and she would win. Serina would be alive, and her crew would have the food they desperately needed.

Just one life. Just one death.

One murder.

Serina stared into Anika's eyes. The girl panted. There was no other sound, save the rush of wind and the thud of Serina's blood in her ears.

Come on, Serina. You've already won.

"Come on, Anika, submit," she muttered. "I don't want to do this."

Anika's eyes narrowed. "If you don't, I will."

It wasn't bluster. The girl was deadly serious. But there was something haunted about her expression. Serina had assumed Anika was one of the violent ones. The ones who deserved to be here. She'd said it herself—she'd killed someone.

Just like you 'stole' something? Serina thought, her stomach lurching. Did *any* of them really deserve to be here? Did they deserve *this*? Her hand holding the knife trembled.

Anika tried to take advantage of Serina's distraction, reaching along the stone, grasping toward one of the knives, just inches out of reach. Serina had only a second or two before the fight began again.

This was her chance to pick her own place. Make her *own* choice. Serina had won this moment.

The knife shook in her hand. But the blade never pushed deeper into flesh.

Her own horror screaming in her ears, Serina raised her hands. "I submit."

Behind her, a collective gasp. Above, on the balcony, an ominous rumble of voices, echoed by another wave of whispers in the crowd.

Anika's jaw went slack. Then she pushed Serina up and off of her.

Serina clutched the knife, her body going numb. But the conviction flowed through her, filling her up. She'd made the right call.

Anika grabbed for a knife, but she didn't attack. She just stood there, staring down at Serina. It was against the rules to kill a fighter who'd submitted, but no one seemed to know what to do instead.

Then Commander Ricci's voice boomed out over the silent crowd. "Get her out of here!"

Before the guards could obey, Oracle and Ember grabbed Serina and hauled her off the stage and out into the deepening night.

TWENTY-SIX

NOMI

NOMI PACED THE tiny room. Two low bunks lined the narrow walls, with one small round window letting in the moonlight. It already felt like a cell.

The boat's movement twisted her stomach. She stared out at the silver horizon. For a moment, she thought she might be sick.

The door opened. Nomi whirled. A lantern threw light across the guard's stony face. And beside him . . .

Asa.

Nomi's breath caught in her throat.

"Thank you, Marcos," Asa said, dismissing the guard. He closed the door and hung the lantern on a hook on the wall. Then he turned to Nomi. The space was small, and her voluminous dress took up most of it.

She was so relieved to see him she almost threw herself into his arms.

"Your brother saw the edge of the letter," she said, a little breathlessly. "I told him it was part of the dress, but when the guard brought me here, I thought it was so Malachi could punish me."

Asa closed the distance between them, his whip-thin body coiled tight with suppressed energy. "You have to be more careful, Nomi. I don't like you risking so much. If anything happened to you . . ."

He was so close. Close enough that he could put his hands around her waist without needing to step closer. She felt the weight of his gaze as surely as she did that imagined embrace. Her own fingers ached to slide up the muscles of his arms, to feel his skin against her own.

The desire frightened her.

"I was stupid, I know." Her cheeks flushed as she stared into his shadowed eyes. "But it's worth the risk. I can't—I can't be Malachi's Grace, Asa. I can't live with my life in the Superior's hands. And Serina . . . This will work, and we will all be free. I will be smarter next time, I promise."

His hands touched her waist, just as she'd imagined. "I've never met anyone as passionate as you in all my life."

Before she could stop herself, her hands were running up across his shoulders. He tightened his grip and then they were kissing, pressed up against the door. Golden sparks flashed across Nomi's closed eyelids. She slipped her fingers into his thick hair as his mouth opened over hers, deepening the kiss. The boat rocked gently under them, urging them even closer.

If Serina were here, she would be horrified by Nomi's behavior. But Nomi didn't stop. She reveled in the spiced heat of Asa's mouth, the soft-rough slide of his skin against hers, the feelings unfurling deep within her, washing the dark room in red.

With a little gasp, she drew back. A crimson light really *was* filtering through the dark. Through the window, she saw the vestiges of fireworks die. Another burst of gold and red exploded into the night sky.

"Look," she said, awed. She'd heard of fireworks, but she'd never seen them before.

Asa wrapped his arms around her waist from behind, and together they watched the show. Nomi gasped at a huge, glittering blast of green and purple, and sighed at the feathery white tails it left as it faded.

Asa kissed the sensitive skin at the back of her neck. The last firework trailed golden threads to the sea. Gradually the smoke cleared, revealing the stars once more.

"They'll come looking for us soon," he murmured.

Nomi leaned her head back against his shoulder. She didn't want to go anywhere. But if they were caught, Serina would never be freed.

She reached into her bodice for the letter. When she tried to hand it to him, he shook his head regretfully. "I'm sorry. I know I said I could deliver it to Trevi tomorrow, but I won't be able to go into town as I'd planned. Father has scheduled weapons training for me, of all things. My swordplay is as bad as my dancing."

"What do we do?" Nomi asked in dismay.

He ran a hand down her arm. "I should be able to leave the palace in three days. But I am at the mercy of my father, just like you. He could change his mind about my activities at the slightest provocation."

Nomi tried to quell the panic rising in her chest. *That's not enough time.*

"The Heir is taking us to the city tomorrow, to a perfumery. Where is your contact? Could I deliver the letter?"

He was shaking his head before she finished her question. "It's too dangerous. If someone were to see you—"

"You're not saying it's impossible," she said, cutting him off.

Asa ran a hand through his hair. "Trevi is in the market in the grand piazza. You'd likely take a carriage from there. So, you *might* see him, but—"

"I can make it work. Somehow, I will." Nomi refused to think about the risks. It was *her* fault Serina was in Mount Ruin. If Nomi got caught trying to save her, then at least she'd be paying for her own crime this time.

"Nomi, I don't know. If we just wait—"

"We can't," she said. "It takes six days to reach Lanos, and six days back. The masquerade is in fourteen days." She touched his face, tentative fingers on the stubbled skin of his cheek. "There's already so little room for error."

He sighed and pressed his face into her hand. "You must promise to be careful. If you can't find my man, or there's no chance to break from the group, you must abandon your effort. Promise me, Nomi. If you can't do it, we'll find another way."

She kissed him lightly in answer.

His arms tightened around her as he said, "Trevi is a small man, older than my father. He wears a blue waistcoat with brass buttons. He works a stall of knives in the piazza. You'll have to find an excuse to wander off a little distance. He won't get close to the carriages. But he won't balk at you giving him a note if you tell him it's from me."

Nomi nodded.

A sudden burst of laughter outside the door startled them both.

"You have to go," Asa said, nudging her toward the door. "I'll follow in a few minutes. If Malachi or anyone asks, tell them you were feeling seasick." He checked to make sure the note was fully hidden in her bodice. "The man who brought you here, Marcos, is loyal to me. If you need to get me a message, you can trust him to deliver it. He has shifts in the Graces' chambers. But don't trust anyone else. Not even your handmaiden. Do you understand?"

Nomi nodded, flustered. Suddenly, everything seemed to be happening very quickly.

"You will see your sister again, Nomi," Asa murmured. "I promise. Now go." With a quick kiss on her temple, he pushed her out the door.

TWENTY-SEVEN

SERINA

ORACLE AND EMBER didn't let go of Serina until they were well away from the amphitheater. Serina stumbled over the rutted path.

The moon glowed, illuminating the hard lines of Oracle's face. In the distance, a strange light burst up along the horizon. Serina couldn't be sure, but she thought it might be fireworks.

The rest of the Cave crew followed. She didn't look behind her; she knew what she'd see—disappointment. Rage.

The slash on Serina's forearm ran with blood.

They were all silent by the time the crew flooded into the cave. Someone stoked the fire, sending sparks up toward the soot-crusted rock.

Serina expected Oracle to pull her off to the side for her lecture, but Oracle turned on her in front of everyone. "You have betrayed us, flower," she said harshly, the standard endearment sounding more like an insult. "You had a chance to win. . . . Petrel *died* to give you that chance. Now we'll starve."

"Because I wouldn't *murder* someone," Serina burst out. She would not feel guilty for learning the line she could not cross. She couldn't kill someone in cold blood. Even to feed her friends. Even to save herself. "Can't you see how wrong that is? The guards are forcing us to kill each other for their amusement. We should be working *together* to make sure no one starves."

Oracle's eyes flashed. "I told you what happens when we refuse to fight. Not just four girls die. *Everyone* does. I will not put all our lives at risk because you were too weak to do what is necessary."

"It is not weak to want to fight back!" Serina shouted. Until she'd come here, she'd never questioned Viridia's laws. Even when she'd first arrived, she'd accepted the fights. They were awful and terrifying and inhumane . . . but they were the way things worked here. They were the reality they were all forced to endure. Just like the reality of the Graces. Just like the reality of Viridia's laws.

Women were forbidden to read.

Women were forbidden to choose their husbands, their jobs, their futures.

Forbidden to dive for pearls or sell goods at market to help their families.

Forbidden to cut their hair unless a man told them to.

Forbidden to think for themselves.

Forbidden to choose.

But *why*?

"My mother raised me to never trust other women because we would always be in competition. But it's *not true*. Look at how we take care of each other here." She found Tremor in the group of women. "We heal each other." She looked at Jacana. "We share food." She thought of Petrel. "We *die* for each other." Tears were building behind her eyes.

"Serina—" Oracle warned.

But Serina couldn't stop. A wave was building in her chest, and if she didn't speak, it would destroy her. "Why do we let them do this to us?" she asked, and she was thinking of more than the guard's barbaric fights. "Why do we let them break us? Starve us? Punish us for being ourselves? Is it because *we* think we're sweet, delicate *flowers* and we let them?" Her voice rose. "I don't think we've ever been what they want. That's why we're here in the first place." She remembered what Oracle had said when she'd arrived, and suddenly, the words meant even more now, because *Serina* believed them.

"We are *not* flowers," she said firmly. "Like you said, Oracle, we *are* concrete and barbed wire. *We are iron.*" Serina stared at the women surrounding her. "We are smart, and we are dangerous. The guards know that. They know we have the power to overthrow them, if we'd just work together. We need to stop killing each other and fight *them.*"

No one said anything, but Ember's eyes blazed. A couple of the women had stepped closer to hear. Serina found Jacana again. Her friend's eyes were wide, her bony hands clenched into fists at her sides. If they worked together, if they just—

"Get out." Oracle's words cut through the silence like a blade.

They pierced Serina to the core. "But, Oracle—"

"You submitted," Oracle growled. "You were weak and you betrayed your crew. The punishment for submission is

205

banishment. You are on your own, Grace. Mount Ruin will have you now."

No one objected.

It was her second death sentence, Serina realized—the Superior had never expected her to survive Mount Ruin, and now, without food, shelter, or water, she wouldn't. Serina pressed her injured arm into her stomach and noticed that somehow she'd held on to the knife. With a last glance at Jacana, at Oracle, she turned toward the tunnel. Women stepped aside to give her space.

Serina couldn't be sorry. She *knew* she was right. She'd die for it, maybe, but dying on her own terms was better than living as a murderer. Her sister would be proud.

Nomi wasn't the only rebel now.

TWENTY-EIGHT

NOMI

IT WAS ONLY Nomi's second time outside the palazzo. The fresh air beyond the palace grounds should have been liberating. Instead, it sat in her lungs, as heavy and thick as oil. Cassia chattered excitedly as the boat cut across the canal to Bellaqua's grand piazza, where the Heir awaited them. Maris looked like she wanted to tell the other girl to be quiet. But Nomi could only stare silently across the water and try to keep her expression neutral.

The note was again in her bodice.

Asa's description of his contact ran through her mind on an endless loop: *His name is Trevi. He wears a blue waistcoat. He works a stall of knives. He won't get close to the carriages.*

She still had no idea how she was going to manage to sneak away and find him. If he sold ribbons or fabric, she could feign interest in his wares. But knives? Why would a Grace examine a stall of knives?

And this was just the first hurdle of their plan. Assuming Luca passed the letter to Renzo with haste, as she'd requested, and Renzo made it back to Bellaqua before the Heir's birthday, there were still several more steps to their plan, each with their own risks and uncertainty.

First, she would have to write another letter with explicit instructions on what to do the night of the ball. Asa would have to find a way to deliver it. She would tell Renzo to make the assassination attempt look threatening but without, in any way, putting the Superior in actual danger. He would have to simulate a struggle with Asa, who would come to his father's aid. In the process, Renzo had to reveal Malachi as the man who hired him. Then he would need to escape the palace.

Second, Nomi would have to plant evidence in Malachi's chambers: a letter from the assassin accepting the job.

And finally, on the day of the party, Asa would have to persuade his father to retire to an antechamber during the festivities, to facilitate the simulated attack.

If all of that happened as planned, Asa would immediately point the finger at Malachi, and subsequently find the additional evidence—the letter—in his room.

She'd thought it a risky, complicated, but reasonable plan when they'd dreamed it up that night on the terrace. But now, in the harsh light of day, with the letter pressing into her breast, it seemed absolutely *ridiculous*. Because all of that, *all of that*, hinged on her having a moment to herself to speak to a strange man in a crowded market. It was the first step, and likely the one that would kill all her hopes.

Nomi fought back a wave of nausea.

"Are you well?" Maris asked, putting a hand on Nomi's arm. "You look quite ill."

Nomi tried to clear her mind, but her stomach still rolled. Dark clouds crowded above the city buildings. "Thunderstorms terrify me," she said faintly, nodding toward the threatening sky. It was true, and a testament to her other worries that she hadn't noticed the weather until now.

Maris rubbed her arm reassuringly. "Those are just rain clouds, and still far away. We've had clouds linger like that on the horizon for days. It probably won't even rain."

Cassia broke in. "You're afraid of *thunderstorms?*"

Nomi gritted her teeth.

With a little thud, the gondolier docked the boat at the piazza. In the square, a large carriage painted in black and gold waited, the Heir and his driver standing at attention beside it. The tall black horses snorted and shook their manes. Beyond the carriage, the piazza was filled with small carts: vendors selling fresh fruit, fabrics, even whole slaughtered pigs.

Nomi was the first off the boat. She wandered toward the market, endeavoring to look interested in the wares being sold, while her eyes searched frantically for a short man in a blue waistcoat.

She saw the knives first.

Silver flashing in the sun, with hilts of twisted metal inset with gems, the weapons were pieces of art. The cart was tucked between a stall of meat pies and one with racks of finely made gloves.

"Nomi!" Malachi grabbed her arm, and she flinched. "The others are waiting."

The Heir led her toward the carriage. Inside her mind, Nomi

wailed. She couldn't risk pulling free of Malachi's grip, but oh, she wanted to. This was her chance, most likely the only one she'd have. She had to put her head down to compose her face and hide her dismay.

The black-and-gold carriage was covered but open on the sides, with two cushioned benches that ran its length and a polished wooden floor. The driver leapt into the seat up front, just behind the two horses.

Cassia was waiting for the Heir. He handed her up into the carriage, and then Maris.

He helped Nomi up last, his hand warm and solid, and then sat beside her on the bench. Nomi was immediately aware of the Heir's leg pressing against hers, their knees knocking together as the carriage moved slowly across the cobbled piazza. She watched the small stall of knives and the small man with the blue waistcoat out of the window until they disappeared from view. She wanted to scream.

You have one more chance, she reminded herself, trying to stave off the wave of hopelessness threatening to crush her. *When the carriage returns. One more chance.*

"How are you this morning, Nomi?" the Heir asked. Today he was wearing a thin white shirt and soft leather trousers. In other circumstances, she might have thought he looked handsome.

"I'm well, Your Eminence," Nomi said, trying to sound as if it were true.

"Ines says we're to visit a perfumery?" Cassia said, edging into the conversation. She leaned toward the Heir, her curves on full display in her orange-and-yellow gown.

Malachi nodded.

"Do you have a favorite scent, Your Eminence?" Cassia asked. "The other day, you mentioned you don't much like fresh flowers." She flaunted her knowledge of the Heir to the girls she saw as her competition, but Nomi knew, even if Cassia didn't, that the blond-haired girl was the only one who wanted to be here. Maris and Nomi would lose no sleep if the Heir showered only Cassia with his attention.

Nomi felt Malachi's imperceptible shrug. "I don't know," he said. "I've never really thought about it."

"Then we'll have to guess," Cassia said coquettishly. "Perhaps one of us will find the perfect fragrance to entice you."

"Maybe," he said, smiling noncommittally. He turned his attention to Maris, and Nomi caught the disappointment in Cassia's eyes before the girl smoothed her expression.

"Maris," Malachi said. "What do you enjoy most about the palace?"

Maris smiled, letting her hair fall back from her face. She looked like a doll: flawless and empty. "The opportunity to spend time with you, Your Eminence."

His arm tensed against Nomi's. "Of course," he replied.

When he made no further effort at conversation, Nomi shifted to watch the city trundle past. The carriage clomped down narrow roadways and clattered over arched bridges. Red-flowered vines climbed along nooks and crannies in the stone houses, and laundry hung above the streets like windless sails. The dark gray clouds built higher on the west side of the city. The carriage would travel down a long stretch of cobbled road with nothing but sun above, only to turn a corner and reveal an ominous creep of cloud.

Nomi hoped Maris was right and it was only rain coming. She'd been scared of thunderstorms since she was a child. She could remember with visceral horror the storms that would come roaring through the valley, flinging rain sideways and shaking their apartment with every crack of thunder. Back then, Serina would climb into bed with her and they would ride it out together. Serina would sing her lullabies, and Nomi would tremble until long after the storm had passed.

With a clatter, the carriage rolled to a stop outside a glass-fronted shop. Malachi climbed down and reached up a hand to help each Grace. Nomi alighted on the cobbles and tilted, her shoe catching on the uneven ground. The Heir steadied her, pulling her a little closer than she liked.

He had none of the coiled energy or liquid grace of Asa. He was strong and solid and intensely focused. She wilted under the weight of his gaze.

How could she sneak off on her errand without him seeing, without him noticing? It would be impossible.

When they entered the perfumery, Nomi flinched at its luminous glow, brighter than the hazy morning outside. The large room was filled with small, mirrored tables arranged in precise rows. More mirrors hung from the walls, reflecting back at each other. It gave the space a surreal feel, as if one could step into the mirrored wall and continue forever.

On each table rested a small cut-crystal bottle, a bowl of coffee beans, and a jar of cotton puffs. Cassia looked around with her hands pressed to her chest and giggled with delight.

Nomi and Maris huddled together near the door.

"Perfume makes me sneeze," Maris whispered.

"That could be useful as a deterrent," Nomi replied under her breath.

Maris made an odd noise, part laugh and part snort.

Malachi glanced back at them. Nomi fought to contain the hysterical laughter bubbling up her throat.

At that moment, the perfumer emerged from a back room and strode quickly to the Heir's side. The man was short and portly, with a tuft of white hair encircling the bald crown of his head and round spectacles resting on his nose. He bowed deeply. "Your Eminence, it is my honor that you have chosen to visit today."

"Thank you, Signor. I'm sorry my father couldn't accompany us, as was his wish," the Heir replied.

Malachi turned to his Graces. "The signor has graciously agreed to share his space with us for a few hours. Please sample the perfumes and find one that suits you. When you've made your selection, inform me and it will be my pleasure to arrange a bottle for your personal use."

Graciously agreed . . . Nomi stifled a laugh. As if the signor had a choice.

Nomi curtsied with the others. She was about to turn to Maris and ask where she wanted to begin, when the Heir stepped in front of her. He held out his hand, all polite gentleman, and gestured to the nearest table. "Shall we find a scent that suits you?"

Reluctantly, Nomi placed her hand in his. She glanced over her shoulder. Maris stared fixedly at the selections on a nearby table, while Cassia dabbed some perfume onto a cotton puff and sniffed delicately.

Malachi held out a damp bit of cotton. "What about this one?"

Nomi leaned a little closer to smell it and wrinkled her nose. "Definitely not. Smells like rotten peaches."

The Heir raised a brow and held the puff to his face. A muscle in his jaw twitched. "You say rotten, I would say . . . overripe."

She forced a laugh. He moved on to the next table. She trailed behind, annoyed and bemused at the same time. She hadn't expected him to sample the perfumes with her. She'd assumed he would stand off to the side and watch his Graces with that terrifyingly intense gaze of his.

Nomi smelled orange oil, which made her skin crawl at the memory of the Superior grabbing her on the boat. When Malachi offered it, she just shook her head. There was plumeria, which was sweet and simple but not popular with the Heir, and a bright, grassy scent that Nomi didn't mind but didn't love either.

Cassia giggled and preened her way through the shop in a veiled bid for attention, but Nomi found herself taking the task seriously. Maybe because focusing on the hints of spice and sandalwood distracted her from the letter hidden in her bodice. The hopeless task she nonetheless still hoped she could perform.

"This one is nice," Malachi said, offering her another cotton.

This scent she couldn't identify. It made her think of cold, snowy evenings in Lanos, with a hint of wood smoke and something crisp and bracing. Tears pricked her eyes.

"May I have this one, Your Eminence?" she asked softly. She dabbed a little on her wrists and breathed in the scent again. "It reminds me of home."

Malachi bowed his head. "It would be my pleasure."

"Thank you," Nomi said, with a small curtsy. "And thank you for bringing us on this outing, Your Eminence. It was very generous of you."

He shrugged. "I know what it's like to be cooped up in the palazzo."

"Don't you mean caged?" Nomi said without thinking.

Her hand flew to her mouth.

Malachi's attention sharpened. "Is that how you feel?"

"No, of course not," Nomi covered quickly. "The palace is beautiful. A dream. It's just been so long since I've left its walls and I've always wanted to see Bellaqua. It's been a gift to see it today."

And suddenly, Nomi knew how to get to Trevi.

"In fact, Your Eminence, I . . . I would like to give you a gift as well," she said shyly. She glanced sidelong at him in time to see surprise flash across his face. "To show my appreciation. May I pick something out for you at the market?"

She held her breath. Would he find a trinket from market beneath him? Would he question her motives?

Please.

"You don't owe me anything, Nomi," he said, and for once his voice didn't sound gruff or distant.

"I know I don't," she said a little too quickly. "But surely I can be kind? You were kind to me today."

He rubbed his chin. "Very well. If you wish."

With a bow, he shifted his attention to Cassia, and then Maris. By the time they had chosen their perfumes, the sky had darkened and thunder rumbled in the distance.

As Malachi helped her into the carriage, Nomi fought her mounting panic. This wouldn't work if it began raining before they arrived at the piazza.

The ride was quiet, the four of them shifting with the bumps of the cobbled street. Nomi kept an eye on the swollen clouds and the shards of lightning that crackled within them.

The carriage stopped a few minutes later. When the Heir helped her down, Nomi didn't pull her hand away so quickly this time. This ruse depended on her acting softened toward him, on him believing she actually wanted to do something nice for him. It might even serve her well for her second task, securing an invitation to his room so she could plant the damning letter.

She remembered something her mother had said once to Serina, years ago: "Your ability to mask your true feelings, your true self, will be your greatest weapon."

"I need a weapon?" Serina had asked.

Their mother had lifted her chin. "Every woman does."

As Malachi helped down the other Graces, Nomi headed to the row of carts in the piazza's center. The air hung thick around her. To her dismay, some vendors had already left, probably to avoid the storm, which threatened to break at any moment. Trevi was packing up his knives.

No.

But the glove vendor next to the knife stand was still open. She hurried over. Malachi would follow shortly, she was sure. He was probably watching her now.

She ran a hand over the soft leather of a pair of black gloves, then glanced over her shoulder. Malachi had turned to speak with the driver. She spun away from the glove vendor, slipped a hand into her bodice, and extracted the letter. Trevi was bent nearly double to place his velvet-wrapped daggers into the shelving built into the lower half of his cart.

She shoved the letter at him, her hand trembling. He looked up in surprise.

"From His Eminence Asa," she mumbled. "It's urgent or he would have brought it himself."

There was time for Trevi to give her a short, wordless nod, when she heard footsteps on the cobbles. She turned back to the glove vendor and caressed another set of gloves, these a rich brown.

Malachi appeared beside her.

She lifted the gloves. "I like these, Your Eminence. Are they a worthy gift?"

She had no money. But she was hoping the merchant wouldn't accept payment from the Heir. That it was the choosing of the gift, not the purchasing of it, that had value.

Malachi nodded at the merchant.

She handed the Heir the gloves, their hands brushing as he accepted them.

"Thank you," he said.

Just then, the first fat drops of rain fell.

They hurried to the canal, where Maris and Cassia were waiting in a large black gondola. As soon as Nomi and the Heir climbed in, the gondolier set off with urgency.

Nomi couldn't help the smile that spread across her face. She'd done it. If all went according to plan, she'd see Renzo in just under a fortnight.

And, someday, Serina.

The rain dinged against her beaded dress, darkening the silver. She flinched when the sky flashed above them. Thunder shook the boat, loud enough to hurt her ears. With the stress of her task relieved, her fear of thunderstorms rose. When the boat docked, she scrambled onto shore before the Heir could help her.

"Excuse me, Your Eminence," she murmured, her voice cracking.

Behind her, she heard Cassia say something cutting, just as a great gust of wind swept her hair back from her face, and the storm shot arrows of cold rain at her. Thunder roared.

She was hurrying frantically toward the palazzo when a hand grabbed her arm. "This way."

The Heir led her along a path to the right of the staircase, into a twisting garden. Lightning raced across the sky. He pulled her under an overhang, out of the worst of the rain. Gooseflesh rose along Nomi's exposed arms. It felt like Lanos in the late summer, when storms lashed the valley and the air cooled, making way for the sharper winds of fall.

She looked around, but they were alone.

"I've found something you're afraid of," the Heir said.

Nomi stared up at Malachi through her wind-whipped hair. "You think *storms* are all I'm afraid of?"

Lightning flashed, sparking in his eyes. "Are you afraid of me?"

Nomi leveled a stare at him. "Don't you want me to be?"

His voice rose against a rumble of thunder. "Why are you like this?"

"Like what?" Nomi swayed. The rain was picking up, great bursts of it pouring onto the garden. The overhang did little to protect them. Her hair and dress stuck to her skin, heavy with water. Her heart beat too fast, urging her to flee.

"*This*. Different. Defiant." Malachi took a step toward her, but it almost looked as if he fought the impulse, a frown thinning his lips. His eyes showed a strain she didn't understand. "I don't know if I'm meant to be punishing you, or—"

"Do your worst," Nomi said madly, the storm egging her on. "You've already sent my sister away. Made me yours."

"You never respond the way I expect." Malachi ran a hand through his wet hair. He looked out at the hedges, streaming with rain. "When I chose you . . . I wasn't thinking. I don't know why—"

"I do," she said, rain lashing her face. She couldn't hold her tongue; she couldn't be demure. Not when she stood in the center of a thunderstorm, her fear and fury raging just as loud. "Because you wanted to break my spirit. Isn't that it? That's what your father said."

"He does not speak for me," he snapped, shocking her. "I am *not* my father."

"No," she said, thinking of what Asa had said. *Volatile.* "You're worse."

"You don't know what you're saying." Frustration filled his voice. Lightning illuminated his reddened cheeks. She cringed at the brightness. "You're—"

Nomi stepped up to him, an inch away, her heart pounding. "What?" she challenged.

He stared down at her through the flashing rain. "Dangerous."

His lips found hers with the force of a thunderclap. She froze for an instant, and then she found herself yielding, slick with

219

rain, fevered and shaking. He gripped her tightly, his embrace both a protection from the storm and its own tempest.

With a gasp, Nomi tore herself away. His full lips were parted, his chest rising and falling quickly, as if he'd been running.

She turned into the driving rain and fled.

TWENTY-NINE

SERINA

IT WAS LATE afternoon, nearly twilight, and Serina had almost
made it to the eastern beach when a storm swept down upon
her. Waves of rain soaked through her thin clothes in seconds,
and the wind tore at her hair, flinging the wet strands against her
chilled cheeks.

Serina kept walking, doggedly ignoring the flashing lightning
and ground-shaking thunder. She was not afraid. If anything,
the storm comforted her; Bruno and the other guards wouldn't
be patrolling in this weather.

Eventually, she reached the eastern beach. Instead of hud-
dling in the small cave she'd found with Jacana, Serina sat on the
wet sand and let the rain wash her clean. She held up her cupped
hands and drank what she could. As she watched the lightning
flash over the tossing waves, she thought of Nomi. Her sister
would be frightened. Serina wished she could be there to soothe
her fears, as she'd done so many times before.

The night before, after she'd been banished, Serina had gone to the cliffs and watched for more fireworks from Bellaqua. She'd thought about jumping. But the next morning, she'd still been there, still trying to figure out a way to get to Nomi.

Now, as the storm pummeled her, Serina let her mind rest. Her empty stomach ached. Her muscles cramped in the needling rain. But she drifted, and it was a gift, this momentary haze.

By the time dawn broke, the weather had cleared, leaving a morning as fresh and clean as any she'd experienced. It was impossible to let the darkness win, when the sun rose from the ocean like a phoenix, draped in fiery orange.

Serina wrapped the gash in her arm with a strip of cloth from her threadbare shirt, and then she glanced around at the wind-swirled beach and worked on developing a plan.

Food, first. She'd eaten nothing the day before.

She scrounged for berries and found the kind Cliff had told her about, that tasted like they would kill her. But they didn't, and she kept breathing.

She examined the trees that framed the beach, and she walked the rocks that built around the narrow strip of sand. The rising cliffs didn't interest her, but the tiny caves that pockmarked their base did. The one she and Jacana had found was one of the largest, probably big enough to hide a raft.

She was heading back toward the trees, hoping to scavenge more food, when the sound of footsteps rose above the constant drumbeat of the waves.

Serina headed toward the trail. It didn't occur to her to hide; she assumed Val had come looking for her. Maybe even hoped he had.

But it wasn't Val—it was Jacana.

"What are you doing here?" Serina asked. Her friend looked even more timid than usual, curled into herself and half hiding behind her stringy blond hair.

Jacana stopped where the waving golden grass gave way to golden sand. "I thought you might come here. I wanted to check on you. Make sure you were okay."

Serina joined Jacana and sat, staring out at the water. "I can't say I'm okay. But I'm alive, so that's something."

Jacana held out a flagon. "I snitched this from the supply. I thought you could use some water."

Serina took it gratefully, tipping a few sips into her mouth. "Thank you."

"I couldn't get any food, but that should last for a day or two. And you can use it to collect more." Jacana glanced back toward the trees. "Oracle is really angry. Most of the girls are."

Serina sighed. "I know. But I don't think I'm wrong."

"I don't think you are either," Jacana said. She took off her flimsy shoes and wiggled her toes in the sand. "But it's dangerous. And we're all hungry."

"And *why* are we hungry?" Serina's anger snapped and growled in her chest. "Because the Superior doesn't send enough food? Or because Commander Ricci keeps it all for himself? I heard Oracle and Val talking. . . . Val said the Commander takes food meant for us."

Jacana shrugged. "But what can we do? We can't all submit. Like Oracle said, the guards would just kill us themselves."

Serina watched the waves slide toward her and suck back out to sea. "What would the guards do," she mused, "if no one went to the fights? If we just stayed away?"

Jacana rubbed her chin. "I guess they would come for us?"

"But are there enough of them?" Serina asked. "They have firearms, but there are hundreds of us and only about forty of them. And we know this island. They don't. They stay in their concrete and barbed-wire towers, hardly patrol. . . ."

"But if we stay away from the fights, that doesn't get us the food," Jacana said softly. "There isn't enough on the island for everyone to eat. You know that. We'd starve."

Serina rubbed at her eyes. "You're right." But she couldn't stop trying to think of a way out. "Maybe we revolt when a ship comes in, take over the ship, and escape."

"Is that more realistic than a raft?" Jacana asked softly.

"*Nothing* is realistic," Serina admitted. But she couldn't let it go. "No matter what the plan is, it starts with getting the crews to talk to each other. Finding common ground. Maybe sharing the food we do have."

"Without letting the guards know we're doing it," Jacana interjected. She glanced over her shoulder again, as if someone might come along to spy on them.

"If they knew we were conspiring together, they'd find ways to drive us apart." Serina thought of the Commander, his eyes narrowed with cruelty. She was sure he would think of plenty of ways to make them pay.

"So how do we get the crews to talk to each other?" Jacana tucked her hair behind her ears. A fading bruise yellowed her jaw, a vestige of training. Serina's whole body ached from the fight.

"Emissaries," Serina said, the word evoking memories of the

palace. "If Oracle were to send a couple girls to each crew, just to start a conversation . . . maybe they could take some kind of peace offering—a little food or extra water. If Cave crew shows they're willing to endure hardship for the greater good—"

"The others might be more willing to hear us out. Maybe even trust us," Jacana finished. A little light came back into her eyes.

"Yes," Serina said. Maybe just focusing on the tiniest of first steps, rather than the ultimate goal, was best. "But I don't think Oracle will go for it. She won't risk her crew."

Jacana rubbed her hands along the tops of her legs and then stood up, slipping her sandy feet into her shoes. "I'll talk to her. Most of the crew was angry at what you said, but some of them agreed with you. *I* agree with you. There are a lot of us who know we'll die when we go to the ring. And some of us would rather take our chances trying to find a way out. Maybe there's enough of us to force Oracle's hand."

"She's going to hate me," Serina said, dropping her head to her hands. She respected Oracle—she never set out to oppose her.

Jacana let out a wispy laugh. "I'm sorry, Grace. I think she already does."

Serina stood up too, clasping the flagon to her chest. "If she changes her mind, if there's anything I can do, please let me know."

Jacana tilted her head. "Maybe . . . maybe you could try talking to the other clans yourself? You *believe* in it. It might mean more coming from you."

225

"Maybe." Serina rubbed the back of her neck. "If the other crews don't kill me. They'll probably think I'm trying to steal food, won't give me a chance to explain."

"True. But they saw you last night, making your stand. They might listen." Jacana smiled, but her green eyes were red rimmed and sad. She squeezed Serina in a quick, tight hug. "Be careful. Mirror said the guards like to go hunting for banished girls. Without crews to protect them . . ." Her voice faded.

Serina's jaw tightened. "Thanks for the warning. And the water. You be careful too."

She watched until the girl disappeared into a patch of straggly trees. The sun was strong, pouring heat onto her shoulders, and she was grateful for the water.

She moved to the cave to wait out the heat of the day. Her stomach ached with emptiness and fear.

At some point, she drifted into an uneasy sleep, nightmares of the fight, of Anika's determined frown, jerking her awake. She dreamt of Nomi too, locked in an embrace with Malachi, golden chains wrapped around her throat. *Help me*, her sister whispered, over and over. But Serina's hands were chained too, and her legs wouldn't move. The harder she tried to get to her sister, the tighter her restraints became.

The man holding Nomi looked up at Serina at last, and it wasn't the Heir. It was Commander Ricci. And he was laughing.

Serina woke, sticky with sweat, tears streaming down her face.

You believe in it.

Jacana's voice slowly drowned out her nightmares. Maybe it was Serina's hunger making her delusional, but suddenly, it didn't seem like such a foolish idea. Going to the other crews . . . making her case for a revolt. . . . A whisper of hope flowed through her. Maybe she could convince them to unite. Even one crew working with the Cave could make a revolt.

And she knew which crew to start with.

THIRTY

NOMI

NOMI COULDN'T SLEEP. Storms ravaged the palazzo until long after midnight, and she flinched with each clap of thunder and flash of lightning, feeling as if she were under attack. Eventually, when the sky finally cleared and dawn crept up her windowsill, she dragged herself out of bed and sat at her dressing table. She stared at her reflection, and it was as if she were looking at a completely different person. Her lips were tender and her cheeks flushed. She stared until her face blurred and her features didn't make sense anymore. Even wrapped in a warm robe, she shivered.

The Heir had kissed her.

Her mind flashed back to the moment, over and over.

The lashing rain, the heat of his mouth, the way her body pressed against him as if it wanted him. But it didn't.

I don't.

Now, away from the rain and the heat and the anger, her stomach turned, thinking about it. Had she kissed him because she knew she had to? Because, with the Heir, it wasn't a choice?

She wasn't sure.

Either way, it felt like a betrayal to Asa.

And to herself.

Angeline bustled into the room, a scrap of material clutched to her chest. "Ines says the Heir has requested breakfast on the beach with his Graces. It'll be nice to spend some time in the sun, right?"

With the Heir? Nomi's stomach balked.

Angeline laid the fabric out on the bed—a black swimming robe. "It's such a beautiful day. The sky is so *clear*. You'd never know we had storms yesterday."

"Yes," Nomi echoed faintly, staring fixedly at her reflection.

"Are you well?" Angeline asked. "You seem a bit pre-occupied. Was yesterday's outing taxing?"

Taxing? *The Heir called me dangerous. And then he kissed me.* The words wanted to form on Nomi's lips. She wanted to talk about it. But she wanted to talk to her sister. Nomi thought of her letter, traveling north to Lanos. She thought of Asa, preparing to launch a false case against his brother.

The Heir is right. I am dangerous.

After she'd donned her swimming robe, Nomi joined the others in the receiving room. Ines led them down through the palazzo and onto the beach. Bleary-eyed and reluctant, Nomi followed Cassia and Maris out into the glaring sunlight.

A wrought-iron table had been set up a few yards from the water, on a black-and-white-checked carpet. Heavy white drapes were staked out above it to provide shade. Next to the table, a row of chaises were lined up like soldiers in the sun.

The Heir sat alone at the table. Cassia stepped forward

quickly to snag the seat next to him, while Maris and Nomi slowly picked their way to the table; Nomi's strappy sandals wobbled and filled with sand. She kept her head down. Her skull felt too full, tight and near to bursting with all that had happened the night before.

Would Malachi expect more of the same?

Of course. You're his Grace.

She was *his*. The thought filled her mind, inescapable. It wouldn't matter that she had feelings for Asa. That she didn't want Malachi to touch her.

She'd comforted herself that Cassia had caught his eye. She'd counted on him responding to the girl's enthusiasm. But what if Malachi chose *Nomi* to grace his bed the night of his birthday? What if her behavior last night had ignited his interest in her?

"What happened to you and Malachi yesterday?" Maris asked quietly. "You both disappeared so abruptly. Cassia was *livid*."

Nomi might have told Maris everything, but not here. Not with Cassia and Malachi so close. So instead, she said as casually as she could, "He helped me get out of the rain. Took pity on me for being so frightened."

It wasn't pity, she knew. It was his volatility. Ignoring her for weeks, then seeking her out. Kissing her in the middle of an argument—in the middle of a storm.

"He went tearing after you," Maris said. "I wish he'd have done the same for us. We got soaked walking up those stairs, and I thought for certain I'd slip and break an ankle."

Nomi smiled wanly. She, too, wished Malachi had gone after the other girls. That he'd never cornered her under the overhang. That he'd never kissed her. That she'd never kissed him back.

By the time the two girls settled themselves at the table, Cassia had already helped herself to several tiny sandwich rounds. For today's outing, she'd piled her shimmering hair on top of her head and secured it with a jaunty pink bow. She wore a flattering, low-cut pink swimming robe. The garment was designed like Nomi's, with stretchy fabric that crossed over the bust and billowed into a short skirt, except Nomi's was black.

Maris had tied her dark hair back in a thick braid and her willowy body into a shimmering gold swimming robe.

"Good morning," the Heir said to the group.

He wore navy swim trunks, leaving the golden skin of his chest and arms bare. His satisfied smile made him look like his father.

He was staring straight at Nomi.

She dropped her gaze to her plate as heat rose to her cheeks.

Beside her, Maris ate a sandwich, her head turned to watch the waves. Nomi drizzled honey over a small round of flatbread and tried to eat it, but her stomach wouldn't settle. Not with the Heir sitting across from her. Not with the memory of last night playing through her mind. She wished Asa were here. He'd distract his brother, send her a secret smile, remind her what they were fighting for.

"How did you sleep, Nomi?" the Heir asked, interrupting her thoughts.

"Very well," she replied, clipping the words. "You?"

"I slept quite well." His voice deepened. "A good storm has a way of clarifying things, doesn't it?"

Maris turned away from the water. Cassia cocked her head.

Nomi could only smile awkwardly and push at her food, her appetite gone. As soon as the plates were cleared, she stood up. "Excuse me."

She escaped to a spot near the water. Her hands shook as she pulled off her sandals and dropped them into the sand. She closed her eyes and tipped her head back, the sunshine bright and hot against her face.

"Do you enjoy swimming, Your Eminence?" Cassia's voice floated out over the crash of waves.

Nomi stepped into the water. It was cool against her flushed skin, and the waves were gentle. Out here, she didn't have to pretend. She didn't have to see Malachi's satisfaction at claiming his prize. Maybe he thought her gift of the gloves meant she had resigned herself to him. But he was wrong.

Suddenly, there was a giant splash behind her. Nomi turned, just as the Heir pushed through the water toward her. "Very refreshing," he said.

Nomi's mouth dropped open. "Your Eminence."

Malachi shot her a little smile before diving into the water, submerging completely. When he surfaced, he shook like a dog, spraying water at her. "Can you swim?"

Nomi shook her head. In Lanos, there had been no need to learn.

He reached out and put his hands on her arms. She was so shocked at his touch, it took her a moment to realize he was drawing her slowly into deeper water. She resisted. Her toes dug into the sand as little swells lapped against her collarbone.

Fear blossomed in her chest. *Too deep, too deep.* "Please, Your Eminence."

Did he enjoy scaring her? Nomi's heart beat faster.

Malachi stopped moving, his hands still loosely encircling her wrists. "When I was five," he said in a conversational tone, "my father threw me into the water. I figured out pretty quickly how to float."

Nomi's breath caught. That was horrible. What if he'd drowned?

Is that what the Heir was going to do to her?

"We've no place to swim in Lanos," she said, her voice trembling. She stood on her tiptoes as a bigger swell pushed at her, sending panic shooting through her. "I've always thought it would feel nice, but—but it's frightening." She took a step back toward shallower water.

His hands released her, but instead of backing away, he moved closer, his skin sliding against hers as he wrapped his arms loosely around her. "That's what I'm trying to say," he said, in a different, softer tone. "I don't think it *has* to be frightening. Here—put your arms around me. I'll show you."

He's toying with me.

Reluctantly, Nomi lined her arms along the tops of his, letting her hands rest on his shoulders. She stared fixedly at his throat, where his wet skin glistened.

"Look at me."

Slowly, she raised her chin. His gaze found hers, as intense as it had been when she'd first seen him, when he'd caught her in the hall. "I promise. I won't let you go."

He pulled her closer, until their bodies slid against each other. Slowly, he moved into deeper water. Heart in her throat, Nomi felt the sand fall away under her feet. Reflexively, she tightened her arms around his neck. *Too deep, too deep.*

But she was floating. His embrace kept her head well above the water, and the rest of her flowed. She kicked her feet a little, feeling the rush of the current.

Her eyes widened.

He smiled. "See?" he said softly. "It's not so bad."

The tightness in her chest eased a little. "I feel so light. Like a—a cloud. I could float away." How she wished she could.

"Well, let's not float away quite yet." He grinned, and for a moment, he looked almost playful. "It was a hard start for me, but I love swimming now." Something about the way he said it, the warmth in his eyes, sent heat through her body. His hands slid down her back and the current pushed them closer together, so close her legs drifted around his hips of their own accord. She was holding on to him everywhere.

Everywhere.

Nomi drew in a breath. She was still looking him in the eye, their faces a mere inch away. Her stomach turned over. His eyes darkened; the intensity was back, all playfulness gone. The world reduced to the silken slide of their skin, the shrinking space between their lips.

"Have you found the gift I left for you?" he asked softly.

"Gift?" she asked stupidly. It was suddenly very difficult to think. What was wrong with her?

"The book."

The book? Nomi's body went rigid. Asa had given her the book. Hadn't he?

"Why in the world would you give me a book?" She tried to sound unperturbed, but her voice shook, betraying her.

"Your sister could read," he said, his body swaying with the insistent prodding of the current. "I thought maybe you could too. I was hoping . . ." He didn't finish the thought.

The moment—any softening she'd felt toward him—shattered.

A trap, a trap, a trap.

Nomi wasn't walking the high wire anymore. She was gripping the line with a single hand. Falling wasn't a question of whether but when.

"No, Your Eminence," she said, her voice hoarse. "I can't read."

The sun lit his eyes to a bright golden brown. Nomi couldn't look away. "I see," he said at last, but she couldn't tell if he believed her. "It was a gift, as I said. Maybe not entirely innocent, but it wasn't intended as poison. If you *can* read—"

Nomi's head swam, and suddenly, the miracle of weightlessness felt like a curse. She couldn't escape from him, not in water so deep. And she needed, so much, to escape. "Please," she whispered, pulling against his arms. "I want to get out of the water."

"Have I upset you?" he asked, and she couldn't tell if he was asking with real concern or mocking her.

"I just—I don't like the water anymore," she said as the panic built in her chest. She yanked herself from his grasp, her head dipping under the water. She sputtered, terror tightening every muscle. But somehow she made it to shallower water. Somehow she made it to shore.

Her teeth chattered. Her lungs ached.

She splashed up onto the beach and reached for a towel from one of the chaises. It was hot in the sun, but she still shivered as she wrapped it around herself. Malachi splashed up behind her. "Are you okay?"

She curtsied awkwardly and bowed her head, aware that Cassia and Maris were watching. "I am, Your Eminence. But I'm cold. May I return to my room for some dry clothes?"

"Of course." He looked as if he wanted to say more, but she couldn't bear it.

The chill didn't leave her for the rest of the day.

THIRTY-ONE

SERINA

IT TOOK SERINA three days to find the courage to approach Hotel Misery. In that time, she spoke to no one, hiding deep in her cave when the guards made their rounds and subsisting on clams she dug out of the sand and berries she found near the edge of the forest.

She hoped that Jacana would bring her news, tell her Oracle had already brokered a truce.

She waited for Val and wondered why he hadn't come to find her. Had he forgotten their conversation about the eastern beaches? Or did he not care, now that she was likely to die anyway?

She thought of Nomi, at the mercy of cruel men. Had the Heir celebrated his birthday yet? She knew what would happen when he did, and how much Nomi would suffer.

Serina tried to guess what Renzo was doing. She closed her eyes and imagined him wandering through Lanos's central market. He passed stalls of fresh meat, skinned rabbits and chickens hanging by their feet, ready to roast. The fruit vendor, with buckets of burgundy cherries, bright bloodred strawberries, and juicy peaches for sale. Next, a stall of dried fruit: sweet pineapple, crunchy dried banana chips, chewy rings of apple spiced with fresh-ground nutmeg. In her mind, Renzo paused before their favorite baker, Alonso, and his baskets of warm loaves of bread. Renzo chose a cornetto and a flaky pastry filled with hazelnut cream. He grinned boyishly, flicking back his dark hair.

Without Nomi there, who was cutting his hair?

Serina pulled her thoughts back to Mount Ruin with an effort. Tears snaked down her cheeks. She stood up. It was time.

Before she left her little cove, she collected as many clams as she could find and twisted them into her shirt. She took a tiny sip from Jacana's water flagon and slung its strap over her shoulder. Her knife, the one salvaged in the fight, hung from a hole she'd cut in the waistband of her pants.

She hiked south along the coast for an hour before heading inland. The island wasn't large—it would probably take a full day to travel from the southernmost point to the northern tip—and it was relatively easy to navigate. Paths crisscrossed the grassy lands and the forest, and the lava fields were open, allowing full visibility. Serina used the guard towers to mark her progress, though she steered well clear of them.

She found a small stream and replenished her flagon. She watched for boar, but found no sign of the animals.

Eventually, she reached the amphitheater. Full of women and death, it was terrifying. Empty, as it was now, it was eerie. Too silent. The air thickened, and for a moment, she fancied the spirits of all the women who had fallen here watching her. Serina shook her head, trying to banish the thought.

By the time she reached Hotel Misery, it was late afternoon.

Just after the turnoff to the half-ruined building, a tall woman stepped into the path. Her hair hung over her shoulders in two long braids and a thick scar ran along the side of her neck. She crossed her arms over her chest threateningly. "We don't take in strays."

Serina unwound the end of her shirt to reveal the clams, heart pounding. "Call this a peace offering. I'm not asking you to take me in. I just want to talk to Slash."

The woman gave her a long look. At last, her hard stance relaxed. "Follow me."

Serina followed her down the rocky path to the hotel. Massive entry columns extended crookedly to the sky, caught in an eternal wave of lava rock. The lobby's carved latticework ceiling had collapsed, and chunks of white marble tile were visible in a few small gaps the lava left untouched. Huge ceramic vases lay broken and half melted, their vibrant blues and reds scorched off. Tattered, charred bamboo walls tapped eerily against each other when the wind blew.

Serina shivered. She'd thought Oracle's cave was a depressing place to live, but this was truly a misery, as its name suggested. It was too easy to imagine the hotel guests running for their lives. Too easy to imagine the ghosts.

The woman led her through the destroyed lobby and to the left, down an open-air walkway bounded on one side by the stone and steel shell of a building and on the other by a brackish, bad-smelling canal. A matching building framed the opposite side of the water. Both structures were three stories high, lined with railed terraces and dark holes where doors should have been. At the end of the canal, a wide, round tower linked the two buildings. Most of the tower had burned, but its curved iron skeleton and ribs of concrete remained. At its base was a shallow marble staircase; Slash sat at the top, sharpening scraps of metal into knives.

She looked up at the sound of footsteps. Her spiky black hair framed an angular face crisscrossed with knife-thin scars. "What's this?"

The lookout said, "She said she wanted to talk to you."

Slash glanced at the woman. "And?"

Serina stepped forward and gently unrolled her clams again, setting them at Slash's feet. She resisted the inexplicable urge to curtsy. "I don't want anything from you but to talk."

Slash raised a brow. "I don't talk to traitors."

"You can talk to the woman who spared your fighter," Serina said, sounding more fierce than she felt. In truth, it was all she could do to meet the woman's eyes.

Slash sat back in the rusted chair and spun the knife in her hand.

Serina suspected she had seconds before that knife flew through the air and buried itself in her chest. "The crews should join together and take the island," she said, words blurring together in her haste to get them out before the woman attacked. "The guards have firearms, but there are fewer of them, and we know the island. If we joined together, we could share resources. We could be *free*."

The knife paused.

"What did Oracle say? Presumably you shared your thoughts with her first."

Serina struggled to hold Slash's gaze, Her mouth was dry as sand. "I betrayed the crew by submitting. She felt she had no choice but to banish me. But that's what Commander Ricci *wants*. He wants us to fight each other, to never question how things work here."

"Why question it? This is our reality." Slash tested the tip of her blade.

"It doesn't need to be," Serina argued. "Commander Ricci put hundreds of women on an island, barely supervised, and told them to learn to fight. He's given us all the tools we need to overthrow him."

Slash stood up slowly and descended the three shallow steps until she and Serina were on the same level. Serina held her breath.

"You're a freshie and a stray, and you know nothing," the woman said finally, twisting the knife in her hand.

Disappointment choking her, Serina turned to go. "Thank you for hearing me out."

From behind her, Slash's voice rang out. "Have you spoken to the other crews?"

Serina glanced back over her shoulder. "Only you and Oracle so far. I started with the strongest."

Slash regarded her through narrowed eyes. "If you can get the heads of the other crews to agree, I'll consider it. But only if there's a plan. A *good* one."

Serina sagged with relief. It wasn't much to hold on to, but it was *something*. "Thank you."

Slash nodded her dismissal. The woman who had brought Serina into the hotel now led her out. As Serina left the ruined lobby, Anika walked in. She stopped dead when she saw Serina.

For a long moment, they stared at each other, and then Serina was past her, out into the fading daylight. The lookout walked her to the main path and then disappeared into the woods.

Serina sipped from her flagon, ignored her grumbling stomach, and began the long trek back to the east beach, a cautious hope pacing her. Tomorrow she would go see Twig. And maybe Jacana would make headway with Oracle.

Serina reached the east beach just as the sun set, sending the night streaking across the sky to find her. She stood at the edge of the water and watched the stars appear.

Someone whistled behind her.

Serina whirled, yanking the knife from her pants, hard enough to rip the fabric further.

Bruno stood a few feet away.

"I've been wondering where you holed up," he said. The darkness hid his face and turned his black-clad body into shadow.

"Go away," Serina snapped.

Her fingers tightened on her knife. She wasn't the submissive girl she'd been the last time they'd met, but she was still scared.

He shifted closer. She fought the urge to step back.

"Why should I?" he said, his voice flat. "You don't have a crew to protect you anymore. I can just take what I want."

"You can try," she growled, and then she lunged forward. She was betting he hadn't seen her knife in the dark, and she wasn't going to wait for him to attack first. She stabbed him in the gut, but it was a shallow wound.

He roared. Without hesitation, he backhanded her, hard enough to send her flying to the gritty sand. She kept her grip on her knife, but it was now slick with blood. As she stumbled

242

to her feet, he kicked her in the side, sending her back to the ground.

"Submit," he muttered. He loomed over her, his feet on either side of her hips. She hooked one of his legs with hers and surged upward into his wounded stomach as she twisted, bringing him down. Her knife slashed his side.

She made it to her feet and was almost free when he grabbed her ankle and yanked.

She went down again, sand filling her mouth. She spit and screamed, her panic and fury all-consuming.

Bruno's grip dug into her skin, shackling her to him. Slowly, he stood up, dragging her toward him. Panic filled her. She kicked and wriggled violently, terror lending her strength. Her arm hit her water flagon. She scrambled for it as something to throw at him, but it rolled out of reach. Her foot finally connected with his knee. His hands slipped, just for a second.

He grunted as she pulled herself free.

Her panting breath screamed in her throat. She scrambled to her feet, backing away from him at the same time. The darkness was disorienting, giving his face a deathly, masklike quality.

Like a snake hypnotizing his prey, his gaze held her. She paused for a split second.

But it gave him an opening. He raised his firearm.

She threw her knife as hard as she could.

Miraculously, it buried itself to the hilt in his chest.

But he still fired his weapon.

A searing pain exploded in her arm as the force of the bullet drove her to the ground. Her head slammed against something hard and the world went black.

THIRTY-TWO

NOMI

BEAUTIFULLY DRESSED WOMEN stood at intervals throughout the small ballroom in the Graces' chambers, their arms raised above their heads in identical poses. Their faces tilted toward the ceiling, with matching expressions of serenity. Except Maris, whose eyes were dulled by grief. And Nomi, who wore a look of fury.

She would *never* master the art of becoming a living statue, because she never wanted to. She wasn't made of clay. Her bones and breath and blood were meant to *move*.

At the far end of the room, Ines gracefully shifted to a new position. In silence, the rest of the Graces shifted too, matching Ines's stance perfectly.

Nomi's muscles shook.

For a week, she had done little but go to dress fittings and dance lessons and endless Grace training. The rest of the time she'd paced her room, driving Angeline to distraction. Asa had sent her no messages, and they'd had no opportunity to speak during the dance lessons. Malachi had appeared a few times to watch the training, throwing all three girls out of sorts, but he had never requested to see them alone.

The moment they'd shared at the beach haunted her. His skin sliding against hers, the way he'd held her in the water, safe and yet at his mercy . . . the fact that *he'd* been the one to give her the book. . . . She knew it was a trap. It *had* to be. But he had called it a gift, and the look in his eyes had almost convinced her he meant it. But how could that be?

And why was she thinking of him when Asa held all her hopes? He was the brother she wanted. He was the one she trusted, that she cared about. The one she was desperate to see.

Maris had tried to speak to her, and Cassia sniped and tittered behind her back. But the haze wouldn't dissipate. Every day that passed without word from Renzo, it was harder for Nomi to concentrate on life in the Graces' chambers.

Had Renzo understood her message? What if he'd decided not to come? What if Trevi had betrayed Asa, and Renzo was even now awaiting the Superior's judgment?

Her mind spiraled further and further into darkness.

And at its center, Serina sat in her cell, thinking she would be there forever. Not knowing how hard Nomi was trying to save her. How desperately impatient she was to see her sister safe and well.

If Renzo didn't get that letter . . . if Renzo didn't come . . .

By the time Ines moved to the next statuesque pose, Nomi's arms were on fire.

"Why are we doing this?" she groused under her breath, dropping her arms to let the blood flow back into her fingers.

"Nomi!" Ines called. "Arms up. No excuses."

With a badly concealed groan, Nomi bullied her shaking limbs into position.

"It is a great honor to be chosen as a living statue for one of the Superior's parties." Cassia held the contorted pose as if made of stone. Not a single tremble.

Nomi's arm dropped again, her fingers having progressed past tingly and into numb. As she shook her hand back to life, she noticed the guard in the doorway slip into the hall. Seconds later, Marcos's stocky form replaced him.

Nomi's eyes widened. Marcos regarded her calmly, but with intent. Did he want to speak with her? Was this it?

She tried to squelch the thrill of hope that shivered up her spine. She'd seen Marcos half a dozen times over the past week. His presence could easily mean nothing.

Still, Nomi's heart jumped when Ines announced, at last, "That's enough for today."

The rustle of fabric and murmur of voices slowly filled the room. Maris shook out her fingers. Cassia twisted at the waist a few times and rearranged her silky blond hair. Some of the other girls sagged, but Cassia's whole body sang with energy.

Nomi rubbed at her aching neck with fingers still smarting painfully.

She left the room with the others, and silent as a shadow, Marcos followed.

He waited until they were alone in the empty corridor of bedrooms before slipping something into her hand.

A letter.

Nomi's breath froze. *N, in care of Trevi* was written in Renzo's hand.

Tears pricked at the back of her eyes. *Renzo.*

"His Eminence asks that you meet him on the terrace. Tonight," Marcos said quietly. When she nodded, he bowed and slipped away.

Nomi hurried to her room. She didn't know how long Angeline would be. She turned the letter over to break the seal, only to find it already broken.

Had Asa read the letter?

A whisper of apprehension swept through her, but she shook it off. She hadn't asked him not to read it, and she was sure Renzo had followed her lead and concealed his identity.

She opened the letter with shaking hands.

Renzo had written her bits of the story about the moon and the man she fell in love with. But some of the details were wrong. She pieced together his message, her hands trembling so hard she could barely read the words.

He was here, in Bellaqua. He would help. He just needed her to tell him what to do.

And he had signed it with a simple *R.*

Nomi sank onto the bed, the letter crumpled into her arms, and wept.

In relief. In terror.

The Heir's birthday was in two days.

Asa was waiting for her when she slipped onto the terrace. There were no words, at first. Only hungry hands and mouths and heat and silence. Nomi clung to him as if, somehow, he could ward off the memory of his brother.

You are who I choose, she thought as he brushed feather-light kisses along her jaw.

This is what I want, she thought as his hands tightened on her waist.

And yet, Malachi wouldn't leave her.

Asa pulled back. "Nomi?"

For a moment, she rested against his chest, her arms tight around him, and breathed.

When she felt steadier, she put a little distance between them.

"You saw my cousin's message," she said. "He's staying at the Fiore. I'll write to him and explain what we need—"

Asa shook his head. "Father has me running errands all over the city for Malachi's birthday. I can go to him myself and explain our plan."

The thought of Asa and Renzo face-to-face made her more nervous than it should have.

"Tell me the plan again," she said. She'd run it through her mind a thousand times, but she wanted to hear him say it. She wanted to make sure she hadn't forgotten anything.

Asa smoothed his hands down her arms, the thin silk of her dressing gown the only thing between his skin and hers. "After the ceremony, my father will retire to an antechamber off the ballroom to rest. The room is private, with easy access from the ballroom if you know where to look. That's where the ruse should take place. We don't want a guard seeing our man and interfering too soon. You and I have promised your cousin that he will come to no harm. We will keep that promise."

"And his exit?" Nomi asked. She wished she could go to Bellaqua with Asa and see Renzo herself. The knowledge that her brother was *so close*, just beyond the canal, was maddening. She missed him so much.

Asa gestured toward the railing. "The ballroom opens onto a patio. He can just walk off into the night. No one will ever know he was there."

"What about a mask? And . . . and a weapon?" Nomi hated the thought of Renzo entering the palazzo with a weapon, but to make the illusion work, he had to have something.

Asa nodded. "I'll make sure he has what he needs. I've got an invitation for him as well so he won't be questioned when he arrives." He kissed the top of her head. "And you, flower, are you ready for your next task?"

"I've written the letter, but Malachi has not requested my presence in his chambers yet. I don't know—"

"He will," Asa interrupted, with a smile. "He will want to meet with each of his Graces once more before the big day. I'll suggest he invite you to his chambers for a game of Saints and Sailors. All you have to do is hide the letter somewhere in his room."

She nodded her head against his chest. She was so tired. It felt as if she hadn't gotten a full night of sleep since she'd arrived at the palazzo.

"I'm sorry you have to risk yourself," Asa went on. "If my handwriting was less recognizable, I could do this part for us."

Nomi straightened so she could see his expression. "It's *our* plan. We must both accept the risks."

"And it will be worth it, in the end," he replied, the mischievous gleam back in his eyes. "We are going to remake this country."

"And save Serina," she added.

"And save Serina." Asa caressed her cheek. "You'll be free too. Of my brother, and all the obligations he has for you."

Nomi told herself that this was right. There was nothing else to say. But she couldn't entirely dismiss her tiny, niggling doubts.

"Asa, your brother put a book in my room. As a test to see if I could read."

Asa stilled, his whole body tensing. "Did you tell him you could?"

"No," she said. "Of course not."

"Good." But he didn't relax.

"I thought you'd left it," she said. "It was about the history of Viridia. About—about Viridia's queens."

When he looked at her, the moonlight illuminated a sudden intensity in his eyes. The expression made him look like his brother. "Malachi is manipulating you, Nomi. He's trying to get into your confidence so he can use the things you love against you."

Nomi's breath froze in her throat.

"Don't trust him," Asa continued urgently. "He'll punish you, just like Father punished Serina. He's done it before, Nomi."

"What do you—"

"Don't trust *anyone* with your secret," Asa interrupted. "It's not safe."

Nomi pressed her face to Asa's chest. Shame slithered through her veins. She'd started to wonder if she was wrong about Malachi. But this sealed her opinion.

And his fate.

"Just imagine," Asa murmured, his breath warm against her hair. "Soon it won't matter that you can read. We can ensure *all* women can. There will be no Graces. Women will be free to make their own choices."

His words were a spell, binding Nomi to him, to his vision of a future she'd give anything to see. "That's what I want, Nomi." He kissed the top of her head again. "That, with you as my queen."

THIRTY-THREE

SERINA

SERINA DRIFTED IN and out with the waves.

Sometimes, the waves were laced with fire, and she burned.

A cool hand on her forehead. The warmth of sun against her cheek.

Water dripped into her mouth.

Velvet night, and Nomi's face—no. Her sister was lost.

When the fire faded, and the world began to make sense again, Serina found Val.

"What, what are you—" The words scratched her throat. She blinked groggily, the darkness pressing close.

He put the cool rim of a flagon to her lips. "Hello there," he said. "You've been trying to become a dead girl on me for real. I'm relieved that you didn't succeed."

Serina licked her cracked lips. "What happened?"

She remembered a fight, a banishment. Bruno's blank face in the darkness.

A gunshot.

"Bruno almost killed you," Val said. His normally clean-shaven face was dark with stubble, and his curly hair had flattened on one side, as if he'd recently slept on it. Only he didn't look like he'd slept much. Too pale, too many shadows under his eyes. "His bullet only grazed you, but you fell down and hit your head. You've been in and out for a few days. I wasn't sure . . . well. I don't have a lot of experience with head injuries. But the bullet wound is healing nicely."

Serina shifted and winced, putting a hand to her side. "It doesn't feel nice."

Val smiled. "I'm sure it doesn't. But you're alive."

"Thank you," she said softly. "You kept me safe."

In the firelight, his cheeks reddened.

As her mind cleared, Serina took in her surroundings. Stone walls, a small fire, the faint sound of the surf. Her cave by the beach. She was lying on a thin pallet, covered with his uniform jacket as a blanket. He sat on another pallet next to her.

He noticed her looking around. "I looked for you by the cliffs first, and then I remembered us talking about the east beach. My rounds only cover the west side of the island, so I couldn't come right away without drawing suspicion. I'm sorry it took me so long."

She shook her head and winced. A dull ache encircled her skull, and every time she moved, it sent off sparks through her brain. It was enough that he'd come. More than enough.

She might have died if he hadn't.

He held up the flagon again and helped her take a couple of sips. "When you feel ready, I've got some bread. It's stale."

She looked at him, her hazy mind filling with wonder. "You came prepared."

He shrugged. "I didn't know what state you'd be in. Bedding, aid kit, food and water . . . it's just the basics."

"Have you been here since the night when—when Bruno—" Her throat closed.

He nodded. "I'd already decided I couldn't wait any longer to come find you, when I heard Bruno talk about the east beach. I followed him at a safe distance so he wouldn't notice. But I was too far away. I couldn't get to you in time." A darkness passed across his features.

"What happened to Bruno?" she asked.

With the back of his hand, Val checked her forehead, looking encouraged. But he didn't answer.

"I killed him," Serina said, staring at him.

"You did what you had to do. He was going to kill you."

"Is—is he still out there?" *On the beach, rotting in the sun,* her imagination supplied.

Val shook his head. "He took a swim. The sharks were grateful."

"You've been here for days. What about Commander Ricci? Hasn't he sent someone to look for you? You can't just leave your post. Won't he punish you?"

Val shrugged. "It was a terrible job. Happy to be rid of it. And he can't punish me if he can't find me."

"Val!" she said, outraged.

"I wasn't going to let you die," he said, looking at her as if this should be no great revelation.

But it was. He had risked himself, abandoned his job for her?

She opened her mouth, but didn't know what to say.

He filled the silence. "The Commander's had us looking for you. I kept the others away from here as long as I could."

A clammy cold sank to her bones. "I thought no one cares about the strays."

"I think he wants to make an example of you. Ricci was furious when you submitted. He called the crew chiefs together and threatened them. He doesn't want anything like that happening again." He helped her sit up and handed her a small, round loaf of bread from his bag. "Time to eat something. You're shaking."

Serina took a tentative bite. When the bread went down without incident, she devoured the strips of dried meat he handed her too. As she ate, some of the trembling receded.

She wondered when Commander Ricci had spoken to the crew chiefs, if it was before or after she'd talked to Slash.

Val put another stick on the fire. The movement caught her attention. Serina watched him for a few moments, trying to puzzle him out. "Why are you doing this? Why did you stay?"

He didn't look at her. "I told you. I didn't want you to die."

Serina wasn't satisfied. "Enough that you were willing to risk your own life? You abandoned your post. Helped a prisoner. They'll hunt you down. They won't let this stand, Val. You've put a target on your own back. Why?"

The more she thought about it, the more inconceivable it became.

Val abandoned his fire and knelt before her. He reached for her hands. "Your life is worth those things to me, Serina. You may not believe that, but it's the truth. I thought—" And for the first time she saw uncertainty in his eyes. "I thought there was something between us, something that maybe justified us fighting for each other. . . ."

The kiss.

The *I think I might die, so why not?* kiss.

Serina knew how she was supposed to act when a man desired her—obedient, submissive, acquiescent. But she'd spent weeks fighting to unlearn all that she knew about the world. Oracle had told her strength was the currency here. Serina wanted to believe she'd found hers.

"I am grateful you came to my rescue," Serina said quietly, and forced herself to meet his eyes. "But I don't know what's between us yet, if anything. And I—I need time to figure it out."

She waited for his anger. Expected him to tell her she owed him. Wondered if he might force payment for his sacrifice.

But he just squeezed her hands. "I understand."

The firelight illuminated his face quite clearly, and she could find no anger or even disappointment in his expression. He released her and went back to the fire, and she felt the irrational desire to follow him, wrap her arms around him, and lose herself in him after all.

But she held her ground.

"You're so different," she mused.

"From other men?" he said, glancing over his shoulder.

"Yes."

Tongues of flame licked his small pile of wood and leaves. He stared at them intently. "My father was part of a trade delegation to Azura just before I was born. He said it opened his eyes to how backward and oppressive Viridia was. So he and my mother tried to do something about it. They started a secret school for girls in the basement of our house. I guess . . . I'm different because of what they taught me. How they raised me."

Before Serina could respond, he stood up and grabbed his pack, returning to sit just in front of her. "I need to change your dressing," he said, pulling out his aid kit.

Gingerly, Serina drew her shirt off her shoulder.

In silence, Val changed the bandage over the bullet wound and rubbed salve on the cut on her arm.

"Were they caught?" Serina asked softly.

"My mother was taken first," he said, staring at her arm even though he'd completed his ministrations. "One of the fathers of the children found out his daughter was learning to read and reported my parents, along with his own wife. My father tried to stop them from taking my mother, but they hit him. Knocked him out, right in front of me."

Serina's heart seized. She couldn't bear Val's story, the way he said the words so matter-of-factly, even as his whole body tensed.

"Two days later, they came for my father. I never saw him again. I think he was probably killed."

"How old were you?" she whispered.

"Fourteen." Val turned his attention back to the fire. "It took me two years to find out where my mother was, another year to pay for my new identity. Six months more to get this job. By then, she was gone. That was three years ago."

Serina could hardly breathe. "Your mother was the one on the cliff. She was the jumper."

Val nodded.

"How did you find out what happened to her?" Her heart ached for him.

At that, Val smiled. "Oracle told me. She remembered her. My mother was too old to fight by the time she arrived. She was going to teach the Cave to read. They didn't have paper or books, of course, but she could do magic with a piece of charcoal and a bit of rock. She was going to contribute. But after she watched a couple of the fights, she . . . she didn't want to stay."

Serina curled her arms around her knees and stared into the fire.

"I'm sorry, Val," she murmured.

He rubbed the back of his neck. "None of the guards know the story. They think I volunteer to bring rations to the crews because I want to prove myself, being the youngest. I'm as gruff and nasty as the rest of them, when they're around. They never questioned it. I paid a lot of money to erase my connection to my parents and their—scandal."

"Why *did* you stay, after you found out about your mother?" she asked softly. "You could have gone back to the mainland. Found another job, a wife . . ."

Val tapped the end of a stick against the ground. "I kept thinking about the families these women left behind. I started doing rounds, and I convinced a few girls not to jump." He took a deep breath, his words halting. "It's hard, watching so many people die. Every time a boat arrives, I think, *this* time I'll leave. I'll move on. But I never seem to do it. There's always another girl standing on a cliff like my mother did. There's another girl showing up at in-processing, so scared she can't breathe."

He looked up at Serina, and for a moment, the only sound was the crackle of the fire.

"I'm glad you thought I was worth saving," Serina said.

"I think *every* woman is worth saving." Val's lip quirked. "You're just especially needy."

Serina bumped his knee with hers, as she might have done to Renzo when he teased her. But the heat that moved through her belly when she looked at him was wholly different. Val threw his stick into the flames, sending up sparks.

Serina's hands tightened into fists. She shouldn't need saving. None of them should. "Commander Ricci knows he's got a precarious system," she said. "That's why he wants to use me as a lesson to the others. If we were to band together, stand against him . . ."

"A lot of you would die," Val said.

"Not enough to stop us," Serina replied. She never would have expected, before she'd come here, that her thoughts would ever run to blood. To revolution.

"Not enough to stop you," Val echoed.

She looked over at him in surprise. "You agree with me?"

He met her gaze squarely, the firelight warming his skin. "I think the women in this prison—in this country—will rise up eventually. My father used to say that oppression isn't a finite state. It's a weight that is carried until it becomes too heavy, and then it is thrown off. Not without struggle, not without pain, but he believed the weight would always, always be fought and overcome. He wasn't the only one trying to change things."

Serina thought of Nomi and Renzo, how they balked at the

strict dictates of their lives. She took a deep breath. "My sister can read."

She'd never said it out loud before.

Val leaned toward her.

"Nomi convinced our brother to teach her, when we were growing up. They hid it from our parents, but I knew. Nomi read to me all the time. They asked if I wanted to learn, but I said no." She swallowed, thinking back to those days, the secrets they shared. "I wish I'd let them."

"Why didn't you want to learn?" Val threw another stick into the fire.

"I was training to become a Grace—there was already so much to learn. And . . . it scared me. It was my duty to uphold the Superior's ideal image of a woman. Learning to read was in direct opposition to that." Serina looked down at her scratched hands and deeply tanned skin. She hardly recognized who she'd become.

"I saw your intake papers," Val said. "I assumed you *were* a Grace. And your crime was listed as reading. How did that happen?"

"It was a mistake. Nomi had a book"—even now she couldn't admit that Nomi had stolen it—"a book we'd loved as children. I was holding it, reciting the story from memory, when the Head Grace entered our room. She assumed I was reading, and then everything happened so fast."

She hadn't told anyone any of this. Not even Jacana. Oracle knew her sister had been chosen, but she'd never asked Serina why she'd been sent to Mount Ruin. Tears ran down Serina's cheeks, and her breath hitched in her throat. "I don't know if

I saved her," she said. "I wanted to help her, but leaving her in the palace, alone, with the Superior and his son . . . I may have secured her a future far worse than mine."

Val reached out a tentative hand and rubbed her back.

Val's comforting touch undid her. She leaned into him and he scooted closer, until they were sitting side by side, his arms wrapped around her. She laid her head on his chest and cried. He hushed her softly, like a child. The last few weeks flashed before her eyes, nightmare after nightmare, too horrifying to be real.

Eventually, she calmed. Her eyes felt gritty and swollen, and her head still ached. Outside the cave, the sky was edging into dawn. Her whole body hurt, bone-deep.

How was it that homesickness could be more painful than a bullet wound?

THIRTY-FOUR

NOMI

"I CAN'T BELIEVE the Heir's birthday is tomorrow," Maris said as she and Nomi strolled through the small garden near the palazzo. Ines had allowed them some fresh air; they were both testy and restless, with the celebration the next day. "I hope Cassia gets her wish."

Nomi hoped so too. Tomorrow would either end with Asa as the new Heir or with her at the whim of his brother, and Serina's future hung in the balance.

Our plan will work, she reassured herself for the hundredth time. She wished she could see Asa again before everything was set in motion. But he was in Bellaqua today. Maybe speaking to Renzo at this very moment.

And she was still waiting for Malachi's summons. What would happen if he *didn't* request her presence before tomorrow? Asa had seemed so sure that he would. If she wasn't able to place the letter in his chambers, everything fell into question. The letter was the key to linking Malachi to their plot. Without that letter, there was no proof the Heir had anything to do with it. And then other suspects would be sought.

Nomi's stomach clenched.

"We'll survive this," Maris said, misinterpreting Nomi's look of concern. "As the years pass and he chooses more Graces, we'll see him less. We'll get a little more space." Maris wore her grief like an iron collar, always there, always dragging at her. She'd told Nomi she felt responsible for whatever had happened to Helena, and the not knowing ate at her every day.

Nomi took Maris's arm. "Maybe one day, our lives can be about more than survival." *This* was why she was risking so much. Because Serina didn't deserve to be imprisoned . . . and neither did the rest of them. "We are not lesser beings, Maris," she said, her voice shaking. "Someday, things *will* be different. I know it. I'm going to make it happen."

Maris patted her hand. "I've stopped giving license to fantasies like that. My father used his cruelty skillfully." But then her gaze sharpened, focusing in on something in Nomi's face, on the force of her conviction. "You *are* speaking of fantasies, right?"

"Of course." Nomi looked away. "It's nothing. A hypothetical."

Maris pulled her to a stop and turned to face her. "What are you planning?"

"Nothing," Nomi said, but she'd never been good with masks. That was Serina's weapon, not hers.

"No one here is worthy of trust," Maris said softly. "The Superior's Graces talk. . . . There are spies everywhere, people watching everything. Nothing is what you think here, Nomi."

"What I think is that we deserve more than this," she whispered. "We deserve to be free."

Maris looked at her for a long time, the defeat in her eyes slowly bleeding into a desperate, unwilling hope. She shook her head, as if shaking off a dream. "Be careful. Please be careful."

"Be careful with what?" A new voice intruded, loud and brash.

Nomi started, guilt written on her face clear as day. She turned to see Cassia stalk toward them, framed by the tall green hedges. How much had she heard?

The girl flicked her silver-blond hair over her shoulder. "Careful with what?" she asked again, raising a brow.

Maris recovered first. She arched a brow. "With the Heir, of course. Tomorrow night."

Cassia licked her lips. "You don't really think he'll choose one of *you* to spend the night with, do you? I'll be Head Grace, you wait."

"What do you want?" Nomi asked, resisting the urge to roll her eyes.

The girl shrugged, her flowing lavender dress rippling. "The Heir has asked to see all of us today. I've gone. Now it's your turn, Nomi."

This is it. The final preparation.

Nomi shuddered with nerves.

"Thank you," she said. She glanced once more at Maris, willing her to have faith. And then she headed inside, trying to convince herself to do the same.

———

The Heir's emissary led Nomi down the long tile corridor and opened the door carved with the leaping fish. With a small curtsy and a stomach swarming with butterflies, she entered the room. She gripped a small bag to her chest.

Malachi was waiting for her on the terrace. She moved to a spot along the railing next to him, not close enough to touch. She watched people move through the piazza, weaving between the stalls of the market. She pictured Renzo moving through the street, and couldn't help but search for his dark mop of hair, his tall, lanky stride.

"You look beautiful," Malachi said.

Nomi curtsied, her shimmering gray dress swishing. "Thank you, Your Eminence." She reminded herself to be pleasant, to keep her anger to herself this time. She couldn't risk Malachi asking her to leave before she'd placed the letter. She couldn't make him suspicious.

Malachi turned and gestured to the closed door opposite his bedroom. "Please join me," he said, and led the way.

Nomi gasped when he opened the door. He had his own library, with floor-to-ceiling bookcases, windows overlooking Bellaqua, and several deep leather chairs. A low table of polished wood was set with a deck of cards, two frosted glasses of orange juice, and a plate of small, star shaped cookies with pale yellow icing.

Nomi drifted to the nearest bookcase. It was filled with leather-bound volumes with titles like *Festival of Corpses* and *The Foibles of Finnigan Hawk*.

"Care for a game of Saints and Sailors?" Malachi asked mildly.

She whirled toward him, her cheeks reddening. "Oh, of course, Your Eminence. I would love to."

Malachi laughed out loud. "You have never wanted anything *less*."

Nomi bit her lip. She'd never heard him laugh before. It softened the harsh lines of his face and the dark glint of his eyes. He looked younger when he laughed.

"If I hadn't suspected before, I certainly would have now," he said almost gently. "Don't let anyone see you around books. Your yearning gives you away."

Nomi took a deep breath, panic unfurling in her chest. "I don't know what you mean."

Malachi's smile faded. "Don't lie to me."

"I'm sorry, I—I—" she stuttered. Asa's warning echoed in her ears.

The Heir moved closer to her. "You lie because you are afraid. But I will not punish you for this, if you tell me the truth."

"Like you punished my sister?" she asked, fire igniting in her chest.

"She was not my Grace," he said, adding, "and that was my father's decision. I had no say."

"But wouldn't you have done the same?" Nomi's pulse pounded in her temples. She wanted to rip him apart. "You left that book to trap me. You wanted to—"

"It was a test, not a trap." His dark eyes held an expression she didn't understand.

Nomi couldn't look away, couldn't stop the words from spilling out. "You gave me a book about women ruling this country.

About a history none of us are ever taught. Why would you do that?"

"Ah," he said, and his face relaxed. "I thought that might draw you out.'"

Despair burned through her. She'd risen to the bait. Now he knew she'd read it. With a breath, she braced for his wrath.

She was not prepared for his smile.

"Why?" she asked. "Why would you *want* me to be able to read?"

His expression softened. "I thought, if you could read, that would confirm something I suspected about you."

"What?" Her heart clamored in her chest.

"I thought you were daring. Persistent. Now I know I was right. Maybe you won't believe me, but I admire your nerve."

Nomi flushed, disbelief radiating through her. Asa had said his brother was incensed by her defiance, not attracted to it. "Are you going to tell your father?"

"Of course not," Malachi said. "But I know now, and that knowledge gives me great pleasure."

Nomi could think of nothing to say.

He cocked his head at the bag she held. "More gifts?"

Nomi shook her head. "Your book."

"You could have given it to the Head Grace," Malachi said. "She's the one who left it for you to find."

"Ines? Your mother?" The woman who'd warned Nomi to follow the rules? The woman who'd turned Serina in for the very same thing? The thought of going to *her* with the book nearly made Nomi laugh in disbelief.

Malachi looked away. "Yes, my . . . mother."

The pause caught Nomi's attention. She thought about what Cassia had said, about Graces not raising their own children. "You don't think of her like that?"

"As my mother?" Malachi's hands clenched once, briefly, before relaxing. "No, not really. But . . . but I do trust her. She would not tell my father about the book."

The book in the bag Nomi still clutched to her chest. Heart in her throat, she asked, "May I return it to your shelves?"

He gave her a casual nod and sank into a chair by the table, with his back to her. For an instant, she stared at him, confused beyond all measure. He'd just confirmed she could read, and . . . that was it? Was he truly not going to call the guards?

Remembering herself, she seized her chance, scrambling to remove the book and the letter from her bag. She slid the book onto a shelf, and the letter between two books on the shelf above, the edge of the letter peeking out the tiniest bit. Not enough for Malachi to notice, hopefully, but enough for Asa to, when he brought the guards to search Malachi's chambers.

Nomi took another deep breath as she turned away from the bookshelf. It was done.

He shuffled the cards. "So, a game?"

"Of course," she said, forcing her muscles to relax even though she desperately wished for an excuse to leave, now that her task was complete. She sat down across from him as he dealt the cards, patterned side up. The other sides varied, with pictures of warty, crooked-nosed Sailors, red-lipped Sirens, uniformed Soldiers, and serene-faced Saints. The deck also had two cards where all the characters entwined suggestively. If one was played, the game reset. Cassia called them the "orgy" cards.

The objective was to end up with only Saint cards or Sailor cards. All Saints was better.

Nomi admired the cards in her hand. She'd never seen a set with such skilled illustrations. The images on the deck Renzo had were simplistic and crude. This set was beautifully detailed, the Siren's eyes filled with murderous seduction, the Saint's face beatific, his gaze turned upward.

The Saint didn't look like he knew all the answers. He looked like he was still searching.

Nomi kept sneaking glances at the Heir. He'd gone to such lengths to confirm that she could read, just as a point of personal satisfaction? Was this part of his manipulation?

Her position felt more precarious than ever. There was so much she didn't understand.

"I want to teach you to ride," he said suddenly, shocking her again. Malachi played a Siren without looking at her, a red flush creeping up his throat.

"I don't know, Your Eminence," she said haltingly. "Those horses in the race, they were so large. I found them quite terrifying."

His lip quirked. "There's a vast difference between riding a pony through the gardens and racing in the Premio Belaria."

"Of course," she murmured, playing her own Siren.

"I saw you speaking to my brother that night."

Nomi looked up sharply, but he was focused on his cards.

"Was he regaling you with tales of his miraculous win?"

"He did mention it," she allowed.

He played a Soldier and drew a card. "He enjoys the attention. Any attention, really. I think that's why he volunteers for the dance lessons." He glanced up at her briefly, before focusing again on his cards. "He thrives when he gets to play the chivalrous hero."

"Volunteer? He told me your father made him attend the lessons," Nomi said slowly.

"Did he, now?" Malachi raised a brow.

"You're saying it's an act?" she asked, suddenly on edge.

He didn't reply.

"Maybe you're jealous of the attention, Your Eminence?" Nomi asked, with a little more bite than she intended.

"Jealous?" He looked up in surprise. "No. Not of that." He paused, and she waited, curious. "Of him riding in the Premio Belaria, yes. I was jealous of that. I wanted to race too, but my father wouldn't let me."

"And then he won."

"Asa's *win* is not something I envy."

"What do you mean?" she asked. She drew a Saint. But she wasn't paying much attention to the game. Tension ran along her shoulders and down her spine. She wasn't sure she wanted him to answer.

Malachi's hands tightened on his cards. "The night of the race, I went to wish Asa luck in the stables, and I overheard him ordering a groom to sabotage the other riders. More died that year than usual. . . . A lot of broken saddles."

Nomi gasped. Asa couldn't have done that. . . . Malachi must have misunderstood.

Malachi's cheeks darkened. "Afterward Asa accused the

270

groom of something—I can't remember what—and had him put to death. I think he didn't want anyone to question his victory."

A chill moved through Nomi, raising gooseflesh along her arms. "That's awful," she said softly. She tried to resolve the brutal story with the gentle man she'd come to know. They couldn't be reconciled. Was Malachi lying? Had he realized that Nomi had feelings for Asa and was trying to undermine them?

"I'm sorry," he said, shooting her a wry smile. "I've never actually told anyone that."

"Why didn't you tell your father?" she asked. "Maybe—I mean, your brother should have been punished, right?"

Malachi shrugged. "I should have told, I suppose. But he's my brother. I—Well, I didn't. That's all."

"Are you and Asa very close?" Nomi stared at the cards in her hand until they blurred.

"No," Malachi said shortly, and played an orgy card. "We were before, but I found it hard to respect him after that."

A wave of fever heat passed through her, sending her blood rushing, making her light-headed.

"I can't imagine feeling that way about my sister. I'm lost without her." Nomi lowered her Saints to the table, winning the game. Tears burned her eyes, threatening to spill over. Everything she'd done, all her plotting with Asa, was to save Serina. If Malachi's story was true, Asa had used that poor groom and then disposed of him without a thought. She *couldn't* believe it was true. But if it was . . .

How could she trust him with Renzo's life?

And if she couldn't trust him with Renzo's life, how would she save Serina's?

She could bear the Heir's presence no longer. His dark eyes, the sharp planes of his face, his strange fascination with her, the confusion she felt when she met his eyes. The things he said about his brother, about *her*. . . . It was all too much.

"I'm sorry, Your Eminence," she said shakily. "I'm not feeling well. May I retire?"

"Of course," Malachi replied. He stood up too, and reached for her. She backed away. "I'm sorry if I upset you," he said, and then something else, but she didn't hear.

She was already out the door.

THIRTY-FIVE

SERINA

SERINA SURFACED OUT of a nightmare, her fists up and her heart thumping in her ears. Someone had grabbed her arm.

"It's just me," Val said, releasing her. "We need to go."

Serina regained her bearings slowly. The sun was high in the sky. She'd slept away the morning, curled into the shade of their small cave. He'd already slung the strap of his pack over his shoulder.

"Where are we going?" She pushed her tangled, dirty hair off her forehead, wincing at the pain in her shoulder.

Val glanced out toward the beach. "It's only a matter of time before the guards find us, and I think you're healthy enough to move now," he said. "I'm taking you off this island."

She gaped at him. *"What?"*

"I told you I was going to save my mother," he said. "You don't think I came to Mount Ruin without a plan?" His smile was crooked at the edges and didn't quite reach his eyes.

She stood up slowly, her legs still weak. She couldn't believe what she was hearing. "Why didn't you say anything last night?"

"The boat's hidden at high tide. And"—he touched her cheek briefly—"you needed to rest a little more, regain a little more strength. I knew if I told you, you'd have wanted to leave right away."

A boat? He really, truly had a way to escape? Serina's pulse raced. After all her plotting—rafts, revolutions—was it really this simple? *Nomi . . .*

"If you'd told me we had to wait for low tide, I would have," she said reproachfully.

"But would you have slept?" His look matched hers.

"Probably not," she admitted. The electricity in her veins, the sudden urge to *move, move, move*, was hard to deny. She would have spent the day climbing out of her skin.

"We've got two hours before the cave is exposed," Val explained. "It'll take us almost that long to get there." He turned north and held out his hand.

"Where do you plan to go?" she asked, without moving.

Val glanced back at her. "I thought we'd head for Bellaqua. Maybe try to rescue your sister?"

Serina didn't know what to say. Her head suddenly felt too light, as if it might float off her shoulders and out to sea. "Is this a trap?"

Val smiled gently. "Not a trap. A way out."

Serina took his hand. His fingers closed over hers, and her muscles melted like candle wax. She'd found her raft and her revolution, all in one. And perhaps more. His grin made her ache.

But she couldn't bring herself to move.

Jacana had defied Oracle to bring Serina water. She'd spent hours trying to help Serina with her escape plans. She'd promised to try to convince the crew chief an uprising was a good idea.

Small, timid Jacana. When she was chosen to fight, she would lose.

Serina knew she couldn't save everyone. But she couldn't leave Jacana behind.

"We have to make a detour," Serina said. "I made a promise to a friend that I would get off this island with her. We have to take her with us."

Val's brows drew together. "There are no detours. You can't get anywhere near the Cave. It's too dangerous."

Serina let go of his hand. She didn't want to anger him or risk her own escape. But she couldn't betray Jacana, not after all they'd been through. "This whole *place* is dangerous. Jacana won't survive a fight. If we don't bring her with us, *we're* the ones sentencing her to death."

He raised his hands, palms up, his expression verging on frantic. "We can't, Serina. I'm sorry. We have to go. Now. We've already waited too long."

Her whole body yearned to follow him. "I can't leave her here," Serina replied, willing him to understand. "She's the only one who helped me. She brought me water—"

"*I* helped you," he said, voice rising. "For a week I watched over you. I spooned food into your mouth, scared you'd never wake. I thought—" He reached for her arm again. "You're not the only one Commander Ricci wants to kill, remember? We have to go."

Serina yanked her arm away, more forcefully than she'd intended. Knocked off balance, he stumbled. She stared at him, wide eyed. But she couldn't back down. "I want to go with you," she said softly, but with a thread of steel. "So much I can hardly stand.it. But I can't leave Jacana. I've taken care of her since we arrived, and I can't abandon her now. *Please* understand."

Couldn't he see how much this was killing her? She wanted to forget Jacana and disappear. But if Nomi had been sent to Mount Ruin instead, if someone had considered saving her, and *hadn't* . . .

Val stared at her for a long time.

"Take the first path to the north beach, then head for the cliffs. I'll get the boat out and wait for you there. Stay away from Beach Camp. Don't let them see you." He shifted his pack. "If you're not there in three hours, I'll have to leave. The other guards are looking for me."

"I understand," Serina said. "I'll be there. I promise."

He gave her a last look, as if memorizing her face. As if he didn't expect to see her again. He turned and headed north without another word.

Serina collected her flagon of water. Then she shoved a handful of sand into her pocket. Jacana was either training or collecting food this time of day. Serina would need to get her attention and draw her away from the others. The sand could come in handy for that.

The hardest part would be finding her and staying unseen. Oracle sometimes posted sentries, but not usually in the middle of the day. It was a brazen time to try to steal their supplies or kidnap one of their fighters, both activities the other crews were known to engage in.

Serina scrambled up the beach to the rocky path. It didn't take long to reach the patch of jungle that bordered the cave. She was grateful for the shade. The day was heating up quickly.

She rounded a bend, the foliage thick on all sides, and stopped dead. "Jacana!"

Her friend was right there, standing in the middle of the path.

Jacana's eyes widened when she saw her. "Serina! Run!"

Before Serina could move, two guards materialized from the thick jungle foliage beside the path. They bolted for Serina. She hardly had time to turn around. With a shout, one of them grabbed her, hauling her to the ground. Her shoulder flamed. Serina whimpered.

For a moment, she tried to struggle, but the guard used all his weight to hold her down. "Hold still," he growled.

The other guard locked shackles around her wrists with an ominous clank.

"That was easy," he said, hauling Serina to her feet. He pushed her toward Jacana, who still stood frozen in the middle of the path, her face ashen and her eyes wide.

"What's happening?" Serina asked, struggling against her bonds.

"They've been waiting for you for days," Jacana said, her dirty face streaked with tears. "They've been using me and Gia as bait. I guess the Commander thought that you'd get hungry and seek out your friends." Her shoulders sagged as they bound her in iron too. "I'm so sorry."

"This is *not* your fault," Serina said. With an effort, she kept her chin up. Despair slipped through her, insidious as venom. How long until Val set sail? Had it been two hours? Three?

The guards dragged Serina and Jacana toward the cave.

Oracle was standing in the clearing when they approached.

The guard at Serina's side yelled, "Everyone to the amphitheater. Now!"

Oracle nodded silently.

Serina couldn't bear to look at her. She didn't fight the guard's tight grip on her arm, even though it dug sore spots into her muscles. She tried to hold her head high as she hiked down the path toward the coast, her hands awkwardly shackled behind her. The rough ground was difficult to navigate in places, and she fell twice. One of the guards hauled her to her feet, sending fire through the wound in her shoulder. She couldn't stifle her moan of pain.

He laughed.

Twilight was falling when they reached the ring. She was sure now. It had been more than three hours. Val was gone. And she was going to die.

THIRTY-SIX

NOMI

NOMI COULDN'T STOP thinking about what Malachi had said. He'd certainly played the part of the responsible older brother, disillusioned by but still protective of his younger brother. If she took him at his word, he was a rebel just like her. Pushing against his father's wishes by choosing her, reveling in the knowledge that she could read. Admiring her *nerve*.

But Asa had said Malachi was manipulative. A liar. He'd spoken of his caprice and volatility.

Which brother was lying?

What if they both were?

She *wanted* to trust Asa. She'd pinned all her hopes on him releasing Serina. She'd pinned her *heart* to his. But every time she tried to envision the sweet, mischievous boy who wanted to make her queen, the laughing man from the night of the race rose instead, boasting of his great golden cup.

She couldn't let Renzo risk himself, not when she didn't know whom to trust. But if she didn't, Serina would be lost to Mount

Ruin. The only solution was to speak to her brother. They could evaluate the risk and decide what to do together.

"Sit still," Angeline admonished. She was twisting Nomi's hair into place, and Nomi kept moving her head and ruining it.

"I'm sorry," Nomi said. "I'm trying." But in truth, Nomi was desperate to flee this chair, these chambers, the palazzo itself. To knock on every door in Bellaqua until she found Renzo.

But instead she was trapped here, getting ready with Maris and Cassia in one of the dressing rooms. From the look of them, they were fighting nerves as well. Maris was staring dead-eyed into the mirror as her handmaiden braided her hair, and Cassia was arguing with her handmaiden over what earrings to wear.

Maris stood up abruptly, rattling the tubes and jars on her vanity. Her sleek black hair was brushed straight and shining, with two thin braids holding back the hair from her face. Her cheeks were pink, her eyes lined with silver shimmer. She tightened her robe around herself as she left the room.

A few minutes later, Angeline stepped back. She'd piled Nomi's hair into an artful swirl on the top of her head. Her makeup was subtle and tinged with gold, to match her gown and the glittering mask Ines had given her.

"Ready?" Nomi asked. She glanced out the window at the horizon, gauging the time by the sun's lowering arc.

Angeline nodded happily. "Time for your dress."

They headed back to the bedroom. Angeline helped her into her gown. It had a massive belled skirt, heavy gold beading, and a corset tight enough to give Nomi curves. It was a dress that would have made Serina look like a queen. She ached for her sister. No matter what Nomi did tonight, it would feel like a betrayal.

It took Angeline twenty minutes to button up the back of the dress. Nomi could hardly move, let alone breathe, but when she looked in the mirror, her reflection glowed back at her, as beautiful and bright as a candle flame.

This was it. In a matter of hours, the fates of Serina, Renzo, and Nomi would be sealed.

The tiled patio was strung with millions of tiny, sparkling lights, strands and strands of them, all coming together at the top of a tall carved mahogany pole in the center. Beyond, the lawn sloped to the ocean. Only a white flash of waves showed through the darkness. The moon rose, bright and gleaming.

Near the arched doorways that led into the palazzo, the Superior and the Heir sat on huge, gold-filigreed chairs. The Superior had not deigned to wear a mask, but Malachi's was ornate, twisted gold and wine-dark gems to match his burgundy velvet coat. Asa stood off to the side, looking restless in his midnight blue coat and silver mask. When Ines, masked in black, led the Superior's Graces onto the patio, he stood up straighter.

Nomi, Cassia, and Maris waited with their handmaidens in one of the doorways. Nomi's beaded dress jingled faintly; she couldn't stand still. The Superior would announce them and then the audience would have ample opportunity to assess and admire the Heir's first Graces before the dancing began. At all the events leading up to tonight, they'd been part of the crowd. There to mingle and practice how to look and act, but not fully on display.

Nomi stared at the gold, beaded brocade of her dress with a fixed attention. Renzo was somewhere out there. She was desperate to find him, but if she saw him now, she didn't trust herself not to cry out. She had to get through the ceremony. Get through one second, and then the next. Then she could look for him and pull him aside privately.

The Superior stood up, his skeletal body moving slowly but precisely. He did not wince or pause. The quiet harp music provided by his Graces ceased.

"Good evening, my illustrious guests," the Superior began, extending his bony hands in an expansive gesture. "I am honored to have you here on this special occasion, the twentieth birthday of my son and heir."

Nomi glanced at Asa. His silver mask hid his expression.

The Superior continued. "Malachi has distinguished himself as an intelligent and conscientious man, one who has the skills and steadiness to one day take my place as the Superior. In the meantime, I welcome his larger role in the running of this country. I believe Viridia will benefit from his insight."

Beside Nomi, Cassia shifted restlessly. Maris didn't move.

"And now," the Superior added, swinging his arm toward the doorway, "my son shall formally accept his first Graces."

Cassia led the way onto the dais. Nomi followed her, with Maris bringing up the rear. They stopped and faced the dance floor, and Nomi bit back a gasp.

There were so many people: Graces, courtiers, and dignitaries.

Servants moved through the crowd, carrying trays laden with food. And everyone, even the servants, wore masks.

How could she possibly find Renzo?

Nomi curtsied in tandem with the other girls, and the crowd applauded. The movement set dresses to sparkling. Nomi was nearly blinded.

What was she going to do?

Malachi bowed to the audience and then, to her surprise, he extended his arm to her. He was choosing Nomi for his first dance. Cassia's face fell.

The music started again. Malachi led Nomi onto the dance floor. He didn't remark on how wooden she was in his arms. As they began to move, for the first time she really studied his face. His mask hid his cheeks and nose, but his sharp jaw, dark eyes, and full mouth were still on display.

He knew she could read, but he hadn't turned her in. He'd kissed her only once, and he'd never punished her for running away . . . or for any of the defiant things she'd said to him.

She kept waiting for him to be the horror Asa said he was, to break her. But had he ever really tried? He stared back at her, his intensity carving a hole into her heart. Over his shoulder, Asa smiled at her. A chill snaked down her spine.

Where was Renzo?

Malachi spun her around. Her gown dragged at her shoulders. Her corset clenched her ribs. "Nomi," he said. "You look absolutely miserable."

Her eyes flew to his face. "I'm so sorry, Your Eminence," she said, trying to school her expression. "I'm just nervous."

283

A flush crept up his throat. "No. *I'm* the one who's sorry. After you left yesterday, I couldn't stop thinking about what you said."

Her eyes widened. What had she said? She couldn't remember.

He continued, softer, so only she could hear. "Of course you feel lost here, especially without your sister. And it's my fault. I chose you without thinking it through. I should have done my duty. Your sister prepared for this. She *wanted* to be a Grace. You never did, and I forced it upon you."

Nomi found herself saying, "I'm sorry," again, as if somehow her lack of enthusiasm was her fault. It was better than saying, *Yes, you* should *have picked my sister, you stupid man.* But she was so confused, so turned around. Why was he saying this to her? Why was he apologizing?

And where was Renzo?

She kept looking over Malachi's shoulders as they spun, but the rest of the dancers were streaks of light and color. No features, no faces clear beneath their masks.

"I've no desire for an unwilling Grace," Malachi said, so softly she almost missed the words. "I will force you no longer."

Her mouth opened, but no sound came out. Suddenly, the problem of Asa and Renzo and Serina fell away. "What are you saying?"

"I'm saying I will free you from your obligation to me." His eyes darkened with something like sadness. "You may leave if you choose."

The words left her speechless.

His lips parted, and the warmth climbed from his neck to the skin beneath his mask. "But I hope you'll stay."

At that moment, something caught the corner of her eye.

Beyond Malachi, in the crowd . . . a figure in a red mask, black pants, and red-threaded jacket paused, head angled in her direction. She could tell in an instant, just by his height, the tilt of his head.

Renzo.

Malachi spun her again, and her brother disappeared into the crowd.

Across the room, the Superior was getting up. Asa was walking beside him, away from the party.

Panic exploded in Nomi's chest.

"Your Eminence, I can hardly account for the honor you show me. May I have some time to consider your offer?" she asked, already stepping away, closer to where her brother had stood.

"Of course." His hands drew her imperceptibly closer, as if he was reluctant to let her go. She wondered what his decision had cost him.

Just then, the song ended with a flourish, and Malachi leaned her back into a graceful dip. For an instant, their lips were a breath apart. Then he straightened, drawing her up with him. "Thank you for the dance."

Nomi curtsied, breathless, and pressed through the crowd, searching frantically for Renzo. She studied every masked face, felt the press of bodies, and didn't see her brother anywhere.

But she did find Maris standing next to the entrance to the patio, waiting for Malachi to ask her to dance. Her gown was a swirl of silver and red, gathered at the bodice with silver netting over her shoulders and arms. Her mask, like Renzo's, was red. Nomi grabbed her and pulled her forward.

"What—?"

"I need your help," Nomi whispered urgently. "There's a man here, in a red mask and black jacket. His name is Renzo. He might be lurking by the hallways or antechambers, I don't know. I need to get him a message. Will you help me?"

Maris nodded, her eyes full of questions.

"If you see him . . ." Nomi said, her heart racing. Malachi's words ran through her mind. She'd resolved to talk to Renzo, to figure this out together. But there wasn't time. "Tell him to leave the palace. Tell him I said to run."

She left Maris gaping behind her and moved on, toward the room she'd seen the Superior head for. Asa had gone with him. If Renzo arrived before she could stop him, there'd be nothing she could do. Renzo would implicate Malachi . . . and she no longer trusted that Asa wouldn't betray Renzo.

She scoured the assemblage for that red mask, but she didn't see it. She headed toward the arches, her feet aching, her heart beating so fast it threatened to escape her chest. Her eyes burned with tears.

There, by the greenery, just inside the doorway—

"*Renzo!*" she hissed.

The figure paused.

Nomi tried to run toward him, but the weight of her gown held her back, thick and impervious as mud.

"Nomi!" His voice reached out to her, infinitely familiar, infinitely comforting. "You shouldn't be here. Asa told me what to do. I don't want you to risk yourself."

"No," she said. Tears streamed down her cheeks. One moment, that was all they would have. "You have to go, Renzo. I was wrong. I've made a grave mistake."

His warm brown eyes widened behind the mask. "What do you mean?"

"I don't think . . . I don't think we can trust Asa after all." Nomi's heart cracked, fissures cutting deep.

"But what about Serina?" he asked anxiously.

"If we do as Asa says, he will break his promise. We're going to have to find another way to help Serina." She couldn't hug him, not here with so many watching, so she reached out and squeezed his hand. She couldn't read his expression behind his mask. "Right now, I'm worried about you," she added, more desperately. "Please go, Renzo. I need you to be safe."

He gave her a long look, confusion turning his mouth into a deep frown. Tears slipped down her cheeks. She pushed him toward the doorway. Then she turned around. She couldn't watch him walk away again.

It was easy to find the antechamber, as Asa had said.

She stepped into the doorway. The Superior sat on a cushioned chair in the center of the small room, surrounded by warm wood-paneled walls hung with tapestries. Asa sat in a chair beside him. He looked up as soon as her shadow crossed the threshold.

Asa raised a brow. He obviously wanted to know where Renzo was. Their window was closing. The Superior would soon rejoin the party.

Nomi slowly shook her head.

For an instant, his eyes filled with something. Hurt? Betrayal?

"Where is your cousin?" he asked brashly, and now it was an ugly thing lurking behind his mask. "What did you do?"

"The right thing," she replied, her chin high. She had *hoped* she was doing the right thing. Now she was sure. "He's not coming."

He won't pretend to try to murder your father so you can save him, she felt like shouting. *He won't name Malachi. He won't help you.*

"Asa, what is the meaning of this?" the Superior began, with ice in his voice. He gripped the armrests with his long, bony fingers and started to stand.

Behind Nomi, footsteps echoed on the marble floor. "Father, are you ready?" Malachi asked as he entered the room.

Nomi never took her eyes off Asa. She saw when the storm broke inside him. Saw him break and become something new.

Saw him wordlessly draw the dagger at his hip and slice his father's throat.

THIRTY-SEVEN

SERINA

THE GUARDS MARCHED Serina and Jacana up onto the stage. The amphitheater filled slowly. The women filing in looked confused, and the crowd wasn't as silent as usual. Oracle, Ember, and Cliff took places in the front row. *Oracle must feel vindicated*, Serina thought. This was exactly what she was afraid of.

The other crew chiefs stood close to the stage. Serina found Slash, and they shared a look. *If I'd had more time . . .* There'd be no chance of revolution now.

When everyone had arrived, Commander Ricci strode onto the concrete stage. The other guards retreated to the balcony, except the two holding on to Serina's and Jacana's shackles.

"Good evening, everyone!" Ricci shouted, spreading his arms in welcome. He seemed to enjoy his showman's role more than usual. "I have a special treat for you."

Serina couldn't tear her gaze from the firearm strapped to his hip. She almost wished he'd dispense with the theatrics and get it over with. But she cherished each breath in and out of her lungs, as fast as they came and went. Her pulse pounded in her temples.

"In our last fight, Cave's fighter made the dubious decision to *submit* instead of winning her crew its well-deserved rations. In fact, she denied rations to all of you, as no winner meant no rations for anyone. She changed the game, and as we all know, the game does *not* change." His voice tightened, the expansiveness gone. A fine tremble ran down Serina's arms.

"She's been busy ever since," he continued. He never once looked at Serina, addressing every word to the crowd. "She tried to incite a rebellion. She killed a guard. And she will, absolutely, pay with her life."

Serina held her back so straight it ached. She didn't know how he knew all of that, but it didn't surprise her that he did. She kept her face perfectly blank. In Viridia, all women wore masks.

She braced for the Commander to raise his gun.

"So," he said, turning to her at last, "you'll fight again. Now."

"F-fight?" she stuttered, confused.

"Oh, you'll die, whether you win or not," he said blandly, his weathered face set in hard lines. "But I'm giving you a chance for revenge first. Who do you choose?" He glanced into the crowd. "You want another shot at last week's adversary? I think she's anxious for a rematch."

The blood drained from Serina's face.

"Or perhaps Oracle," he suggested. "After all, she *did* banish you." He twisted his lips into a grotesque pout as he turned his attention toward Jacana. "Or perhaps you'd like to fight our rabbit, here. She provided the perfect bait, it seems. She, you might actually kill. Then I'd get to kill you, which of course I'd enjoy."

Jacana bent her head, her shoulders shaking with her sobs. One of the guards unshackled her so she'd be free to fight.

"It's time," Ricci said, his voice taking on an ominous tone. "Who will you fight?"

Serina glanced at Jacana. She'd come back so Jacana wouldn't *have* to fight.

Her gaze shifted to Oracle. It was true the crew chief had exiled her. But more important, Oracle was one of the most skilled fighters here. She could kill Serina quickly and rob the Commander of some of his spectacle. Rob him of the chance to kill Serina himself.

Anika would kill her quickly too. Serina knew she didn't have the strength to gain the upper hand with her a second time. Not with her injuries.

"Oh," Commander Ricci added. "Submission is not an option this time. But I'm sure you realized that." He nodded at the guard who stood behind her, and suddenly, with a clank, the weight of her chains was gone.

Serina closed her eyes, just for a second. She'd made her stand already. She'd refused to kill another woman. She'd *meant* everything she'd said to her crew, about being strong. Working together. Being iron.

If she chose to fight a woman now, those words would all be empty. Nothing would change.

Serina lifted her gaze and stared Commander Ricci straight in the eye so he could see her fury. "I won't do it," she shouted, because it was the only way to mask the shake in her voice. "I won't play your game."

His face purpled. Serina reminded herself she was dead no matter what. Val's boat was gone. Nomi was gone. Hope was gone.

But maybe she could leave a little defiance behind.

"If you want me to fight, then I choose *you*," she screamed. "Kill me now, with your firearm or your fists. But I won't raise a hand against my sisters."

Commander Ricci roared. The guard beside Serina moved, but Ricci waved him back. "Stand down. Nobody move. She's mine."

He rolled his shoulders. Pounded one massive fist into the other hand. Widened his stance and stared her down. "You want to fight me? Well then. We shall fight."

Staring death in its craggy, terrible face, Serina waited for a sense of peace to steal over her, or a numbness. But all she had left, burning from within, was fury.

He came at her, fast as a striking snake. She scrambled in her pocket for the sand she'd planned to use to get Jacana's attention, and threw it in his face. He paused, pawing at his eyes. It didn't slow him for long.

She was able to duck away from his first punch, but the second caught in her in the stomach, stealing her breath.

Then he punched her in the face, and she went down.

Serina prayed for Nomi. It was too late to pray for herself.

Ricci stood over her, terrifyingly massive. He kicked her in the side. She howled as her rib broke, a fiery pain streaking through her. Crying now, gasping for breath, she struggled to her knees and backed away, blood dripping from her mouth. He paced her, taking his time. All he had to do was kick her in the head, or reach down and break her neck, and it would be over.

He knew it. She knew it. But still he played with her, giving her time to regret her brave speech. He reached down and grabbed her arm—the one Anika had cut—and dug his fingers into the wound, drawing new blood.

She threw a desperate punch as his stomach, but it was like punching a wall. He didn't even flinch. He lifted her until her feet dangled, and pulled her close, until their noses were an inch apart. "Women think they're strong when they're fighting other women," he growled, his moist, stinking breath clinging to Serina's cheeks. "But when a man fights them, they know the truth. You are weak. All of you. And you always will be."

He dropped her. Serina crumpled, her legs unable to support her.

That was Ricci's victory speech. He was done playing.

With her last remaining strength, Serina stood up on shaking legs, put her head down, sucked in a breath, and barreled into him as hard as she could.

It was like trying to move a mountain, and yet he did move, a little. A few steps back. He hadn't expected her to try to shove him. He braced against her and thrust his hands under her arms and threw her across the stage. She hit the concrete hard, her ankle twisting under her.

He stalked toward her, murder flashing in his eyes.

A roar built throughout the amphitheater. Serina had time to note that the women watching weren't cheering. They were *screaming*. And then, with a bloodcurdling shriek, Oracle and Ember stormed the stage.

Oracle flung herself at the Commander, latching onto his back with an arm around his throat and her legs locked around his waist, blocking his access to his firearm. He coughed and twisted, trying to throw her off. Someone on the balcony fired off a shot, but the Commander waved an arm. "My fight. My kills," he roared.

He bent forward sharply and Oracle almost went over his head. But Ember slid beneath and drove a makeshift knife into his belly. He reached for her, but she danced out of range. Oracle kept choking him, and no one moved.

Shock crashed over Serina in waves. Oracle and Ember had come to her rescue. They had revolted. The women surrounding the stage screamed and shouted, their banshee voices drowning out the Commander's strangled gags. Out of the corner of her eye, Serina saw movement. Slash was leading her Hotel Misery crew around the edge of the stage.

Onstage, Oracle shrieked again. A hunting cry. The Commander's face went purple as he scrabbled against her arm. Ember yanked out her blade. He sank to his knees in a puddle of his own blood. He scratched Oracle's arm, leaving deep gouges, but she never let go.

Serina took a shivery, painful breath just as Commander Ricci's eyes rolled back in his head. His body slumped to the side. Oracle wrenched his neck until it cracked, just to be sure.

She straightened and met Serina's astonished gaze. A smile flickered at the edge of her lips.

Then a bullet hit her square in the forehead, whipping her head back. Her brown eye went as unseeing as the white one.

Serina screamed.

Chaos erupted.

A wave of women crashed across the stage. Gunfire blasted out over the cacophony. Serina struggled to her feet, her broken rib sending spikes of pain through her body. Guards fell from the balcony to the concrete below. It took her a moment to realize why—Slash's crew had snuck up the stairs, coming at the men from behind.

But the gunfire didn't slow, and women continued dropping.

If Oracle and Ember could run onto the stage and attack the Commander, Serina could find the strength to keep fighting. She yanked a knife from the hand of a lifeless member of Slash's crew and staggered up the stairs. The screams and concussion of gunshots echoed eerily in the stairwell. She dodged a body tumbling down the stairs.

By the time she reached the balcony, the guards had turned and were fighting the surprise attack in earnest. There wasn't much the women below could do but wait for more guards to fall. If the impact didn't kill them, the women waiting would.

Before Serina could intervene, a red-faced guard shot Slash. Serina lunged at him, yanking the firearm from his hand as he fell. She fumbled with the weapon for a second, trying to figure out how to use it, but a strong arm hooked around her throat. She thrust an elbow back and the man grunted, but he didn't loosen his hold.

"This is all your fault," he growled. He punched her in the kidney without easing his grip on her neck. She had no air to groan.

Serina sagged, black spots dancing before her eyes. She

elbowed him again, but it was a feeble effort. Her strength was fading. Her lungs were screaming.

Suddenly, through the haze, she saw the guards nearest the edge of the balcony crumple. No one had touched them. They'd been shot.

The arm around her slackened for an instant. She twisted and became deadweight, slipping away. Then she buried her knife in his belly. Two more guards went down. There were only a few left now, and the women fighting them seemed to be gaining the upper hand.

Serina peeked over the broken railing.

Below, in the center of a circle of uneasy women, Val lowered his firearm.

THIRTY-EIGHT

NOMI

NOMI HAD NEVER seen anyone die before. It wasn't peaceful, and it wasn't quiet. The Superior's hands scrambled ineffectually at his throat as he gagged on his own blood. Malachi rushed into the room and tried to stanch the flood. There was so much, a red river running over his hands, his velvet coat. She couldn't see the stain spreading; the jacket was the same color as the blood.

Belatedly, Nomi realized she was screaming.

Asa nodded approvingly at Malachi. "The more blood on your hands, the more believable this will be." He turned back to Nomi. "Now you, my flower. You're going to need to be quiet."

And he lunged at her with the dagger.

Nomi's scream became a strangled cry. The point of the knife rammed into her beaded gown, but the heavy fabric and whalebone of her corset became unlikely armor, deflecting the blade. She stumbled backward.

Malachi knocked Asa to the ground with a thud. From beneath him, Asa twisted and bucked. Malachi was larger, but

Asa had a weapon. He slashed Malachi's arm. Malachi groaned. Nomi watched, horrified, uncertain what to do.

Asa spit and scrambled. He was suddenly a stranger, someone she had never really known or understood. Everything she'd believed, all the feelings she'd harbored, crumbled to dust. He had manipulated her.

He had lied to her. Preyed on her. He'd taken her rebellion, her agony for her sister, and twisted them into something he could use. It was so obvious now.

Asa wanted to be the Heir. He wanted the power, the adulation, the attention. He wanted everything his brother had, and she hated him for it.

Fury bubbled up inside her, hot as lava.

He had betrayed her.

Tried to *kill* her.

Malachi punched Asa in the face, knocking off his silver mask. Asa's eyes rolled back in his head and his body went limp. Malachi started to rise.

But it was a ruse. Asa surged up, thrusting upward with his dagger. He caught Malachi in the stomach. Malachi never made it to his feet. Instead, he crumpled.

Nomi dropped to her knees by his side. He had no corset to save him. She pressed her hands to his jacket, against the wound. He moaned. Behind them, Asa staggered to his feet.

"It's okay, you're going to be okay," she whispered, crying.

But she knew the truth. Nothing was okay. Blood seeped over her hands.

Asa stood over them. "Nomi, you shouldn't have warned off your cousin," he said reproachfully. "But this will work out fine.

Why an attempted assassination when you can have the real thing? Thank you for leaving that note in my brother's room. You behaved beautifully."

Nomi's heart twisted. She'd *trusted* him. He'd promised her everything she wanted, and it was all a lie. Every kiss, every touch they'd shared became poison. She swallowed back bile.

Footsteps clattered through the doorway. Nomi looked up.

Eyes wide, Maris slammed to a halt. She stared, mouth open, at the bloody body of the Superior, still slumped in his chair. "I—I was looking for Nomi. What—"

"Marcos!" Asa called. "If you would."

From a shadowy doorway at the opposite end of the room, the stocky, mountainous guard and a few of his friends appeared. Asa gestured to Maris. "Can't have witnesses wandering off, can we?"

"Run!" Nomi shouted.

Maris turned, but the guards reached her before she got more than a few steps. Marcos pulled Nomi to her feet. Through the doorway, the faint sounds of the party grew louder, pressing ever closer. Nomi prayed it was a convoy coming to check on the Superior, that there would be witnesses to Asa's crime.

Malachi groaned at her feet. She reached for him, but Marcos yanked her back up.

"You can't kill us all," Nomi said, struggling against the guard's iron hold.

"Of course I can." Asa brandished his dagger.

The distant voices were getting louder.

"Asa killed the Superior!" she shouted, as loud as she could. "The Superior is dead!"

She could hear footsteps now, speeding up.

Asa faltered only for a moment. "Well," he said, nodding to Marcos. "I did promise you would see your sister again, didn't I?" Nomi stared into his brown eyes and wondered how she'd misjudged him so entirely.

"Get him up," Asa ordered, gesturing toward Malachi. "Put him on the boat with the girls. When he dies, throw him overboard."

The Heir's eyes were closed, his breathing ragged. Nomi cried out as one of Asa's guards hauled him over his shoulder, his head rolling on his neck.

Maris stood frozen, watching everything with eyes so wide Nomi could see the whites all around. Her chest heaved faster and faster with every breath.

Marcos pushed Nomi from behind. The other guards hustled Maris. As they were herded through the door in the back of the room, Nomi heard Asa shout, "Help me! My father!"

The door slammed behind her just as the footsteps thundered into the room.

THIRTY-NINE

SERINA

SERINA HELPED THE women on the balcony secure the handful of surviving guards with their own shackles. One of them lunged forward, shouting.

Anika shot him in the face.

The rest were quiet after that.

"We should kill all of them," Anika said. Her cheek and one of her arms were streaked with blood, and a bruise marred her temple.

"We can't." Serina put herself between Anika's firearm and the guard she was pointing it at. "We might need them for leverage. They might have special ways they communicate with the mainland, or codes to unlock the rations or something. We should wait."

Anika lowered the weapon, a little too slowly for Serina's taste, seeing as it was pointed at *her* belly now. "Fine," the girl said. "I'll wait for now."

But she spit on the nearest guard as she stalked over to help lead them down the stairs.

Serina collected all the guards' weapons and left them in a pile in the back corner of the balcony. She'd have to ask Val if there was a safe place to store them in the guards' compound. She prayed no guard had remained behind during the fight. She had no desire to continue this war.

Serina turned back to the carnage. Slash lay crumpled over the body of a guard, her eyes unseeing. Serina knelt next to her body and put a hand on her shoulder. Today was Slash's victory.

Serina helped carry body after body down the stairs. They laid each out carefully on the stone stage, now sticky and red with blood.

Thirty-two guards were dead, including Commander Ricci.

The death toll among the women was higher. Oracle lay with at least forty other women. Ember sat in the blood next to her and held her hand, sobbing. Serina had never seen the fierce woman look anything but in control.

Val stood a few feet away. He didn't move much; maybe he didn't want to draw attention to himself, now that he was the only guard not dead or restrained. The women seemed to understand he was on their side. But Serina noticed from a distance that he kept a hand on his firearm.

Serina stumbled across Jacana's body at the edge of the stage. She was curled into a ball, looking even smaller in death. Tears slipped down Serina's cheeks. The girl had been so scared of the fights, so convinced she would die here, and Serina hadn't been able to save her.

Val made his way to Serina. They stood with Jacana's body between them, and Serina wondered if it was a distance they could breach.

"I should have—" she began.

"I couldn't leave—"

They stopped.

"They used her as bait," Serina said. The tightness in her chest hadn't loosened. "To get to me."

Val's jaw tensed. "I shouldn't have told you what to do. I should have respected your choice."

Serina walked around Jacana to meet Val on the other side. "You didn't leave without me."

He held her gaze. "You launched a rebellion."

She wasn't sure how to feel about that.

Had she saved lives by upending the system? Or cost more? What happened when the Superior found out and sent forces to take them all out?

Serina looked around. A lot of women were milling around without purpose. Others were wrapping the bodies in sheets retrieved from Hotel Misery. There no longer appeared to be separations among the different crews.

"We'll need a system to distribute the rations Commander Ricci was hoarding," she said, staring at the gaunt faces. "And a place to keep the captured guards. And a way to deal with the boat guards when new prisoners arrive." Maybe, somehow, they could keep the Superior from finding out. At least until they were ready to defend themselves.

"I can get you access to the rations, and there are a few holding cells in the guards' compound. The boat . . . well, we probably have a week or so before the next one arrives. We'll figure it out." He gave her hand a brief squeeze. "The worst is over."

Serina eyed him, but didn't reply. The worst might be over on Mount Ruin. But she wasn't planning to stop here.

She led him to the far side of the amphitheater, where Anika and several other girls from Hotel Misery were training firearms on the captured guards.

"Anika, this is Val," Serina said. "He's going to show you where to take the guards. He also knows where there's extra food. Bring it back here and we'll split it evenly among the crews." She expected the girl to question her, to smile a dangerous smile. But to her surprise, Anika gave her a short, business-like nod.

"Traitor," one of the captive guards hissed, glaring at Val. Anika elbowed him in the nose. With a moan, he subsided. The other guards stared into the barrels of their own firearms, still trained on them by Anika's comrades.

"You've got this?" Serina asked, shifting her gaze from Val to Anika. Would Val be safe with these women, who were so ready to kill all the guards who'd oppressed them?

"We've got this," Val replied firmly. He ran a hand through his unruly hair.

Anika nodded. As Serina turned away, the girl added, "I thought you were weak. But you had a plan this whole time, didn't you? It only took you a few weeks to take them all down."

Serina would never have expected Anika to look at her with respect. And she knew enough not to tell the girl the truth—there had been no plan, save getting the crews to talk to each other. There was no plan now.

"Mount Ruin burns the weak out of you," she said instead.

Anika smiled a little. They were both fighters now.

With a last glance at Val, Serina headed back down to the stage. She found Cliff sitting on a bench a few feet from the array of bodies. She was twisting her hands together, triumph and fear flitting across her wide, plain face.

"Cliff," Serina called, drawing the woman's attention. "You know any of the women in the other crews?"

Cliff nodded, returning her focus to the dead.

"Can you organize a group to take the dead guards to the cliffs and commit them to the sea?" Serina asked.

Cliff stood up abruptly. "I can do that."

Serina patted her shoulder. Then she went looking for Ember.

The hike up the mountain was harder that night, with the weight of Oracle's body on her shoulders. But Serina felt lighter too. The stars burned holes in the sky, and the greasy flicker of torches lit a long line through the darkness. There were many sisters to honor tonight.

But Oracle was first.

Fire, breathe
Water, burn
Terror, wane
Your reign is over.
Fire, breathe
Water, burn
Stars, lead the way
Your sister is here.

Serina sang the words for Oracle and Jacana.

But they were also for Val's mother, and Petrel, and Slash, and all the women who'd fought and died here.

And they were for the living too.

When the last body sent up its last shower of sparks, a voice, hoarse from singing, asked, "What do we do now?"

In the red glow of the volcano, Serina saw face after face turn to her.

She took a deep breath. She'd managed to survive Mount Ruin by bringing these women together. But there was still so much more to do.

Someday, when she saw Nomi again—it was *when* now, not *if*, she was certain—she would apologize. She'd always thought there was no value in fighting back, that it did no good.

But Nomi had been right to rebel. It *was* worth it. Fighting back could change the world.

No. It *would* change the world. Serina would make sure of it.

FORTY

NOMI

ASA'S GUARDS SAID nothing as they hauled Nomi, Malachi, and Maris through the halls of the palazzo. Malachi's labored breath filled the silence, and his blood dripped to stain the floor.

"Please," Nomi begged Marcos. "He's going to die. Help him."

The guard ignored her.

"What happened?" Maris asked, terror turning her face bone white and her eyes black holes. "The Superior . . ."

Nomi choked on a sob. "Asa killed him. He—he staged a coup. He used me—Malachi—" She couldn't get the words out.

It was so obvious now, how profoundly he'd manipulated her. Maybe he'd never intended for the Superior to die. But she was *certain* now that Asa would not have let Renzo escape after their charade. He would have convinced everyone Malachi and Renzo had worked together. Maybe Nomi too. He'd have had

Renzo put to death, just like that groom. And he would have done it without a second thought.

Asa had taken advantage of her grief, her desperation, her *nerve*. He'd taken advantage of everything, even Renzo's absence, turning it to his own purpose. Now he wouldn't just be the Heir. He'd be the Superior.

"What are they going to do to us?" Maris moaned. She couldn't keep up with the guards' fast pace and kept tripping. Nomi could see how much the girl wanted to just collapse, but the guard yanked her up, over and over again.

"I don't know," Nomi replied, only because she didn't want to frighten Maris more.

I did promise you would see your sister again, didn't I? Asa had said.

Marcos led the bloodstained group to a part of the palace Nomi had never seen, and then outside to a wharf. Several large boats bobbed in the black water.

Moonlight illuminated Malachi's growing pallor.

"Get the chains," Marcos ordered, and one of the guards peeled off into the night.

Nomi's stomach roiled.

Maris suddenly yanked away from the guard holding her. She caught him unprepared and was able to break free for a moment, but only a moment. He grabbed her again, pulling brutally on her hair. She cried out.

"I'm so sorry." Tears streamed down Nomi's face. "I should never have asked for your help. I'm so sorry."

"The man you were trying to find," Maris said, wincing as

the guard hauled her onto a boat by her hair. "Who was he?"

Nomi stumbled as Marcos pushed her onto the boat. It was a large workboat, with iron gunwales and a stained wooden floor. The sailors who manned it scrambled belowdecks to get the boiler going.

"Someone very important to me," she said. Would Asa hunt Renzo down? Would he go after her family? "I was trying to keep him safe. But now I've imperiled you."

The guards chained the girls to the gunwale of the boat. Maris sagged to her knees, hands trapped above her head. The red in her dress looked like blood.

"I'm so sorry," Nomi said again. "He promised to release my sister. . . . I trusted him."

The guard carrying Malachi dropped him onto the hard wooden flooring like a sack of grain.

"You there," Marcos yelled to one of the sailors. "When he stops breathing, throw him overboard." Then he leapt off the boat, untied the heavy mooring ropes, and pushed them away from the wharf.

The boiler belched steam. Soon Nomi couldn't hear the lap of water over the *shush-shush* of the boat's pistons. Slowly, they moved away from land, out into the vast dark sea.

The shackles around Nomi's wrists clanked against the rail with every swell. She stared fixedly at the reflection of the moon bobbing on the water; if she looked down, she'd see the rusty stains of blood on her bedraggled golden dress.

Maris swayed with the movement of the boat, her head pressed into its cold metal sides.

"I'm so sorry," Nomi said again, the words her mantra. Her prayer for deliverance.

Maris's curtain of hair blew back from her face in the sharp sea wind. "Nomi, this is not your fault."

Bitterness coated the back of Nomi's throat. Yes, it was.

The Superior was dead, Asa had engineered his rise to power, and Malachi—

She stared at the lump of blood-soaked fabric, so motionless in the bow of the boat. Was that the faint swell of his breath, or the rock of the boat?

One of the guards approached him.

"He's breathing! He's breathing!" she screamed.

To her relief, the man backed away. For now.

Malachi hadn't opened his eyes since they'd left the palazzo. Hot tears dripped down Nomi's cheeks. He would die. Likely soon.

She'd done this to him, as surely as if she'd been the one to plunge the knife into his gut.

And Renzo . . . oh, Renzo.

She'd sentenced him to life as a fugitive.

She prayed he kept running.

Nomi curled forward toward her hands, the agony unbearable. In trying to save Serina, and herself, she'd destroyed them all.

The night stretched on and on, the ocean throwing them through the darkness with savage abandon. Nomi's stomach revolted. Maris sang a lullaby under her breath, her voice hoarse from weeping.

Malachi's chest rose and fell, slower and shallower with each passing moment.

And then, at last, as dawn bled up from the horizon, Mount Ruin slowly rose from the mist, blackened and ominous.

Nomi took a ragged breath.

Serina, I'm here.

ACKNOWLEDGMENTS

It was an absolute honor to work with the incredible teams at Alloy and LBYR in bringing Serina and Nomi to life. Huge cupcake-sprinkled hugs to my editors, Pam Gruber, Lanie Davis, and Eliza Swift, and to my story gurus, Josh Bank, Joelle Hobeika, and Sara Shandler. To Les Morgenstein, Romy Golan, Matt Bloomgarden, and the rest of the team at Alloy, thank you for everything you've done to support me and this book. To Megan Tingley, Alvina Ling, Emilie Polster, Katharine McAnarney, Carol Scatorchio, and the whole amazing team at LBYR, thank you so much for taking a chance on my sisters and being so enthusiastic about them! And to the wonderful designers who brought them (and the cover in general) to beautiful life—Karina Granda, Mallory Grigg, and Liz Dresner—thank you!

My sincerest thanks to Kirsten Wolf at Emerald City Literary Agency for helping me with my contract, and to Linda Epstein, who somehow always knows what to say (no, *you're the rock star*). I feel so lucky to be one of your authors, Linda, I can't even tell you. Thank you so much, Mandy Hubbard, for encouraging Linda to check her e-mail.

To my dear friend Michelle Nebiolo—thank you for helping me with my Italian and for generously suggesting Serina, your grandmother's name, for my first sister. Serina would literally not be Serina without you. *Grazie, amica mia!*

Dr. Jody Escaravage, Aimee L. Salter, Morgan Tucker, Rachel Hamm, and Natasha Fisher: Here are some big, awkward squishy hugs for being such insightful early readers and such amazing friends. This process would have been so much harder without your encouragement, feedback, and emotional support.

To my writer and editor friends who listened to my angst, who cheered for me, and who sent me hilarious gifs—Jax Abbey, Paige Nguyen, J.D. Robinson, The Wonder Writers, Crystal Watanabe, and Morgan Michael—thank you and a dark chocolate cupcake for each of you!

To my family, thank you so much for your support and encouragement. It has been thrilling to share this experience with you.

Ollie, I love that you're already telling your own stories. My favorite is the one about Risky Pupperniss. Remember that one. I think it's got legs.

To my husband, Andy, without whom none of this would have been possible: Thank you for making me laugh, for comforting me during stressful deadlines, and for always, always being there (except, you know, when the Army needs you to be elsewhere. Ha!). You are an incredible husband and father, and an incredible man. You inspire me daily. Not only do I hope Ollie grows up to be like you . . . I hope someday I do too. I love you.

And finally, dear reader, I'm so honored that you've spent your valuable time with Serina and Nomi. You are magical and wonderful, and I love and appreciate each and every one of you. If I could, I would bake *all* of you cupcakes. Thank you!